LUCIFER'S PRIDE

Soulkeepers Reborn Book 3

G. P. CHING

CONTENTS

Books by G.P. Ching   vii

1. Burn it All Down   1
2. Revelations   9
3. The Devil's Dilemma   17
4. The Secret Society   25
5. The Visit   37
6. Connections   41
7. Aunt Millie   51
8. Call Me Liam   59
9. Confessions   67
10. Ultimatum   73
11. The Coven   85
12. Our Greatest Fear   95
13. You Slay Me   103
14. Demiurge   111
15. The Second Test   119
16. Hero   131
17. The Initiate   137
18. Reunion   147
19. The Deal   155
20. Things Left Unsaid   161
21. Free Lunch   167
22. Technothrob   173
23. The First Time I Died   181
24. Malice   191
25. Lost Boys   199
26. The Broken Tree   209
27. The Deal   217
28. Introductions   223
29. Gone   233
30. The Sacrifice   239

31. Theodor   245
32. Battle   253
33. Finn   259
34. The Fall   265
35. The Soulkeepers   271
36. Ever After   279
37. Paris High School   285
    Epilogue   291
    About the Author   299
    Books by G.P. Ching   301
    Acknowledgments   303

GROUNDED

Prologue   307
Chapter 1   313
Chapter 2   323
Chapter 3   335

Lucifer's Pride: Soulkeepers Reborn, Book 3

First Edition: May 2018

eISBN: 978-1-940675-36-7

ISBN: 978-1-940675-37-4

v. 2.0

BOOKS BY G.P. CHING

Soulkeepers Reborn

Wager's Price, Book 1

Hope's Promise, Book 2

Lucifer's Pride, Book 3

The Soulkeepers Series

The Soulkeepers, Book 1

Weaving Destiny, Book 2

Return to Eden, Book 3

Soul Catcher, Book 4

Lost Eden, Book 5

The Last Soulkeeper, Book 6

The Grounded Trilogy

Grounded, Book 1

Charged, Book 2

Wired, Book 3

❧ 1 ❧

BURN IT ALL DOWN

Unforeseen consequences were the heartburn of life, the jellyfish sting during a swim in the ocean, a paper cut from a love letter.

As Finn Wager sat across from Hope on the bus to Revelations, he felt like a hero. He cradled Theodor's pocket watch in the web of his fingers, Mike and Wendy's souls contained inside. He'd saved them from Hell, and soon his friends would be safely back inside their bodies. Once that happened, Hope and Ms. D would have no choice but to welcome him home to Revelations with open arms. Everything he'd done, all the sacrifices and risks he'd taken, would make sense to them considering his ultimate goal.

But when the bus passed between the twin dragons that guarded the gate to Veil Island and Revelations Institute, everything took a turn for the unexpected. Although the familiar sifting of his soul had produced a small amount of discomfort in the past, this time it caused him heart-stopping pain. He gripped his chest and sent a pleading glance in Hope's direction. But what could she do? A million pins impaled him, accompanied by the fading of his flesh. His cells came apart, swept backward through the dark electric tunnel of the bus's magic portal.

He'd been rejected. The dragons that guarded the gate to Veil Island allowed only Soulkeepers inside. But Finn *was* a Soulkeeper. He had passed inspection before. Both the angel Gabriel and Hope had confirmed his status as a Horseman. What had changed? And where was he going?

A voice in his head, the kind that kept a person awake at night mulling over the things they should or shouldn't have done, called to mind the ruined tree in the cemetery and the spells he'd used to turn it into a portal to Nod, spells he'd bound like enchanted tattoos to every square inch of his flesh. When he re-formed in the heart of the cemetery in New Orleans, the one he'd pictured in his mind, those tattoos were still pulsing and burning in the wake of his travels. He wasn't sure exactly why he'd been rejected, but one thing was clear:

He wasn't a Soulkeeper anymore.

"Ignite!" Theodor's tone, high-pitched and frantic, reverberated off the surrounding tombs. Finn reoriented himself to face the tree. At a run, he wove between the graves, reaching his mentor in a few quick strides.

Theodor had vowed to destroy the tree hours ago and the bridge between worlds it represented. In Lucifer's hands, it could reconnect the Devil with the source of his power. But the twisting branches of the ancient oak remained stubbornly intact. Despite the magician's spells, the bark resisted any damage.

"What's wrong? Why isn't it burning?" Finn asked.

Theodor whirled, his shiny dress shoes kicking up loose gravel. The magician always wore the same black tuxedo. Usually, this formal attire, along with his waxy complexion and stoic personality, served to camouflage his reaction to whatever trouble he encountered. Not today. The magician had broken a sweat, and his usually impassive expression looked strained by exhaustion and frustration.

"Finn! I thought you were taking the pocket watch back to Revelations." He glanced at his wrist. "You're almost out of time."

"The watch is still on its way." Finn hesitated, but there was no hiding from the truth. "The guardians at the gate to Veil Island rejected me. I guess I'm not a Soulkeeper anymore."

Theodor stilled, assessing him. One of his cards flipped over his knuckles and between his fingers. "No. I don't think so. From what I've learned, being a Soulkeeper is genetic. It cannot be taken from you. I suspect it is your skin that was rejected by the guardians, and since you cannot harmlessly be separated from it, your entire body was transported here."

"So, Ms. D was telling the truth. The symbols are an affront to God and nature." Finn's heart pounded, his anger rising like a red tide. "Great. That's just great."

"Some of the symbols. Not all." Theodor took a deep breath. He gestured toward the tree. "I suspect the portal has something to do with it as well. This wasn't supposed to happen. I'd intended my spell to transport me once, open and shut. Not to build a bridge between worlds."

"You don't say," Finn snapped. "It seems as if a magician with your level of experience would realize this was a bad idea. Or that placing a binding spell in my skin might corrupt more than my flesh." He held out his arms. "When exactly were you going to warn me about the consequences of what we did, Theodor?"

Theodor lowered his chin. "I did warn you, Finn. And by

what you've told me, Hope and Victoria warned you as well. Your choices were your own. Don't deny it."

Finn pointed at Theodor's chest. "I had no choice. I had to save Mike and Wendy, not to mention your sorry ass."

"Mike and Wendy may be the reason for your choice," Theodor said. "But a choice you did have. You made it. I made it. And now we are paying the price." He tugged at the sleeve of his tuxedo. The thing looked new again, although it had been scorched at the collar and cuffs only a few hours ago. Nothing but magic explained its freshly laundered state. "Now, help me destroy this tree before the consequences become much, much worse."

With more grumbling than was necessary, Finn approached his side. "What have you tried so far?"

Theodor held up half his deck.

"Let's try again. We'll be stronger together," Finn said. Side by side they tried to ignite the tree, then eviscerate it, then reduce it to dust. Methodically, they worked their way through Theodor's deck, trying every spell with any hope of ending the bridge. Nothing worked.

"It must be resistant to magic," Theodor said. "All magic."

Finn arched an eyebrow at his mentor. "You're a genius." With a snap of his fingers, he conjured a chainsaw and pulled the cord, firing it up. "Nothing magic about this." Finn lowered the blade to the base of the tree, but no matter how hard he pressed, he couldn't even nick the trunk.

"It's not working," he said, sending the chainsaw back to where it came from.

"Only a blessing can break a curse," a smooth voice said.

Finn and Theodor pivoted to find Damian Bordeaux glowing behind them like some kind of white-winged lighthouse. "How would you know?" Finn asked. "You've had your nose up the Devil's ass for centuries. Excuse me if I don't trust that the goose feathers and incandescence you're putting off isn't a highly tuned illusion."

"Can't you feel it, Finn? This tree is cursed. It's surrounded by dark energy. Even the roots under our feet are cursed. Only divine intervention can undo the damage. I can show you." He pointed at the tree. "I can do it."

Finn groaned. "We don't need your—"

"Please!" Theodor said, cupping his hand over Finn's mouth. "We would appreciate your help."

Damien stepped forward and raised his hands toward the heavens. Finn pushed Theodor's hand away and curled his lip in disgust as the angel mumbled a prayer that made him glow more brightly. Where did this guy get off playing the angel after what he'd done to Hope? When he was still a fallen angel, he'd deceived her, played with her emotions. And now, he acted like those actions occurred in the distant past rather than days ago. Redeemed or not, he should have to pay for his crimes. Finn's only recompense was that the guy was barred from Revelations too. No angels allowed. Only Soulkeepers.

Glowing like a star, Damien lowered his hands toward the bark but stopped short when the tree began to change. A human-shaped knot formed like a cancer on the trunk. Damien hesitated, as confused as Finn about what was happening.

"Theodor, what is that?" Finn asked.

"I-I don't know. There was no one else where I was," Theodor said. "Damien, finish this! Nothing good can come from the other side of that bark."

But he was too late. Like a pimple popping, the bark split and a blur of hot pink hair whooshed past the angel. In a flash, Kirsa's fist connected with Finn's jaw. Theodor cast a card toward her, and she froze, her hand reaching for Finn's throat. Finn ran to Theodor's side.

"That won't hold." Theodor shook his head. He turned Damien back toward the tree. "Continue. Don't stop, no matter what."

The angel made no comment as he began again, raising his hands toward the sky.

Finn regarded Kirsa in her temporary catatonic state. "What was she doing in the tree?" Finn asked, his skin prickling.

"I don't know." Theodor smoothed his mustache.

"But... this means something," Finn pressed. "Kirsa has been helping Lucifer for weeks. If she's here, it means Lucifer has been here too! He must have sent her through. That's why she wasn't with him and Ravenguard at the warehouse."

"Lucifer can't set foot on hallowed ground," Theodor said. But the words seemed to tempt fate. A dark fog rolled into the cemetery and coalesced on the pebbled pathway a few feet in front of them: Lucifer and Ravenguard.

"Correction, this *was* hallowed ground. Now it's mine." Lucifer raised his hands and released a pulse of dark energy toward the tree. Damien swiveled but couldn't dodge the blast in time. Pummeled by Lucifer's power, he broke apart into a spray of shimmering light that rained down at the base of the tree.

"No!" Finn yelled. He'd never been a fan of Damien's, but he didn't want him dead. How would he explain this to Hope? How else would they fix the tree?

Reflexively, Finn shielded himself while Theodor's hand gripped his arm. He had a heartbeat to digest that Lucifer had raised his hands again and the look on his face was pure death. And then they were gone, incorporeal and traveling through space at Theodor's direction. Finn didn't know where the magician was taking him, but he knew this: they'd failed. Lucifer now had access to the bridge to Nod.

Wherever they were going, he needed to find a way to contact Hope. Finn and Theodor had made a mistake, and the greatest consequences were still to come.

❧ 2 ❧

REVELATIONS

M ike Carson had never intended to come back to Revelations. Even the thought of roaming these halls again, a place where he'd suffered and drowned at the hands of resilience instructor Kirsa Hildburg, seemed inconceivable. Yet here he was. Not only walking the halls but also training in them, participating again. Crazy how life could turn on a dime. He'd wanted normalcy. What he got was a pedestal with his name on it.

"Try again," Hope said. "Push yourself. You need to move faster." She hurled an apple at him. Pressed into the meat of his palm, the triquetra pendent Hope had given him pulsed. The blessed object came alive inside his fist, sending an arc of razor-sharp light over his knuckles. It was a chakram of pure energy, a circular weapon that drew on the power of the heavens above. He had no business wielding it.

His blow sliced through half the apple as it flew past him, not deep enough to cut in half. Hope winced.

"I'm moving as fast as I can," Mike told her, wiping sweat

from his brow. "I'm a three-sport athlete, Hope. I'm not dragging ass over here."

She picked another apple from the basket. "No. I get that. You're fast for a human." She frowned. "But you're not human anymore. Healers—all Soulkeepers—are naturally faster and more agile than any human alive. It's part of our genetics."

"I guess my genetics haven't kicked in yet." He thumped his chest. What did she want from him?

"When you move, try to connect with the base of who you are. Open yourself up to the light. Accept everything good and bad about yourself and channel that into your blow."

Mike stopped and stared at her in unveiled annoyance. "I have no idea what the hell you are talking about." They were in the armory, the same place where Kirsa had once tortured him hour after hour. To his left, there was a bloodstain on the mat of the fighting ring. He was almost certain that was his blood. He remembered Kirsa stabbing him there.

This place left him rattled. No, he didn't want to open himself up in here. In fact, if it was possible for a soul to erect reinforced steel walls, Mike had those suckers in place times three. "If I'm off my game, this place ain't helping." He pointed to the bloodstain.

Hope tossed the apple she was holding straight up and caught it in her hand. "I have bad memories of this place as well. That's why it's the perfect place to train. When you face the Devil or his devotees, the situation is never optimal. You might be weak or injured. You'll probably be too hot or too cold or wearing the wrong clothes. Your battles won't take place in a controlled environment. Believe me. I know."

Mike groaned and shook his head. "You don't know. You were born for this, trained for this from the time you could walk. You have parents who did this before you." He straightened and moved his neck in an exaggerated circle. "You had your own angel following you around like a puppy dog. That's not me. I don't belong here. I don't want to do this."

"Mike..."

"No. Listen to me." He charged her, finger pointing at her chest. "I don't have parents. I have an aunt who is fifty-two years old this year and is the only family I got. I can almost guarantee she isn't eating right with me away—won't waste the food budget on herself. I have a truck that needs fixin', a job that needs doin', and I live in a house with paint peeling off the siding. *I* didn't ask for this. So excuse me if I'm not performing to expectations." Mike opened his fist and removed the triquetra. He looped the chain over his head to return it to his neck. "I'm done for the day."

Hope grumbled, "No way. We have so much more to do. You will never survive against a demon given the shape you're in."

Ignoring her, he headed for the creaky metal stairs that led to the platform overlooking the training ring and the only exit to the main floor of Revelations.

"Mike," she called. "I know this is a lot. I didn't mean to be critical."

He paused at the door. All he wanted to do was get out of there, away from the weapons, the scent of dried blood, and his own deficiencies. Couldn't she see he wasn't cut out for this? "I need some time."

"I've never trained anyone before," she said. "As soon as we are off the island, Gabriel will help you the same way he helped me. He's better at this than I am."

There was a note of regret in her voice. She'd tried hard to teach him, and Mike had taken out all of his frustrations and insecurities on her. It wasn't her fault God had chosen him to take over for her. Or did Fate choose him? As he understood it, he was born with the Soulkeeper gene, which was science, not magic. He turned back toward her. Hope was a friend. He couldn't let her dangle like this.

"No," he said firmly. "I didn't mean it like that. You didn't do anything wrong." He rubbed the back of his neck. "I'm not sure I'm cut out for this. Maybe whoever decides these things has the wrong guy." There, he said it. There had to be some mistake. Deep in his heart, he didn't feel right about this. Couldn't she tell he was an imposter?

Propping the wicker basket on her hip, Hope began collecting the apples they'd used for practice. For a long time, she didn't say anything, and Mike wondered if she'd heard him. But once she'd tossed the last one in, she turned toward him.

He stepped to the metal railing. It was weird, looking down on her from the upper platform of the metal stairs. It was a position of superiority, only he had nothing on Hope. She was brave and accomplished and had a future. She'd probably attend some fancy college and get an overpriced degree to do something vitally important for humanity. He needed to do what he needed to do to feed himself and his aunt. He didn't have choices. She and the others, they were from a different world. She didn't understand.

"There's something I have to tell you," she said tentatively.

"I'm listening."

Her eyes might as well have been made of diamonds the way her stare cut right through him. "You have a choice."

"Huh?"

She made a grunt deep in her throat. "I was born a Healer. You were made one. That means you are a potential until you are initiated by the immortals."

"What does that mean? Initiated?"

"It means to achieve full Healer status, you need to cross over to the In-Between—that's a different realm, a place between Heaven and Earth—where you will be tested. You'll only become the Healer if you're worthy. I can't tell you more than that because I don't know more. Malini never talks about her experience." She sighed. "I did go through a trial when I earned my current powers. But it wasn't the same thing. I've heard it's different for everyone anyway." She smoothed the hem of her T-shirt.

"Where does the choice part come in?" Mike chewed his bottom lip.

"I think... if you don't complete the initiation or you tell Gabriel no, I think the Healer status passes to someone else. The Soulkeepers can't operate without a Healer. God *eventually* finds a way to replace you."

"Eventually." Mike couldn't miss the way she'd stressed the word.

"It will take time. Time we don't have."

Mike snorted. "That's not my problem."

Hope climbed the metal stairs, her feet stomping with each step, and met him at the top. "Finn didn't make it through the guardians at the gate. He's not a Soulkeeper anymore."

"So you said."

"He's not a Soulkeeper anymore because of what he did... for you." She said the last through her teeth.

Mike balked, narrowing his eyes at her. Where did she get off blaming him for Finn's choices? He had no control over the guy. He certainly hadn't asked Finn to do what he did. He cursed. "None of what Finn did was because of me!" His voice rose with each word and his head felt hot.

Hope pushed him in the chest and he took a step back.

"Seriously? You're going to wash your hands of any responsibility for Finn's predicament?"

"Responsibility? Why would I be responsible for Wager's predicament?" Now he was angry. "Finn did what he did for Theodor and Wendy. I might as well have been along for the ride. In case you haven't noticed, we haven't exactly been best bros lately. Not since the day he got me involved with this place. If anyone is responsible for what's happening to you now, it's Finn."

"You were invited to this school because Finn was looking out for you. Yes, Revelations turned out to be a horrible experience, but Finn didn't know that. He thought he was helping you."

"Almost killed me." Mike used his fist to brace his chin and cracked his neck.

"Yes, Kirsa almost killed you, and she would have succeeded if Finn and the rest of us hadn't saved your ass." Hope's grip on the edge of the wicker basket tightened until her knuckles turned white. "The only reason Lucifer targeted you was because he knew you were Finn's friend. He was trying to flush us out. And it worked. Finn risked his life to save you. If it weren't for him, we wouldn't have had your body here to put your soul back into. Ever think of that? That had nothing to do with saving Theodor."

A heavy feeling formed in Mike's chest. He remembered seeing Finn locked in Kirsa's grip. That dumbass had challenged Lucifer to try to save him and Wendy. He scowled and shook his head. He didn't want to hear this.

"Yeah, you're starting to connect the dots now, aren't you? Good, I'll keep going." Hope wagged her finger in the air. "Finn put those spells into his skin so he'd be strong enough to perform the ritual that brought you, Wendy, and Theodor back to Earth. Not only did he save your body, he saved your soul."

"I'll buy him a fruit basket." Mike sneered. "He did those things for Wendy. If it had been me alone, he wouldn't have bothered." He never asked Finn to do any of those things. Any sane person would have run the other way in those circumstances. Finn knew what he was getting into. There was no way to make something like that up to another person. What did she expect him to do?

"Save the sarcasm. You don't believe that for a minute. Finn loves you like a brother. He always has." Mike opened his mouth, but she shut him down. "I'm not done! All of what Finn did for you, it corrupted his soul. It's the reason he's not a Soulkeeper anymore."

"Oh?" Mike shifted uncomfortably.

"And because he was performing the spell to bring you back, he wasn't helping us with our mission, which I believe is why I'm not the Healer anymore. So our already small team is down a Horseman and a Healer—"

"Because of me?"

"Because of you."

Mike stared at her for a beat, her sharp features becoming ugly with her anger. She was right and he knew it, but he wasn't ready to admit as much. It was a lot of weight to bear on his shoulders.

"So, you can choose not to be initiated as the Healer." Her head shook in disgust. "You can deny what you've been called to do and go back to working construction and having a normal life, whatever that means. But at least accept responsibility for putting the rest of us in a deadly position." Hope stepped in closer until the basket in her arms hit him in the stomach. "Lucifer is still out there. I have power but not like I used to. I'm too weak now to face him alone. Paul is still crippled. Jenny is a Helper and can't fight. That leaves Damien, if he doesn't ascend to Heaven, Jayden, and the instructors who, aside from Ms. D, haven't faced demons yet because they were too busy adjusting to a completely new life in the real world. Untrained. Leaderless. Not exactly optimal when you're up against the ultimate evil." Her words stung and the heaviness in Mike's chest was almost to the point he couldn't breathe.

"I see your point," he said, clearing his throat.

"Do you? Because there's one more thing you need to think about."

He didn't want to know. He really didn't. "What?" he asked.

"Lucifer knows who you are and where you live. Where your aunt lives. We've been protecting her but if he gets much stronger, who knows if it will hold. He used you once, Mike. I'm fairly sure he won't hesitate to use you again."

His jaw dropped, memories of Hell flooding his brain. The burning, the anguished souls. He rubbed his eyes. "I don't want this. I don't want any of this. Tell Gabriel I pass. God can give it to someone else."

She stepped back from him, a look of absolute disgust on her face. Grabbing the door handle, she threw it open with unnecessary force. It slammed against the doorstop, then bounced back. She held it open with her foot. "Tell him yourself. I'm going to find Victoria. It's time for us to hit the road. Once we're off the island, you can talk to Gabriel directly about your decision. If you're not going to be our Healer, there's no sense in wasting our time training you."

She stormed out, allowing the door to close slowly behind her.

✣ 3 ✣

THE DEVIL'S DILEMMA

Lucifer needed to feed again. The power he'd used to fight the Soulkeepers and that traitor Damien had left his cheek and thigh aching and his illusion in need of repair. It had been a mistake to pause to nourish himself after the battle in the warehouse, damaged or not. But Hope's trick with the vines had taken the life of one of his hunters, Applegate, and he was afraid he'd lose Ravenguard too if he didn't care for him. Even with the meal, Ravenguard showed signs of strain. Beside him, the hunter's fangs were extended and his face sagged around rheumy, vacant eyes. If he didn't know better, he'd think the man was grieving his long-time partner. But of course that couldn't be the case. You had to have a heart to grieve someone, and Ravenguard was far beyond such vital organs.

He should have known Theodor would try to close the portal. The magician was smart enough to understand the implications, even if he was too slow to finish what he started. Luck was on his side. He'd shown up before Damien could do any real damage.

"Bring us someone to eat," he said to Kirsa, who was huddled against the chipped plaster-and-brick wall of a mausoleum, conspicuously silent. Her clothes were charred and stained and she blinked as if the light was too bright for her. She raised her chin. *Dead inside*, he thought. If he blew in her ear, would the wind howl in the empty cavity that once held her soul? Good. It was about time he broke her spirit.

With a shiver, the woman found her voice. "You," she said through her teeth. "You pushed me into that tree. Do you know where I've been?" She pointed her finger toward the tree accusingly.

"I have an inkling." He gave her a dark look but backed off, allowing her room to speak. Once she confirmed what he suspected, he'd make her do his bidding.

"It was dark. So dark. A desert filled with thorns. It took me ages to make my way blindly down the path to the city. A ghost town. Empty buildings and empty cages. Filthy cages. There was nothing there. No food. No water. It was Hell!"

"No. Not Hell but close to it. It's a place called Nod. A very important place that has been hidden from me for a long time." He rubbed his hands together slowly. "Tell me more. I need details. Did you see where Theodor was staying?"

Kirsa shook her head, the spark returning to her eyes with her burgeoning anger. "If you wanted to know, you should have gone yourself! I'm not telling you anything. I'm not your guinea pig." She crossed her arms and started for the gate.

Lucifer stilled, and when he spoke again, his voice was quiet and his thoughts were lethal. "You signed your soul over to me. You will do as I please." With a twist of two fingers, he stopped her in her tracks, her body tensing under his control, unable to advance.

She whirled to face him, her teeth clenched, her bottom lip trembling.

"The dilemma I face, Ms. Hildburg, is if I cross over this bridge, I may not be able to return. Believe me, if I could have gone myself, I would have, but alas your help was required." He gestured toward himself and she slid along the pathway without moving a muscle. He stopped her when her face was only inches from his. "I'll tell you a secret. The tree helps me. Now that I know what's on the other side, I can use its proximity to strengthen my power. It is a thread connecting this world to the next, a tiny tear in the fabric that separates realms. But for me to come into my full power, I'll need more than a tear—I'll need a gate. I'll need ancient magic, strong enough to break my curse and widen this tear into a hole big enough to merge worlds. Still, this is a start." He swept a hand toward the tree. A bit of drool oozed from the corner of Kirsa's mouth and he loosened his grip on her, allowing her to swallow.

Ravenguard sniffed, looking like he might keel over from exhaustion at any moment. "Where do we find this ancient magic powerful enough to merge worlds?"

Rubbing his jaw, Lucifer wished he had a Scotch and a young soul to ease his own growing fatigue. But, he didn't dare leave the tree, not for anything. "It starts with the obsidian blade. Once we find it, we can capture the Healer and complete the ritual to end my curse. The energy we'll create will merge dimensions. All we need to do is destroy something of Heaven's using something of Hell's. A Healer's soul will make the perfect sacrifice. The obsidian blade, the perfect tool to do the job."

"Now that Hope is no longer the Healer, who will we use in the ritual?" Ravenguard asked.

"What's he talking about?" Kirsa asked softly, still recovering from his hold on her. She curled her lip. "Since when is Hope not the Healer anymore?"

Was Lucifer mistaken or did the woman seem disappointed? Although Kirsa was indestructible on the outside, he occasionally wondered if her inner workings were more vulnerable than she let on. "Did you have feelings for Ms. Laudner? Will you miss her?" he asked, tone dripping with contempt.

"No," she responded defensively. "But I didn't think it was possible to kill a Healer. Don't they come back or something? How did you do it?"

"Hmm. Well, she isn't dead, unfortunately. Damien decided to redeem himself using her power and become an angel of God again. Idiot fallen angel upset the balance between good and evil and cost her the Healer status. She's still alive, still a Soulkeeper, but not the Healer."

"Then who is?" Kirsa asked.

"That is the question, isn't it?" Lucifer scowled. "Even if we find the dagger, it will take some doing to find the new Healer. It could be anyone. It's possible that even the Soulkeepers don't know who it is yet." There was something else as well... one more ingredient he needed to awaken the ancient magic and complete the spell. But it wasn't his way to tip his hand. Letting Kirsa or anyone else know exactly what he needed was unwise and left him vulnerable.

Kirsa scoffed. "You said you need something of Heaven. Why not sacrifice Damien instead of the new Healer? You said he was redeemed. That means he's a full-fledged angel now, right? Sounds like something from Heaven."

Tired of her questions, Lucifer rolled his eyes. "You underestimate the angel's abilities. If I had the power to restrain or control an archangel, I would not have to perform the sacrifice."

"But—"

He stepped in closer to her, cutting her off. "Enough! Ravenguard and I are hungry and require rest. You will find us souls to consume and bring them here. Go, now."

She ran a hand through her hot pink hair, and Lucifer made note of her sunken cheeks and the wear her clothing had sustained during her time in Nod. With a curse, he realized he needed her strong as well. "The bus is in the same place it was before. Clean up and get yourself something to eat." He handed her a wad of cash. "I doubt you'll find anyone of value if you remain dressed like that."

Eyes widening, she snatched the money from his hand and bolted for the exit without another word.

"I won't take that personally," Lucifer mumbled around a wry smile.

"My lord, about the dagger," Ravenguard said, looking tired. The man staggered and Lucifer caught him by the shoulders.

"Come. Rest near the tree." Lucifer led him to the patch of grass near the roots of the giant oak, which was now a portal to another world. Gently, he helped him lie down. He wasn't sure exactly what was happening to Ravenguard, but his health had deteriorated since Applegate's death. Were they connected somehow, or was it grief that yellowed his skin and darkened the area under his eyes? At the moment, he looked like a fresh corpse.

"When she died, something of me went with her," he whispered in answer to the unasked question.

"Oh, Perhaps all those years on the island bonded the two of you." The Devil perused Ravenguard, analyzing the dark stuff he was made of. "Never mind. Whatever the cause of this ailment, I will not allow you to end until I have what I want." Lucifer placed a hand on the hunter's chest and passed a dark seed of power into him. It left Lucifer even weaker, but the expense couldn't be helped.

Ravenguard groaned and curled on his side. His eyes closed. He winced in pain.

"You were saying about the dagger?" Lucifer leaned his head closer.

The hunter blinked rapidly and grimaced. His voice was a burly thread when he answered. "When the wind blows just right, I can smell it."

"You smell the dagger? Here? Now?" Lucifer looked right, then left.

"Not always, only when the wind blows."

Lucifer tensed. "Are you sure?"

"As sure as a hunter can be. It is the same scent as was on the mattress in the house in Colorado. It smells of sin and darkness, sulfur and arsenic." The old man's voice slipped away, his eyes closed again, and Lucifer felt his consciousness slip through his fingers. His body drifted into a deep sleep. Lucifer was tempted to force him awake, but in Ravenguard's weakened state, he was afraid the magic necessary to do so would end him. Whatever effect Applegate's death had on Ravenguard must be ameliorated. Rest was necessary. Lucifer needed the hunter. He'd wait until Kirsa was back with sustenance and have the man feed before he probed further.

But if Ravenguard's senses were to be believed and he truly smelled the obsidian blade on the wind, that meant one of two things: either the blade was close but not too close, perhaps hidden in one of the businesses or homes outside the wall of the cemetery, or the blade was here, shrouded by Soulkeeper magic. Either Theodor or Victoria Duvall must have cloaked it. That would explain why Lucifer could not smell it, but the hunter could. As admissions counselor, he was partly immune to the magic of Veil Island. This immunity was why Juliette's song had little effect on Ravenguard and he was the only one other than the Devil who could overpower Kirsa.

Lucifer stood and sniffed the air experimentally, but all he could detect were the smells of the city: Cajun cooking, beignets, the remnants of alcohol and vomit from Bourbon Street, all layered under vehicle exhaust and suspended in lingering humidity. Closer still, he smelled the sweetness of flowers left at a few of the graves, and under it all, the plaster and dried bones of the graves themselves. Not a hint of obsidian.

As he scanned the mausoleums, a plan formed in his brain, ugly and genius. It curled the corners of his mouth. As soon as he was strong enough, he'd make this cemetery his home. A little magic, a little sorcery, and the humans would forget it ever existed. He'd erect a cabin here, close to the tree, and leave only to use Juliette to attract new souls. He'd grow stronger here.

Yes, it was all clear now. New Orleans had welcomed its newest resident. If the obsidian blade was here, the Soul-keepers would do anything to retrieve it. The one thing he could count on when it came to Soulkeepers was their frustrating propensity toward self-sacrifice. One of them would come for it. They'd risk their life to keep it from him. And when they came, he would be watching, waiting. They'd lead him right to it.

He leaned back in the grass next to Ravenguard, his head resting in the web of his threaded fingers, and smiled at the clear blue sky. The trap was set. All he had to do was wait.

❧ 4 ❦
THE SECRET SOCIETY

Finn stumbled forward as he and Theodor materialized on a sidewalk near a weathered yellow building with a wrought iron balcony. Although he was proficient at disseminating now, he'd never done it with someone else in the driver's seat. Being broken apart and towed through space and time was a disorienting experience, and he caught himself on his knees, breath coming in quick gulps as his heart pounded in his chest.

"I had to get us out of there," Theodor said. "Whatever he did to Damien, Lucifer would do far worse to us."

"Where are we?"

"Dumaine Street. Not far from the cemetery, but far enough." Theodor glanced toward the setting sun. The gas lamps along the buildings flickered to life in the twilight.

"Is Damien dead?" Finn recalled the look on the angel's face as he'd blown apart into a shower of sparkling light.

"Angels are immortal. I do not believe what Lucifer did to him is permanent, but I have a feeling it will be some time before we see Damien again."

"Great. So… why are we here?" Finn frowned at a shop window to their left. It was filled with voodoo paraphernalia. The shop door was open, and Finn spied a selection of carved wooden statues and hanging herbs. A dark and unsettling vibe made the hair on the back of his neck stand on end. Were those dried entrails? A shrunken head?

"This city is one of the oldest in America. These walls harbor *old* magic. Voodoo magic." Theodor took a step toward a separate door to the right, lit with a gas lamp. A few mail-boxes were built into the wall, each with their own number. Apartments. "We need a place to stay and this place is safer than most from Lucifer's power. Come with me."

"How do you know there's a room for rent?" Finn didn't see any signs.

"Perhaps I read an ad in the paper this morning while you were getting ready," Theodor said. Finn narrowed his eyes on his mentor. There just so happened to be an ad for a rental in the very building with voodoo magic in its walls? He didn't think so.

"What the hell is going on?"

Finn and Theodor whirled to find Wendy standing beside them. "Wendy! You're back!" Finn jogged toward her and swept her into a hug, which she thankfully returned.

"You shaved your head!" she said, her smile widening.

Finn ran a hand along the smooth skin of his crown. "Uh, yeah."

"I like it! You look tough."

"So, the transition was successful… for both you and Mike?"

"Ms. D put me back into my body on the island and lo and behold, I got kicked out again. Ended up here. Sorry, I don't know about Mike. I saw a flash of Ms. D hovering over me, and then I was gone."

Theodor rubbed his chin. "It's possible Michael returned home. Finn, when you were ejected, you said you thought of me and arrived by my side. Michael would likely think of his aunt."

Finn agreed, which meant that Wendy, for the second time, had thought of him. He smiled at her, warmth blooming in his chest, and pulled her into his side. Her freckles fanned out across her nose when she looked up at him. Sweet.

Behind them, the door to the building opened with a long, slow, creak. Theodor hadn't even knocked. "Can I help you?" The foyer inside was dark. Finn could barely make out a silhouette beyond the door, but the voice was distinctly male, a double bass that seemed to reverberate in the narrow space.

"We're here to rent the apartment," Theodor said.

"Come in. I've been expecting you. Watch your step." A dark hand pointed toward the legs of a coat rack that extended into the walkway.

Theodor entered first and Finn followed, wondering how the man could possibly be expecting them. Had Theodor planned for this? Why? If he'd believed he could close the portal, why would he need an apartment?

There was a click as Wendy closed the door behind her and the dull lights took over for the gas lamps that lit the streets. Finn blinked until his eyes adjusted. The man inside was dressed in a flowing white shirt and khaki linen pants. Despite the dim lighting, he wore sunglasses, and it didn't take long for Finn to guess he was either fully blind or close to it.

"I am Dr. Louis Beauvoir, landlord of this building and owner of Beauvoir's Voodoo Emporium." Finn wondered what kind of doctor the man was.

Theodor extended his hand. "Theodor Florea, and this is Finn and Wendy, my students."

"I smell magic on you like ozone after a rain. What have you three been up to?"

"Fighting with the Devil," Theodor said flatly.

Dr. Beauvoir grinned slowly and broke into a laugh. "A worthy pastime. Come. I'll show you the apartment. You do know it's a studio flat? Plenty of square footage but only the one room." He turned in Wendy's general direction, his nostrils flaring.

"That will be sufficient," Theodor said.

They followed him to a set of doors at the back of the building and up a flight of stairs. "There's a small courtyard out back. We share with the neighbors. No magic allowed."

"I understand." Theodor tugged at his collar. The stairwell was hot and dark. At the top was a metal door that looked heavy and out of place. The man produced a key and let them in.

"Wow," Finn heard Wendy say from behind him. He was thinking the same thing.

The space inside was wide open, with a wall of windows that faced the balcony. Aside from a galley kitchen and a single bathroom with a pedestal sink, there was nothing but space. Not even a bed. There was, however, a small loft.

"You have access to the roof. View of the quarter and the river. It's twelve hundred a month," Dr. Beauvoir said.

Theodor walked to the windows, his lanky silhouette breaking the light from the street. "We'll need protective wards," he said. "Ones that our enemies cannot detect as our own."

"I already have a few in place, but if you're expecting me to keep out the Devil... Fifteen hundred dollars per month. And the rule is if you shed blood in this space, you cleanse the area of all negative energy after you finish."

"Deal." Theodor reached out and shook the man's hand, then produced a wad of cash from his pocket.

"A pleasure to have another practitioner on the property. Welcome." The man nodded and retreated from the room with careful, measured steps.

Once the door was closed, Finn spoke up. "I thought you were confident you could destroy the tree this morning? When did you have the time or the inclination to line this place up?"

Theodor glanced at Wendy who was hugging herself in front of the windows.

"I didn't line this place up. I saw an ad for it in the paper this morning, and when I disseminated from the cemetery, it was the first place to pop into my head."

"But Beauvoir said he'd been expecting you."

Theodor shrugged. "He's the preeminent voodoo practitioner in New Orleans. We've never met before, and I didn't call to say we were coming if that's what you're wondering."

"But if that's true..." Finn frowned. "Creepy as hell."

"Powerful," Theodor said. "Exactly what we need to mask our whereabouts, especially once we start practicing again."

Wendy pivoted to face them. "So, this has been fun, chaps, but I guess this is when we talk about how I get home. Unfortunately, I don't have any money or power, so... Can one of you spring for a bus ticket? I don't think calling my parents will go over well."

A wave of disappointment washed over Finn. He liked Wendy a lot and had hoped she would stay for a while. But he supposed she had to go home to her parents.

"I'd like you to stay and help us," Theodor said.

"What?" Wendy's eyebrows shot up and Finn's head whipped around.

Theodor glanced between the two of them. "You may not be a Soulkeeper, Wendy, but my experienced eye tells me you have the potential to practice magic. If you'd like to learn, I would like to teach you."

Wendy's mouth dropped open. "Are you serious? Me? You think I could learn magic?"

"Yes." Theodor grinned. "You were able to learn to fly on the island. Soulkeeper or not, you have potential for the extraordinary. I can teach you the craft."

Finn's stomach twisted. "No. I don't think this is a good idea."

"What? Finn!" Wendy shot him a scathing look.

"It's dangerous. There are side effects... consequences."

"Dangerous?" She laughed. "How is it any more dangerous than falling off a high wire or starting myself on fire? After Revelations, I imagine magic will be a piece of cake." She pushed her hair out of her eyes and tucked it behind her ear.

"I didn't shave my head," he blurted. "Using magic did this to me!"

Wendy balked at that. For a few minutes, she stared at him, taking him in. Then she stepped closer and cupped his face in her hands, turning it left, then right. "Your eyes are different too. Silver..."

Finn looked down at his toes.

"They're beautiful." His gaze snapped up to find her smiling. She placed a kiss on his forehead. "I'm staying."

At once, Theodor clapped his hands together and announced, "It's settled. We will train here and become a coven. Lucifer won't stand a chance against us."

"You don't have to do this," Finn whispered and touched his

forehead to hers, her brown hair falling like curtains on either side of his face.

"No, I don't. But I want to." Her breath smelled like cinnamon gum. Finn breathed it in and allowed the happiness that was filling him to creep like a blush all the way to his eyes.

She pulled back abruptly and looked at Theodor. "Hey, before we become a coven, can we get something to eat? I'm starving. This body hasn't eaten in weeks." Incredibly, Finn hadn't noticed until then how peaky her complexion looked.

He held out his hand to her. "I know just the place."

"Finn?" Theodor cast him a sideways glance.

But as soon as her fingers met his, he carried her away.

* * *

AFTER A MEAL THAT STARTED WITH GUMBO AND ENDED WITH pecan pie and plenty of flirting in the middle, Finn returned to the apartment with Wendy to find that Theodor had done some decorating while they were gone. There were three chairs: one made of ornately carved wood, one plush leather, and one upholstered in a floral fabric with sleek nailhead trim. There were beds too—one upstairs in the loft for Wendy and old-timey ones with curtains for privacy in the main room for Finn and Theodor.

"Excellent. Where did you find all this?" Finn asked Theodor while Wendy tested the floral chair.

Theodor cleared his throat. "Found the chairs in a local antique shop. The rest I conjured. That was the best I could do... left to my own devices." The magician gave him a harsh look. Conjured products came from somewhere, which meant the beds were stolen. He was sure the magician would have preferred to obtain them the traditional and legal way but clearly couldn't do so on his own.

"Sorry about that," Finn said guiltily. "Wendy and I needed time to catch up, and I thought you'd want some time to yourself anyway." In fact, Finn hadn't thought of Theodor's feelings at all. It was unlike him. Only now did he consider the man might have wanted to go too.

"In any case, I must dine now. I'll leave you to settle in." If he was upset with him, Finn couldn't tell. His face was thoroughly impassive, his complexion waxy again. With a curt gesture in lieu of goodbye, Theodor departed through the front door.

Wendy stood and stretched. "Thanks for dinner. I'd love to stay up and chat until dawn, but I'm beat. Going to Hell and back will do that to you."

He smiled and kissed her on the cheek. "Go lie down. I'll still be here when you wake up." She disappeared up the stairs to the loft bedroom.

Finn turned the leather chair to face the window and sat down, suddenly exhausted himself. He wasn't sure why he chose the leather, but everything in him knew this chair was his. The floral was Wendy's, and without a doubt, the wood was Theodor's.

As he watched the streetlights flicker outside his window, a bitter taste filled his mouth. His time with Wendy had distracted him from the day's events, but now, in the quiet and stillness of being alone, it all came back to him. He'd been rejected from the island. He was no longer a Soul-keeper. Hope must have tried to call him by now, to assure him she was successful with Mike and to make sure he was okay, but he'd been cast from the bus with nothing but the clothes on his back. His phone was still on board. She'd have no way of reaching him or even knowing where he ended up. No matter. With magic, he would rectify that situation post haste.

He held out one hand and concentrated on a symbol that resided over his heart. It was a five-pointed star, the representation of conjure, and it allowed him to fold space. This was how he'd summoned the chainsaw in the cemetery. He'd concentrated on the thing he wanted, activated the symbol, then plucked the item from an array of choices that appeared before him like pins on a Google Map. It took more energy to pull something from far away than it did to retrieve it from the next room.

He concentrated on his backup earpiece and activated the symbol. The electronic device appeared to him in his room in Beaverton, where he'd left it, next to his gaming console. He experienced a brief pang of homesickness for his father, before sweeping the device into his metaphysical hand and returning fully to the leather chair. He tucked the earpiece into his ear and tapped. HORU formed beside him.

"Finn! I've been so worried!" She blinked large anime eyes at him, her tail wagging.

"Sorry, HORU. When I was... ejected from Revelations' bus, my earpiece stayed on board. I'm only now getting a chance to check in."

"Why would Bus eject you?"

Finn suppressed a giggle at how HORU thought of the bus as a sentient being. As an artificial intelligence, she often did not understand why other systems weren't as smart or as sophisticated as she was. "It's complicated. It has to do with magic."

"Oh." She pressed a holographic finger to her lips. HORU never understood magic.

"HORU, I also left my phone on board. Can you check if I have any messages or missed calls?"

Her ears twitched. "No. Your last call was from your father, three days ago. You called him back. The call lasted three minutes."

Finn bristled. "Are you sure? No texts or messages? Nothing from Hope?"

"No. Nothing."

But how was that possible? It had been hours since he was unable to pass through the dragons to get onto the island. Surely Hope would call to make sure he was okay. She could have called from the island's one working phone or used HORU to contact him or even taken a trip back to this realm on the bus to text or call. Why would she leave him hanging?

Unless she was too busy thinking about Damian to care what happened to him. He rubbed his stomach, which had started to ache. Maybe the Soulkeepers were glad to be rid of him. He'd broken the rules after all. Ms. D had looked terrified when she'd found out about his tattoos. They were probably celebrating not having to deal with him anymore. What could he contribute now that he was corrupted?

He scowled. "HORU, can you access the copy of your database on Bus?"

"Yes, Finn. The network we set up is still in place. The connection is slow, but it is there."

"Delete everything they have. Everything. The analysis of the scrolls, the data on the demons. I want the only copy to be right here with us." He pointed at his earpiece.

"This command cannot be undone."

"I know. Delete."

HORU stilled, her body blinking as she did what he asked

her to do. After several long moments, she gave him a wide grin. "Done. Is there anything else I can do for you tonight?"

Finn leaned back in his chair, brimming with smug satisfaction. "No. That will be all." He snorted as she blinked out of sight. The Soulkeepers had never appreciated him. Ms. D thought he was a kid and Hope treated him like he was disposable. Not anymore.

The Soulkeepers were about to learn what life was like without Finn Wager.

❧ 5 ❧
THE VISIT

Back on Veil Island, Hope Laudner waited to leave for the earthly realm. The sounds of Ms. D, Amuke, and Orelon doing a final check filtered through the window above the booth where she sat on the bus, and she could hear Fuse humming to herself in the driver's seat. People surrounded her. So why did she feel completely and utterly alone?

As disappointed as she was in Mike, she was equally disappointed in herself. She'd been the Healer for long enough to understand what he was going through. Why couldn't she find the words to help him? And if she couldn't help him, she had to convince him. They couldn't wait for another Healer, not when Lucifer had gained more power than they'd ever imagined and now had access to the portal Finn had opened.

"Hope, we have a problem." Jenny Pendleton appeared in the aisle and sat down across from her.

"What kind of problem?"

Jenny slid her tablet toward her, tapping on the database that held all the information on the demons they were targeting. HORU had scanned all the scrolls on the island to find students who were killed at Revelations. The team was now aware that students who Applegate and Ravenguard killed were cloned and possessed by demons, who reentered the students' lives seamlessly using the students' identities. Finn's AI unit had cross-referenced the students' previous addresses with public records and found where all 185 known demons now lived and what they did for a living. That list was imperative. Not only did it help the Soulkeepers prioritize their missions, it contained vital information on the enemy, especially now that they didn't have a Healer to offer guidance and direction.

"Where is the list?" Hope asked. The database was empty. No names appeared in the indexed catalog.

"They're gone. And before you ask, the backup is gone too. HORU is also gone. Finn's earpiece was left behind when he, uh..."

"Right. It didn't go with him when he was, er, removed from the bus. Same thing happened to Wendy when she was using HORU and was ejected."

"Well, I have the earpiece, but there is no one in it."

"Are you saying all the copies are gone?" Hope frowned. How was that even possible? They'd stored copies on several different devices.

"That's exactly what I'm saying." Jenny fiddled with the ends of her hair.

"You don't think that Finn..."

Jenny shrugged.

"He wouldn't do that to us."

"Have you talked to him since the, uh, incident?"

"No. There hasn't been time. I was training Mike and meeting with Ms. D and the council about what happened."

"Crap."

"What?"

"Well, Jayden and Paul didn't either. They said at breakfast that they felt awkward about it. They didn't want to embarrass him by calling attention to it."

Hope's eyes widened. "Calling attention to it? It's not a pimple. Finn was sucked out of the bus!"

Jenny shrugged. "I doubt Mike had time to text him either."

"So, basically Finn, wherever he is, thinks none of us care about him and has wiped HORU out of anger and resentment."

With a heavy sigh, Jenny said, "It's a theory."

The front door opened and Ms. D jogged on board. "Bus is ready. We'll drop Michael off in Beaverton, so he can do what he needs to do."

"That bastard," Jenny said under her breath.

Hope shook her head. "I tried my best. He honestly does not want to do this." She squirmed in her seat, more annoyed than ever that Mike planned to turn down his role as Healer as soon as he could meet with Gabriel. It left them all vulnerable.

"And after we drop off Mike?" Jenny asked.

"Then, we'll go on to New Orleans." Ms. D adjusted her glasses.

"Back there again?" Hope asked. They'd just left there and it was the last known whereabouts of Lucifer.

"Yes. Technothrob's website says Lucifer will be in Atlanta for a concert tonight. I want to retrieve the obsidian dagger from the place where I hid it while he's onstage. When it comes to Lucifer, it's always best to act when we know exactly where he will be. No surprises."

"Why move it?" Jenny asked. "I thought it was safe on hallowed ground."

"Yes, it is. Only, someone other than myself knows where it is, and I'm not sure I can trust that person."

Finn, Hope thought. *Now that he's not a Soulkeeper.*

"There's something you should know," Jenny said. Hope wanted to stop her. This looked bad, like Finn was sabotaging their success. She didn't want Ms. D or the others to think of Finn as the enemy. But before she could stop her, Jenny had handed the tablet to Ms. D.

The older woman shook her head. "Unbelievable. From friend to enemy in less than twenty-four hours. We need to get that blade."

"Let me talk to him," Hope said. "There must be some mistake." She met Ms. D's gaze and held it. The older woman's tough-as-nails exterior softened slightly. She wanted to believe in Finn as much as Hope did.

"Okay. But be careful." Knocking on the wall, she gave Fuse the go-ahead, then found a seat in the back near Orelon and Amuke, leaving Hope and Jenny to themselves.

"I hope you know what you're doing," Jenny said.

"Me too."

The moment the bus transitioned into the earthly realm, Hope texted Finn.

You okay? Where are you?

Several long minutes passed before her phone buzzed to indicate a return message: an address in New Orleans.

6

CONNECTIONS

Hope tipped her Uber driver and let herself out of the car in front of the address Finn had sent her. She'd come alone. Ms. D planned to retrieve the dagger, and everyone else was in waiting mode while Mike declined the Healer role and God called a replacement. They'd dropped him off at his aunt's house before coming to New Orleans. They were giving him space to do what he needed to do. Hope snorted bitterly. She'd never had space. She'd never had a choice. Secretly, she prayed Gabriel would refuse his resignation and knock some sense into him.

Still, the delay gave her time to meet up with Finn. She prayed she could find the words to earn his forgiveness and hopefully convince him to let them use HORU again.

The door opened of its own accord. "Would you like to come in, young lady?" a deep voice said. "I believe your friend is waiting for you upstairs."

"Uh, yes, I'm looking for Finn Wager?" She entered the dark foyer, tripping over the leg of a coatrack protruding into the narrow passageway. Lanky fingers caught her upper arm and sent a shock through her torso. She looked up into the cloudy eyes of a blind man. The door slammed shut, making her jump. Behind him was an open door with a sign for "Beauvoir's Voodoo Emporium." The room within brimmed with books and bones, wooden statues, herbs, stones, and other magical artifacts.

"Careful," he said, helping her to her feet. "This place is full of hazards if you don't watch your step." The smile he gave her was crooked and yellow and made her spine tingle. "Your friend is upstairs." He pointed toward stairs at the back of the hall.

"Thank you," she said, rubbing her nose against the scent of mold and old books. She hurried to the staircase and jogged to the second floor, knocking three times on a metal-plated door. It opened almost immediately.

"Well, well, well, if it isn't the girl I used to sleep next to every night," Finn said. He winked at her over a tight smile that didn't go all the way to his eyes.

She gave a light laugh and raised her eyebrows. "In a separate bed."

"Still worth a mention."

She decided there was only one way to start this conversation. "I'm sorry," she said. "I should have texted you sooner. There's been so much. I'm not the Healer anymore and we lost you." She shook her head. "I was overwhelmed."

He considered her, his gaze seeming to weigh the sincerity of her words. She must have passed inspection because his expression softened and he pulled her into a hug. "Come on in. It's just us. Wendy and Theodor went out to get provisions."

"Wendy?"

"After you put her back in her body, she came here. She's decided to stay. Theodor and I are teaching her magic."

"Magic? I don't understand…"

"Anyone can learn magic, Hope. You don't have to be a Soulkeeper to tap into the power all around us."

Dangerous, she thought but held her tongue. This conversation was not about chastising Finn. He ushered her into the apartment and closed the door behind her.

It was a charming flat with an open floor plan awash with natural light. To her right was a galley kitchen and to her left two beds and a set of stairs leading to a loft. "This is so different from downstairs. The voodoo shop is creepy. I think I saw a shrunken head in the window."

Finn laughed. "That's Walter. At least, Dr. Beauvoir calls it Walter. I've never asked if it's real. I don't want to know."

Hope raised an eyebrow. "So…" Where did she start? "I'm sorry about what happened to you. I wish I could have stopped it."

He shrugged. "What would you have done? I did what was necessary to rescue Theodor, Wendy, and Mike. If I could go back and do it all over again, I wouldn't change a thing."

That was surprising. She was expecting him to regret what he'd done considering the consequences.

"Did Mike make it home okay?" he asked.

Hope considered telling him what Mike was but thought better of it. What was the point if he planned to turn down the role of Healer anyway? Why muddy the waters with something that wouldn't matter? "Yes. He's fine. Home with his aunt."

"That's a relief."

Hope rubbed her palms together. "I came here for a reason, Finn. Ms. D said you could join the troupe again now that we're off the island. We need your skills, and she's committed to helping you undo the damage." She gestured at the skin of his arm where she knew some of his spells resided. In fact, Ms.

D had been hard-pressed to make such an offer, but Hope convinced her before she left the bus that it would be in the best interest of the Soulkeepers to keep Finn close. "Theodor is welcome as well. She'd never admit it, but I think she misses him."

Off balance, Finn staggered backward a step and took a seat in a lustrous brown leather chair. "Of all the things I thought you were coming here to say to me, this was not what I expected."

"No? Why not? You didn't think we'd kick you out of the show simply because you're not a Soulkeeper anymore. Everyone understands why you did what you did." She removed her purse from her shoulder and sat down in a wooden chair across from him. Oddly, there were only three chairs in the place, positioned in a circle at the center of the room. There was no coffee table, so she placed her bag on the floor near her feet.

"I can't. We can't." Finn's gaze darted around the empty apartment as if Wendy and Theodor were there in spirit.

"Why not?"

"I don't know how to tell you this, Hope, but Theodor and I failed to close the portal we opened."

"Huh?" Hope tried to wrap her mind around what he was saying. She knew that Finn had opened a portal to bring their friends back from Nod, but he'd also said Theodor made sure that it closed. What type of portal didn't close? The one he'd opened at the school had run its course in a matter of minutes.

"When I performed the ritual to bring Theodor back, we used a tree. An ancient tree. Very powerful. Theodor was using magic as well. Together we built a bridge between here and another realm."

"Nod." Hope remembered her mother and father telling her about the ugliness of the world between this one and Hell.

"Yes. I didn't know it at the time, but apparently it's a bad place."

Hope nodded. "It's close to Hell. I'm sure Lucifer was licking his lips when he heard about it at the warehouse."

"Well, Theodor couldn't close it, even with my help. And then Damien came."

"You've seen Damien?"

"Yeah. He showed up and tried to bless the tree. Said it was the only way to close it. But he never had a chance because Lucifer showed up."

All the air rushed from Hope's lungs. "But you all got away, right?"

"Yeah. Obviously." Finn shifted in his seat and took an interest in a loose thread at the hem of his T-shirt.

Slowly the feeling returned to Hope's extremities. Why had she reacted like that? Damien had lied to her. Angel or not, there was a lot that was still unsaid between them. She looked down at her fingers and tried to push all thoughts of the angel from her mind, especially the memories of being alone with him, the ones that made her feel like someone she loved had died.

"So, you guys couldn't close the portal. And Lucifer was there?" Her skin prickled. This was bad, but she wasn't sure how bad. It felt like she was missing something, like she hadn't quite put two and two together.

"Yes. So, you see, I can't go back to being part of Revelations' troupe until we figure out how to destroy the bridge. The three of us have formed a coven. We're going to fix this."

Hope allowed that to sink in for a moment. "Lucifer has control of the tree, doesn't he?"

"Yes. He's sent Kirsa through, obviously to test it, but I don't think he can go himself for some reason. I don't fully understand why."

"He can't leave Earth." Hope tipped her head back to stare at the ceiling. "If he leaves Earth before his curse is broken, the ancient magic may lock him out so that he can't return." She groaned and slapped her thighs. Her head pounded with the implications. "Why didn't you guys use more caution? You must have known what you were doing was dangerous." Despite her best efforts, her voice was rising. Not the best way to garner Finn's cooperation. She reined herself in.

"We *were* careful. I opened the portal on hallowed ground. I didn't realize what we were doing would desecrate it."

A dark, creeping thought came to her. "Hallowed ground? Where is this tree?"

"Saint Louis Cemetery."

All the blood rushed from Hope's face, and she had to grip the armrest of her chair to keep from falling out of it. "No."

"What's wrong?"

"That's where Ms. D hid the dagger."

Now it was Finn's turn to go white. Hope actually felt sorry for him. He looked like he might be sick. "She hid it where I told her to hide it." He cursed.

"Hallowed ground."

Finn swallowed hard enough for Hope to hear it. "I don't know how to tell you this, but Lucifer, Ravenguard, and Kirsa have taken over that cemetery."

"No."

"When we opened the portal, it desecrated the grounds. He has full access to it and has been guarding it since our first failed attempt to destroy the portal."

Hope stood and paced to the window, feeling sick to her stomach. "Do you think he's found the dagger?"

"I don't know. The three of us haven't had time to plan another attempt on the portal."

Pressing her forehead against the window, she tried to absorb the coolness from the glass, pulling long deep breaths into her lungs.

"What happens if Lucifer finds the dagger?" Finn asked.

"From what we know, if Lucifer sacrifices the Healer with the obsidian dagger, it will create a blast of metaphysical energy possibly strong enough to break his curse. That in and of itself would allow him to move between Hell and Earth unencumbered. But with the power of the tree in the mix, it's quite possible he could bring Hell here."

"What—what does that mean—bring Hell here?"

"It means a world flooded with hellhounds and demons. The veil between life and death will thin to the point of making them indistinguishable from one another. Every living person would instantly become a citizen of Hell."

Finn rubbed his head with both hands. "Not good."

"No. Not good."

"Wait. You said he needs the Healer. You're not the Healer anymore. That means, he doesn't have the ingredients for this spell, right?"

"I may not be the Healer anymore, but there is a Healer. There is always a Healer."

"And the Healer is...?"

Hope shook her head. There was no reason to tell Finn about Mike. No good could come of it. Mike wasn't going to accept the role and the more people who knew he was a potential, the greater the chance his life would be at risk. "No one knows. A Soulkeeper will have to be called and then accept the call. They'll need to pass an initiation. No one has done that yet."

"Damn. Whoever it turns out to be, we need to protect them. They may be all that stands between us and Hell on Earth."

"Oh, we will. Finding the new Healer is our top priority." It wasn't a lie. Hope removed her phone from her pocket, intending to text Ms. D but paused when Finn spoke up again.

"We need to get the dagger back." His jaw twitched.

"That's why we're here in New Orleans. Ms. D was going to move the dagger. She was afraid—" Hope stopped short.

"She was afraid because I knew where it was."

"It was a risk," she said quietly. "She wasn't sure about your intentions after the incident with you running away from us."

"I had to—"

"I know."

They stared at each other for a moment, and Hope saw her old friend Finn behind those strange silver eyes and that newly bald head. He was a good guy. Caring. Kind. There was no way he would do anything to hurt them.

"I don't know what to do, Finn. If, as you say, Lucifer is there, retrieving the dagger might be risky. Maybe it would be safer to leave it where it is."

"With Ravenguard on his side? He'll find it eventually. The man's a hunter. He can probably smell it."

"I need to talk to the council."

He put his hands on his thighs, his eyes narrowing. "Yeah. I'm sure you guys will come up with something."

"So, I can't convince you to join us again?"

He shook his head. "No."

Hope retrieved her purse, her phone firmly gripped in her

hand. "I'd better go. This is something I should explain to Ms. D in person." She headed for the door.

"Haven't you forgotten something?" Finn asked.

"Huh?" Hope turned back to him, confused.

"HORU." He handed her an earpiece. "Isn't that why you came?"

She shook her head, tears clouding her vision. "One of the reasons. Not the most important one."

"What's the most important one?"

"You. Our friendship." She shook her head. "I still care about you, Finn. You're my friend."

He looked down at his fingers and murmured "friend" under his breath. When he looked up again, she could feel the distance widen between them. "The earpiece has full access to all of HORU's functionality. If you ask her, she can repopulate the databases for you." He pointed to an identical earpiece in his own ear. "Of course, I have full access to her as well. But I don't mind sharing her."

She nodded. "Thank you. We needed this. It's going to help so much." She took a step forward and kissed him on the cheek.

"I think hero is the word you're looking for," he said, his cheeks reddening.

"Ha-ha. Maybe." With a strange ache in her heart like she might not ever see him again, Hope pulled open the door. "Goodbye, Finn. Talk to you soon?"

"Anytime."

She gave him a little nod and strode toward the exit. Someone had to warn the team. The dagger had been compromised.

7

AUNT MILLIE

M ike Carson pulled his aunt into a tight hug. He didn't think it was possible, but she seemed even smaller than when he'd left, nothing but skin and bones and a thin gray bun tied high on the crown of her head.

"Well, if it isn't my long-lost boy come to pay me a visit." She placed cold fingers on his cheeks and tilted his face down so she could look him in the eye.

"I'm sorry I didn't call, Aunt Millie. They have crazy rules at Revelations. This is the first break we've had since we went on tour."

"That's all right. It's just good to have you home." She dropped her bony hands, tucking them into the pockets of her dress. The garment looked big on her. It used to fit.

"You haven't been eating enough. You're wasting away," he said.

"Oh, bother. I have my cheese sandwiches. You know me."

For as long as he'd lived with her, Millie had displayed a fondness for overstuffed grilled cheese on white bread with Campbell's tomato soup on the side. She passed this off as a luxurious and healthy meal that made up for the fact that she hardly ate for the rest of the day.

"Well, now that I'm here, we'll have my favorite, okay?" Mike sat her down at the small Formica table and dug some chicken out of the freezer, still untouched for the entire time he'd been gone. He preheated the oven and moved to the pantry for some potatoes.

"Tell me how it's going," she said. "You could have knocked me over with a feather when I received your letter. My Michael, joining the circus."

He slid the chicken into the microwave and set the defrost function. "To be honest, the change took me by surprise too. It's like you always say, when opportunity knocks you've got to take it."

"The checks you send... they're too much. I don't need all that money. I've put it in the bank for you. You can have it anytime you want it. I haven't spent a dime."

He turned toward her, resting his hands on the back of his chair. They always sat in the same spots, which left his vinyl seat cracked from his above-average size. He hadn't realized that Revelations had been sending her checks. Jenny had mentioned taking care of her, but he'd assumed that meant protecting her from Lucifer, not paying the rent.

"I have plenty, Millie. That's all for you, to help out around here. You need to hire someone to paint this place, fix the roof and the stairs. Do you think I sent enough to cover that?"

Her eyes widened. "Lord knows I could buy a whole new house with what you sent me. But that should be for you, for college."

Michael had to turn away and close his eyes. They'd sent her a lot of money. This was good. *If* he could get her to use it. But then a thought crossed his mind. If he decided not to continue as the Healer, would he have to pay the money back?

"Revelations has a scholarship program. My college is covered. That money is for you." He said it toward the microwave door to reduce the likelihood of her detecting the lie.

She clapped her hands together. "Lordy, that job gives and keeps on giving. What are you doing for them anyway? What's your act?"

He thought for a minute. "Uh, it changes. Mostly illusions. They want me to take on more responsibility, but I'm questioning whether I should."

"Why wouldn't you? It seems like they've been treating you right. They must think you have what it takes to do more."

"Yeah, they do."

"Then why haven't you accepted the new position?"

He sighed. "I'm not sure I'm good enough. The people who did this before me were better suited for this type of thing. The last one had parents who were both... performers. She'd been training since childhood."

"Hmm." He recognized that throaty grunt she made. A lecture was coming.

"It isn't—"

"You think because we never had any money that you can't be as good as someone who has? No, you didn't have basketball lessons, but you played at the park from sunup to sundown. No coach. No rules. Whoever wanted to play you, you'd play. And when you made the Beaverton team, you were first string as a freshman."

"Basketball—"

"And track, and football. You have always had a God-given edge when it came to sports. God-given, Michael. It says in the

Bible not to hide your light under a bushel. You have an obligation to use the talents God gave you."

"But what if I'm not good enough? What if I make a mistake?" He pulled out the chair and sat down. "I'm comfortable the way things are."

She leaned back in her chair. "It sounds like you're afraid."

"In the circus, we perform dangerous acts with pyrotechnics and heights. If I advance before I'm ready and make a mistake, I could be the reason someone gets hurt."

His aunt nodded slowly. "Mmmhmm. Accidents happen. Only, I wonder if the next person to take the role will be as careful as you. Will they care as much about the risk? Or will they be more likely to get someone hurt? You care. You're afraid, which means you'll be careful."

He chuckled. "Or, they could be better at the job than I am. I appreciate your confidence, but if someone were going to do surgery on either one of us, I'd choose the experienced person, not the scared newbie."

"You didn't tell me that. Is there a more experienced person available and willing to perform this role?"

He cleared his throat. "No. Not really."

"So it's you or whoever's behind the mystery door."

He shrugged.

"Oh, Michael, didn't you learn anything from all those Sundays I made you sit in the pew next to me at church? God chose the foolish things of the world to shame the wise; God chose the weak things of the world to shame the strong. He doesn't call the ones qualified: he qualifies the called. It sounds like this role has fallen into your lap for a reason. You've got to rise to the call, son."

"But what if it's not *safe*?" Michael groaned. She wasn't

getting this. If she understood the risks, she'd never be encouraging him to do this.

"Safe?" She made a face. "Safe? Nothing in life is safe. Your mother was shot on the way to the store to buy you milk."

"I don't want to talk about this." He buried his head in his hands. He hated this story.

"She thought she was safe. Wasn't doing anything risky."

Mike shook his head. He didn't want to hear this again.

"Stray bullet caught her in the head, and you know how they found her? Cradling that milk because she knew you needed it. She fell down bleeding but protected the damned milk. That's how much she believed in you."

Tears welled in his eyes. He was too young when it happened to remember much about that day. He had the faintest idea that it was a woman with red hair who came to get him from the house. Social services. His mother had left him home alone that day.

"They tried to find your father after it all happened, but he was long gone. So you came to me. And I was scared. I didn't know anything about raising a son. I was scared just how you are scared. But I trusted. And it wasn't always easy, but look at the blessings I received." She cradled his hands in hers. "I got you."

The microwave chose that moment to beep. Mike stood and removed the chicken, dumping it into a glass baking dish. He added some potatoes and carrots and slid the whole deal into the oven. As long as he was here, Aunt Millie was going to eat well. He wiped under his eyes before turning back around.

"Promise me, no matter what happens, you'll take care of yourself while I'm gone and use the money I send you to fix this place up. I won't be able to accomplish anything if I'm worried about you."

"I'm a grown woman. You shouldn't worry about me."

He gave her a firm and pointed look.

"Oh, all right. I will eat more and fix up the house if that will make you happy." She leaned her cheek on her fist.

"It will," he said.

"Now that we have that settled, I want to hear all about Revelations. How are your friends doing?"

Michael spent the entire forty minutes of cooking time telling Millie about the show, everything Hope had told him. He talked about Jayden and Jenny and even Finn, although he put a positive spin on his words. He refused to lie outright to his aunt, but it wasn't difficult to mislead. All he had to do was tell her enough to satisfy her curiosity and no more. Jayden performed an outrageous act filled with pyrotechnics. Finn was studying to be a magician and currently taking a break from the show to complete intensive training with a mentor. Jenny was the brains of the operation. Hope was an overall talent.

Soon, he had turned the tables on the conversation, and she gossiped about the other ladies at the library. She described the considerable number of books she'd read since he'd been gone. They didn't stop gabbing until both their plates were empty and his aunt could barely keep her eyes open.

"Are you staying the night?" she asked hopefully.

Mike nodded. "Yeah. You should get some rest. We can talk more in the morning."

She stood to clear their plates and kissed him on the cheek. "Good. And Michael, if you're still not sure about this new job, ask God for a sign. He'll give you direction if you ask."

He sighed. If only it were that easy. "Thanks." He watched her walk to her room at the back of the house. He missed this —being home. Rising from the table, he washed the dishes and locked the doors. Then he climbed the stairs to his room on the second floor.

"She's a smart old bird."

Mike leaped back as Gabriel stepped from the shadows, his pearl-white wings arching over his shoulders.

"What are you doing here?"

"You know what I'm doing here. You've been called."

Lowering himself onto the bed, Mike leaned forward and braced his elbows on his knees. "I need more time to think about it."

"More time?" Gabriel growled. "We are out of time. Even now, Lucifer is gathering forces, growing stronger, and planning to wipe the Soulkeepers from the face of the Earth. The team must have a leader."

"Hope said I had a choice."

The angel became eerily quiet. He paced the room, eyes locked on Mike, body giving off a slight glow. "Everyone has a choice. Even I have free will. But you should know that a choice against something can be a choice for something else. There are unintended consequences to our choices."

"I need more time," he said again, then remembered what his aunt had suggested. "I want to pray to God for a sign."

Gabriel's eyebrows shot to the ceiling. His derisive snort preceded a laugh Michael feared would wake his aunt. "Are you asking for more of a sign than an angel standing in front of you? I am the messenger of God. What other sign do you need?" He spread his hands.

Shifting under the angel's stare, Michael tried to think of an excuse to put him off. His aunt was right; he was scared. So what? What they were asking him to do was scary! It was worth taking a moment to think about. He rubbed his eyes with his fists.

"I just need..." Mike shook his head.

But Gabriel wasn't listening. He sniffed the air, then looked over his shoulder at the door. "Michael, grab your triquetra," the angel warned.

Mike looked up at him, confused.

That was when he heard Aunt Millie scream.

8

CALL ME LIAM

Hope was about to call Ms. D and tell her everything she'd learned from Finn when the smell of citrus and cinnamon made her freeze. She spun around to find Damien standing behind her. Despite herself, a sense of relief washed through her. She'd been worried about him after hearing he'd faced Lucifer again. Why? She wasn't sure. He was immortal after all... and there was no reason for her to care as much as she did, was there?

Standing on the street beside her, wings tucked away, he might have been anyone. He was as beautiful as always with dark hair that flopped lazily over his forehead and eyes the color of ripe wheat. Remarkably human looking.

"Damien," she said.

"Call me Liam."

"Why?"

"Because the name Damien reminds me of someone I no longer am."

She turned back to her phone. "That's the thing about life. We can change our future, but there's no rewriting the past."

"Have coffee with me. Let's talk."

She whirled on him. "What will we talk about? How you deceived me? How you owned a school with the sole purpose of killing off Soulkeeper potentials and replacing them with demons? That won't change if we talk about it. Shining a light in a sewer doesn't make it stink less."

"But it shows you where to clean." He rubbed the back of his neck. "I can't change what I did. I can only ask your forgiveness and keep asking until you give it to me."

She winced. "Forgiveness takes time and distance. You need to give me room to breathe, to process everything." She tapped her phone, annoyed the app wasn't responding fast enough. "I have to get back to the bus and tell them what's going on with Lucifer. It's worse than any of us thought. The portal Finn opened is right next to the dagger's hiding place."

"I know. I tried to eliminate it for them, but I didn't have enough time. We need to consecrate the tree or the portal will remain open. I can do it if I can get close enough."

"Finn says Lucifer is guarding the portal. Ms. D needs to know. It's going to be harder than she expected to retrieve the dagger and more important than ever that she's careful if she does."

She tapped the app on her phone. Completely locked up. She needed a new phone. She powered her phone off and then on again. As the smell grew stronger and she felt the warmth of Damien's body behind her, she cursed.

"Did you hear a word I said about distance?" she snapped.

"How long do you want me to stay away?"

"Maybe forever."

He recoiled.

"You hurt me. You lied to me. You pretended to be human

and used me for your own gain. I think that means I get to be angry and resentful for as long as I need to be."

"Did I?" He spread his hands. "Was it in my best interest to allow you to redeem me?"

She frowned and turned away from him. "I noticed you made sure to keep all your money. I bet that shell company you set up is rolling in it by now. I hear Damien Bordeaux's estate was worth billions."

He circled until he was facing her again. "Would it help if I gave all the money to Revelations? To you? I personally don't have a need for it anymore. You can do with it what you will."

Hope's head popped up. "I'll keep that in mind."

His hands came to rest on her shoulders and the warmth they infused made it impossible for her to shrug them away. Why wouldn't he leave?

"Please forgive me, Hope."

"Why? Why does it matter if I forgive you?"

The look of hurt on his face made a spot in the center of her chest ache. "Because I love you."

Hope shook her head, tears forming. If the ground could open up and swallow her, now would be a good time. She didn't want to hear this. Nor did she want to feel the breathless squeeze in her torso that made her close her eyes and want to hear him say it again. She was split in two, her heart and brain running in opposite directions. If she didn't do something, she'd be decapitated by the wrench of it.

He kept going. "You know it's true. And I don't expect you to love me back. If you don't, I understand. But I will never be at peace if you don't forgive me."

She looked down at her fingers. Forgiving him was something she wasn't prepared to do. Her phone vibrated as it powered back on and she stared at it dumbly.

Damien held out his hand to her. "If you need to get to Victoria quickly, don't bother with the car. I will take you."

Light shone between his outstretched fingers. Beautiful, multifaceted light. It came from his skin, she knew, and from whatever it was that flowed under it. She'd heard angels bled silver, but to her, Damien had always had a gold aura. A tremor started somewhere deep within her.

She didn't want to touch him.

She desperately wanted to touch him.

He both was and wasn't the man who had deceived her. This situation was impossible, their relationship doomed. From where they'd begun there was nowhere to go, was there?

"I won't hurt you," he said. His expression was a mask of pain.

"I know," she said.

"You're shaking."

"There was a time you wanted to kill me."

"I'm not him anymore."

"So you say, Liam not Damian."

"Exactly."

"I don't know you."

He stepped closer to her but didn't touch her. "Hello, my name is Liam." He offered her his hand and a reassuring smile.

She looked him straight in the eye. "No. You are Damien. And if I ever forgive you, it will be because I accept you for everything you are, not for something you wish you were."

He scowled at that, but she placed her trembling fingers in his and allowed him to wrap his arms around her. His wings, translucent, hidden, but as soft as they'd ever been, enveloped her. They broke apart and traveled on the light.

Hope rejoiced in his warmth, in the golden brightness of

his soul melded with hers for a few glorious moments before coming back together in front of the bus.

"Here you are," he said, releasing her.

Her gaze met his and the corner of her mouth turned upward. "Thanks for the ride." She opened her mouth but her next word caught in her throat. Did she owe him anything? No. But there was something she wanted to say, for herself, for her own sanity. She tried again. "Damien, I told you, I need space and time. I can't work out what happened or forgive you if you're constantly hovering over me."

"I understand." He blended into the light and was gone.

The doors to the bus opened, and Ms. D stepped off the stairs. "Hope! I've been looking all over for you. We need to discuss the show tonight."

Hope placed a hand on her shoulder and turned her back toward the bus. "We need to discuss a lot more than that."

"WHATEVER HE'S DONE TO IT MAKES MY HEAD HURT." HOPE stood at the gate to the cemetery with the rest of the Soulkeepers, watching tendrils of fog worm their way between the crypts. Fuse, Amuke, and Orelon had stayed behind on the bus as backup. It was twilight and the sky above them was clear, the weather temperate. But behind the gate, the atmosphere had gone all sorts of funky. The entire cemetery had taken on an unnatural hazy quality, and she could feel a cold wall of air extending a few inches past the metal bars of the gate. Cold air aside, the place oozed ominous energy. Her head throbbed and her skin prickled.

Ms. D reached a mottled hand toward the lock, then

snatched it away with a curse. "He's warded it off. Strong magic."

"I can't feel anything alive beyond this point," Hope said. "Not a root or a vine. If there is one, I can't connect to it."

Ms. D frowned and turned to Damien, who despite promising to give her space, was behind her. Not his fault, she supposed. The team needed him, especially now that they were operating without a Healer. "Can you fly over and see if you can get in from above?"

He nodded and bent his knees to launch himself into the air.

"Discreetly!" Ms. D said. The angel disappeared, but Hope felt a brush of feathers as he took off on his invisible mission.

Ms. D looked over her shoulder at the traffic and people bustling in and out of shops across the street. "It seems all of us could use a little discretion. A cloaking spell should do the trick." She circled her hands and Hope watched a shimmer of magic fall like rain around them.

Emboldened, Jayden stepped to the lock. "The air is cold here. Let's see if a little fire has any effect." His hands burst into flames and he thrust them at the bars. With a crackle and zap, his feet left the ground like he'd touched an electric fence and he was blown back from the gate. Only Paul's quick thinking and even quicker movements stopped him from flying beyond the cloaking spell and into the street.

"Thanks, man," Jayden said after Paul set him on his feet again. Hope breathed a sigh of relief.

"If Damien is going over, I'll try to go under," Paul said. He crouched down as Hope and the others averted their eyes. In a few heartbeats, a rat poked its head out of a pile of Paul's clothes and scampered toward the wall where it burrowed into the ground.

Not to be outdone, Jenny stepped as close to the wall as she could bear and tapped the earpiece Hope had given her after visiting Finn. HORU's hologram formed, flickering in the middle.

"Hello, Jenny. Please excuse my state of being. The energy field next to you is interfering with my projection." HORU's ears twitched and she wrinkled her nose.

"HORU, can you tell me anything about this place? We can't get in."

"Accessing satellite." Her oversized eyes blinked rapidly. "This isn't science, Jenny. It is magic. This entire cemetery is no longer visible by any networked equipment. The way the video feed bends around it, I must conclude that it exists inside a bubble."

"A bubble?"

"A reflective bubble. From space, nothing appears to be missing. That is only possible if the light is bending around this place. A bubble."

Paul scampered back to his clothes, his whiskers twitching as he burrowed into his shirt. The boy formed where the rat had been, quickly arranging his clothing and brushing dirt from his hair. "It's impenetrable from below. I tried everything. The other animals have fled. There isn't so much as a worm down there."

A rush of air confirmed Damien's return. He came into view beside Hope, who rolled her eyes at his persistent nearness. "There is no access from above. Even when I tried to use my power, I was thwarted."

Ms. D sucked air through her teeth. "No choice then. We cannot retrieve the blade. Our only chance is that he does not find it."

"There's something else," Damien said. "He's erected a cabin next to the tree. Smoke is billowing from the chimney. That's not fog you're seeing. It's smoke."

Hope's brow furrowed and she turned to Ms. D. "I thought you said he was performing tonight. Why would he leave a fire burning?"

Damien sighed. "Because it is no ordinary fire and this is no ordinary magic. Lucifer has used the power of the tree to conjure hellfire. It is the fire of Hell that burns in that cabin and fuels the magic protecting this place. Smoke like that will detect anything holy. It is the opposite of everything we are made of, everything we stand for. You might say it is a litmus test for evil. There is no way in for any of us."

In silence, Ms. D dropped the cloaking charm, and the team started back toward the bus. Once the others had crossed the street, Ms. D grabbed Hope's arm. "I need to talk to you." She lowered her chin. "Alone."

Hope nodded. "Yes. Of course."

❦ 9 ❧

CONFESSIONS

A cross the street from the cemetery, in a place called the Voodoo Café, Hope sat at a table with Ms. D, staving off the remaining chill from the cursed cemetery with a hot cup of tea. Ironically, it was a hot and humid day, but the sun's heat couldn't reach the place left cold by Lucifer's actions.

"You wanted to talk to me?"

Ms. D stared out the window at the place where they'd just been, rubbing her outer arms. She peered over her glasses at a man who seemed to cross the street to avoid it. "I don't think they can even see it," Ms. D said. "Look how he avoids the cemetery without even realizing." They watched a woman walk directly at the gate, only to trip, become disoriented, and veer to the right.

"Do you think Lucifer has already found the dagger?" Hope asked. It was a question she wanted to ask before but was afraid it would upset the others.

Victoria shook her head. "I sense the protective enchantment I put on it is still in place. I did not leave it unguarded."

Hope's head throbbed and she looked away from the window, down into the swirling tea leaves in her drink. Maybe it was the newfound power within her, but she seemed connected to those leaves, as if her soul was tumbling in the belly of the teacup, the tides of change spinning her life in every direction. She needed to settle, to anchor herself to something, or she'd slip away.

"I asked you here because I wanted to speak with you privately about something." Ms. D ran a finger around the lip of her mug.

Hope gestured for her to continue with a tilt of her head.

She cleared her throat. "How was Mr. Wager when you saw him?" Ms. D adjusted her glasses.

Hope had already shared the basics of their meeting. Jenny had HORU, and Ms. D knew about the portal. This wasn't about any of those things. She wanted to know about Finn. How he was personally. Hope took a deep breath.

"He's damaged, Victoria. I can smell it on him, a darkness that scares me. He's not a Soulkeeper anymore."

"You told him he could return if he wanted to? And Theodor."

She nodded. "He doesn't want to. They've formed a coven: Finn, Theodor, and Wendy."

"Yes, Wendy. You mentioned her. She's learning magic as a human." Her lips thinned.

"Finn has this idea that the three of them will become powerful enough to stop Lucifer with magic. They want to do it their own way."

Ms. D huffed. "Because that's worked so well in the past."

"At least we're on the same side." She gestured toward the cemetery. "We are going to need all the help we can get.

Without a Healer, we have no guidance from above. We're flying blind."

Victoria swirled her coffee. "I don't suppose you could ask Liam to, you know." Her eyes flicked toward the ceiling. She lowered her voice. "Ask God directly."

"Damien. His name is Damien," Hope corrected. She shrugged. "Sure, I can ask him. But can we trust him? He's an angel now, but who knows what that means. He's Lucifer's brother. He has free will. He fell once—he can fall again."

"I can see why you'd be skeptical of his motivations, but have you ever thought that his past could be an asset? He has insight into Lucifer's mind that the rest of us will never have."

"And you think we can trust him?" The question came out more accusatory than she intended.

"I think we should hear him."

Hope drank the last sip of her tea. "You hear him. I'm too busy staying away from him."

Ms. D grunted and tapped the side of her mug. "There's another, more obvious answer to our problem." Her eyes shifted sideways toward the cemetery and her lips thinned, tiny wrinkles forming around the corners of her mouth.

Hope squinted. "What?"

"We can't retrieve the dagger, you understand. It's only a matter of time before Lucifer finds it."

"That's the fear."

"Based on what we know from when he tried to capture you, he needs more than the dagger to complete the spell. He needs the Healer." Ms. D lowered her chin and peered at Hope over the top of her glasses. "What if we don't create a Healer for him to sacrifice?"

"God calls the Healer, not us. What are you suggesting?"

Victoria leaned forward. "Michael is rejecting the role. It will take time for another Healer to be called. Once we know who it is, we can force the person to stay on Veil Island. Lucifer can't sacrifice what he can't find."

Hope frowned. "True, but the person also won't be capable of acting as our Healer. Only the Healer can cross to the In-Between. That's something I wasn't able to do before from Revelations. We need a Healer. Without one, the Soulkeepers have no anchor or direction."

She waved a hand in the air. "We could get by without one. We have no Healer now, and we are surviving. Slowly, we will make our way through the list of demons, isolate Lucifer, then somehow force him through that portal and let the curse do its dirty work."

Hope shook her head. "Even if the Soulkeepers could continue to operate successfully without a Healer—and as the former Healer, I'm not convinced that's the case—what you're suggesting is tantamount to keeping whoever Michael's replacement is a prisoner. It could be years before we kill all those demons. No one is going to give up their freedom to live on that island willingly."

"There are things more important than a potential Healer's happiness," Ms. D said quietly, although she looked disgusted by her own words.

"We have time. Mike is with his aunt now. He told me he is going to refuse the role as soon as he can talk to Gabriel. He won't be the potential much longer, but as I said, it will take awhile for another to be called." And hopefully, by then, the Soulkeepers would think of another way to thwart Lucifer other than imprisoning their leader.

"Right. When will we know for sure?" Ms. D leaned back in her chair.

"We're supposed to stop by Mike's house tomorrow to confirm he's rejected the role. I can't call Gabriel anymore—that was a gift of the Healer. We will have to ask Michael if the angel gave him any guidance or direction."

"Or you could ask Damien."

Hope frowned. "Fine. If Michael doesn't have a message from Gabriel, I'll ask Damien."

Ms. D glanced toward the window and inhaled sharply. "Look who's leading a cemetery tour?"

Hope followed her gaze across the street to find Kirsa leading a group of ten adults through the gate. Her stomach clenched and she stood from her chair. "We have to stop her!"

"It's too late." They were through the gate, the fog closing in behind them.

"She's luring them to that cabin to feed to Lucifer, isn't she?" Hope felt sick.

Ms. D sighed. "It appears Kirsa is now doing his dirty work while he's onstage. She's bringing him souls so he can spend less time away."

"How do you think she's passing through the enchantment? How are the people? We tried everything to get inside."

"He must have cursed her somehow. Or it's possible the enchantment sees her specific genetic makeup as a key. It's sophisticated magic."

"Keeping a spell like that going has to be a drain on his resources. Juliette must be working overtime to keep him fed."

Ms. D pursed her lips. "Only, he's scheduled fewer concerts, not more. The portal and the hellfire must be strengthening him."

Hope rubbed her aching head. "I wish I knew what to do."

"Yes, hmmm." Ms. D folded her arms over her chest. "Well, we've learned one thing today. Lucifer may still be performing, but he's not living on a bus any longer. That cabin and those people are there for a reason. It appears the Devil has taken up permanent residence in New Orleans."

10
ULTIMATUM

"Aunt Millie?" Michael shot Gabriel a confused look before ignoring the angel's advice and leaving the triquetra around his neck. He didn't know how to use it anyway. He opened the door and ran down the stairs.

His aunt's scream came again from her bedroom. The door was open. What Mike saw inside stopped his blood cold. A man held his aunt in the corner of the room, a knife to her throat. Wait, no. That wasn't a knife. Michael looked more closely at the sharp extension protruding from the man's knuckle in abject horror. That was a talon.

"You're a demon." A chill ran the length of his spine.

"Very good, Michael." The man's bright red tongue licked his bottom lip, his dark eyes shifting from his aunt to him and back again. "You need to come with me. Lucifer would like a word."

Lucifer. Mike cringed. Hope had warned him. The Devil knew where he lived and he was supposed to be in Hell. Aunt Millie's eyes were wild. Her small, bony hands gripped the demon's forearm helplessly.

"Michael, do you know this man?" she asked shakily.

"Let her go," Mike said through his teeth.

The demon snorted. "This is not a negotiation, *human*." The talon sliced across his aunt's chest, drawing blood and eliciting another scream.

"No!" Mike yelled, rushing forward. But the demon stopped him in his tracks with a talon to her throat.

"The next one slices her jugular."

He held up both hands. "Okay, okay. What do you want me to do?" The demon reached a hand toward him, shifting his bleeding Aunt Millie to the side.

Light rushed through the room, knocking the demon against the wall and throwing his Aunt Millie toward the bed.

"Michael, now!" Gabriel yelled.

Mike fisted the triquetra and tore it from his neck, watching the arc of energy fan across his mahogany knuckles. The demon attacked. This wasn't apples or a training ring. This was an honest-to-goodness fight. He ducked slashing talons and punched the demon in the gut with his glowing fist. The ring of energy sliced through the man's lower abdomen, almost cutting him in half. Mike danced backward with small steps, hands raised like a boxer against the retaliatory strikes. The thing's mouth spat black blood.

As Mike dodged, the hole in its abdomen widened. He waited for guts to pour out. Instead, a black tangle hatched from the body like an egg. The thing became a scorpion of darkness with claws and barbs.

Mike howled as one of those claws snapped toward his head. "Gabriel, a little help here!" Mike swiped with the triquetra again, sending one claw crashing to the carpet. Black blood splattered his shirt.

"You're doing fine, Michael. I'm amazed, considering you refused my training," Gabriel said.

Between punches and slices of his chakram, Mike saw the angel lean against the wall and inspect his fingernails.

"Aren't you going to help me?" Mike yelled, dodging a potentially deadly sting and slicing through the side of the scorpion's tail.

"I would, but you refused our relationship. I'm not supposed to meddle in human affairs."

The demon charged and Mike barely escaped by dive rolling over its elbow and across the room. He whirled and took another nick out of its hide. "I don't think I ever gave you an answer," Mike said. "But I can't be the Healer if I'm dead!"

"Oh, so we're still discussing the possibilities. I see." Gabriel didn't move.

Slice. Punch. "Gabriel!"

A ball of fire passed over Mike's shoulder and lit the scorpion's head on fire. Mike did not waste the opportunity. Positioning himself on the clawless side, he put all of his weight behind a final blow to the thing's middle and sliced it in half. He watched the entire demon explode into black confetti, peppering the room with sulfur-smelling filth.

"Very good," Gabriel said, clapping his hands. "I'm impressed."

Mike ignored the angel and rushed to his aunt's side. Something was wrong. She was barely breathing. Eyes staring at the ceiling, she lay sprawled on the bed. Her wrinkled hands clutched the wound in her chest.

"Aunt Millie?" He shook her shoulder. "Aunt Millie!" She stopped breathing. Michael wasted no time and started CPR.

"It's amazing what we take for granted until it's gone," Gabriel said from behind him.

"Call 9-1-1." Michael delivered two big breaths into his aunt's mouth, then returned to chest compressions.

"9-1-1? You're a Healer, Michael. If you accept what you are, you can heal her, no ambulance required. You won't need CPR. You have the power, waiting inside you."

"How?" Mike turned on Gabriel. "Tell me how to help her, right now, or I will rip those wings off your back and shove them somewhere they won't be nearly as pretty."

Gabriel took a step back, his mouth twitching. "There's a saying, *Don't shoot the messenger.* I'm a messenger angel, Michael. I didn't do this to your aunt and I can't stop it from happening. But you can. If you accept the role you were meant to fill."

"I thought I had a choice!"

"You do. You can deny the call, but then your aunt will die. The demon poisoned her. The poison is killing her."

"That's not fair."

"Then save her. Become the Healer."

Mike's eyes burned. He had no choice. He couldn't let her die. Not like this. "Fine," he yelled. "How?"

"Simply choose it. Decide, right now, that you will take on the role of Healer."

"This is blackmail."

"This is how it works. You've been called," Gabriel said. "You can deny the call, but you can't deny the consequences."

Michael cursed.

"What will it be?"

Mike compressed his aunt's frail chest, feeling her ribs crack under the pressure. "Yes. I'll do anything."

Everything stopped. It was as if time itself had taken a coffee break. His aunt's ceiling fan stopped spinning. The dust stopped floating in the air. His aunt stayed exactly where she was.

Gabriel picked the triquetra up from the place on the bed where Mike had dropped it and dangled it in front of Mike's face. "I promise you, she will be fine, as long as you pass the initiation waiting for you on the other side."

"I really hate you right now," he said to the angel.

"I never said I was here to make you happy." Gabriel brought the pendant closer to his face. "Try to relax. Stare at this and let your mind go."

"You'll take care of her?"

"God will take care of her. He wants you in this role, Michael. He won't let anything happen to her if you cooperate."

Heart pounding in his ears and breath coming in pants, Mike did as he was told. He stared at the triquetra. Gradually, the silver ovals blurred and spread like liquid mercury. Scales morphed and shingled around him, reflecting light as if he'd entered a hall of mirrors. Gabriel was gone, and Michael was falling, sliding down the smooth silver, until he crashed into a hard surface and came to an abrupt stop. His teeth rattled. His body ached. He blinked rapidly, but the reflective room had left him temporarily blinded. What his senses could pick up was ticking, layers of it, as if he were in a room with a hundred clocks. He rubbed his eyes with both fists and was relieved when his vision cleared.

One hundred was an underestimate. Michael wasn't in his aunt's room anymore, but he was surrounded by clocks. Cuckoo clocks of all sizes lined an entire wall: this one carved to look like bears in the forest, that one a log cabin with lumberjacks. There were shiny gold grandfather clocks with pendulums that swung in time with the ticking. Kitschy kitchen clocks filled another section, one with an hour hand painted to look like a carrot and a minute hand like an asparagus stalk. An hourglass rested on an end table. Strange silver orbs spun like revolving planets in the corner. Aside from a fireplace and two empty chairs, every visible surface of wall and table was covered with a timepiece. As he took it all in, he realized with some amount of horror, they were all about to strike midnight.

He pressed the heels of his palms over his ears as the world exploded into a dreadful cacophony of chirping birds, cathedral bells, and tinny alarms. Even through his hands, the noise was deafening. He closed his eyes against it as if closing off one sense could dampen another. The chiming rattled his bones. He curled into a ball and screamed.

* * *

"ARE YOU IN PAIN?" A FEMALE VOICE ASKED. THE CLOCKS HAD struck twelve; they were back to ticking again.

Michael shut his mouth and opened his eyes. There was a girl there among the clocks. Young, Latina, maybe nineteen, with a pierced lip and a hot pink streak that ran from her widow's peak to her chin. She was cute but definitely not normal. Her eyes were weird, like her pupils took up most of her eye. And her presence felt too large for her body. She filled the room. It was almost as if she were part of the ticking clocks and they were a part of her.

Mike smoothed a hand over his hair and then his shirt. He climbed to his feet.

"Hi. Uh, not in pain," he said, trying to regain his composure. He gestured toward the walls. "It's loud in here with all the clocks."

She furrowed her brow, an action that made her nose wrinkle adorably. "Is it? I don't even hear them anymore."

There was something wrong with the girl's eyes. Not just the large pupils but... Mike stepped closer to get a better look, extending his hand toward her. "I'm Mike... Carson."

With a glance at his hand, the girl pointed at the red velvet wingback behind him. "I know who you are. Have a seat. We have much to discuss."

Mike lowered himself into the opposite chair. "Who are you?"

"When I was human, they called me Mara. You may call me by that name if it makes you comfortable, although here, now, I am called Time."

So, she was one of the immortals. "Time. Like Cronus..." Mike muttered, remembering his Greek mythology.

"Who's Cronus?"

"Never mind. My mistake. You said we had something to discuss?"

"As Gabriel must have told you, you have the potential to be the next Healer."

"So they tell me."

"Did they also tell you that you must survive an initiation before you can be deemed worthy to fully accept the role?"

"Gabriel and Hope might have mentioned it, but they were sketchy on the details."

"That's appropriate, considering the initiation is different for every Healer. If they'd given you details, they would most certainly be wrong."

He rubbed his palms on his thighs. "I'm here. What do I have to do?"

"For you to become what you were born to be, you must face and overcome your greatest fears. You must release what you desire most, and you must choose your course based on your wish to serve, knowing you may do so alone."

"Okay. That sounds... cryptic."

"Mind you, Soulkeeper, should you fail, you will be returned to your body. Unfortunately, that hasn't ended well for others in the past. Full disclosure: it is common for failed Healers to suffer premature death or insanity."

"Great. I'm surprised people aren't lining up around the block for this gig," he scoffed.

Straight-faced, she scrutinized him, as if she were discerning if he was joking or not. He squirmed in his chair. This close, he could tell that Mara's strange eyes were not a trick of the light. Her pupils were filled with twinkling stars, universes revolving around each other, galaxies exploding and colliding, eternity and the power of a split second all contained in the body of a girl who looked small enough for him to throw.

She leaned toward him. "With that in mind, do you choose to attempt the initiation?"

Mike thought of his aunt. "Yes," he said, attempting to keep the sarcasm from his voice. It wasn't like returning to his life was an option. She'd made it clear that death or insanity was probable, and that didn't even begin to take into account what could happen to his aunt if he didn't become a Healer. If that wasn't good enough reason to continue, there was something else, something he wasn't ready to admit to himself. A tiny niggle at the back of his brain thought he could do this, and that maybe, the Soulkeepers needed him. "I'll do it."

Mara smiled and nodded. "Then I have a gift for you." She stood and moved to a table of clocks behind her. After shuffling a few, she reached between a gold carriage clock and one made entirely of gears and withdrew a pocket watch.

"Hey, that looks like—"

"The watch that once protected your soul? It is an exact copy. The original is in Victoria's office at Revelations." She opened the face and closed it again. "I believe there are no coincidences in life. There's a certain poetry to you having this now. Time protected your soul once. Time was chosen as the guide to your initiation." She pointed at her chest. "And I believe time will be both guide and teacher for you. Keep this with you always, and consult with it when you feel lost and alone."

Michael accepted the gift from her and was shocked that when he reached for it, the sleeve of a pinstriped suit covered his arm. Confused, he turned toward the grandfather clock behind him and checked his reflection in the glass. He was wearing an old-fashioned suit, with a vest that included a pocket for the pocket watch. His hair was slicked back on the sides and left natural near the front.

"Why am I dressed like this?" he asked.

"Every immortal who welcomes an initiate is allowed to give him or her guidance in the form of a gift. I'm giving you time. Not all of it, of course. You wouldn't be able to survive if I loaned you the power I carry inside me. No, this is a taste. The watch and your clothing are a link to your past. The past can give us power over the present, and our command of the present can frame our future."

He was beginning to think Mara was speaking in code. He understood what she was saying, but not what it meant. "What does this have to do with the suit?"

But Mara didn't answer him. "You have three days to pass three tests. Look at the center dial on your watch."

He removed the pocket watch again and this time noticed a small gauge on the face with a needle pointing to the number one. The gauge ended with a four, the start of the fourth day. In between, markers representing days one, two, and three were depicted as the sun in various stages of passing over a moon.

"Three days to do what?"

Mara frowned. "Follow the path and survive."

"Survive." He sighed. "That's vague enough to not be any help at all. Which way to the path?"

"I'll show you out."

At first, Mike was confused because the room did not appear to have any doors, but as Mara passed him, the clocks seemed to part for her. Seemed to. He never noticed any movement. It was more like the path out of the room couldn't be seen until she was walking on it, like the space was folded, and her presence opened it.

He followed her from the room of clocks to a foyer of blown glass and sand, the smooth, translucent walls giving way to grit that crunched under his shoes. Once she led him outside, he could see where the sand came from. Her home was in the middle of a desert. She walked with him a few yards along the stone-lined path that led from her glass castle. When she stopped, he looked back at the place, finally taking in the panoramic view.

"Oh, it's a sundial," Mike said when he noticed the shape of the place and the shadow it cast. He chuckled at the desert around him—the sands of time.

"Aren't you a smart one?" Mara tipped her head and smiled. "I hope that serves you well out there."

"I keep following this path?" he asked.

Mara faced him and became brutally serious. "What you are about to experience is both truth and illusion, the In-Between world and the magic of who you are. Make no mistake. If you die on this journey, you die in real life and nothing can bring you back. Follow the path, face the three challenges, and return here before you run out of time. Or don't, in which case I will say my goodbyes now. Goodbye, Michael."

"Goodbye," he said, wishing he could think of something else to ask her. But she was gone. He was left standing in the sun, sand blowing against his pant legs and sweat blooming beneath his jacket.

He turned and continued down the stone path into the blowing sand, thumbing the watch in his pocket and wondering what was to come.

❧ 11 ❧

THE COVEN

"**G**ood work, Wendy." Finn watched the takeout container hover in the center of the circle with delight. Although Theodor tapped his fingers on the arm of his chair as if he found the spell underwhelming, he knew as well as Finn did that she was coming along faster than either expected. They'd been practicing three times a day, almost since the moment they'd rented the place, and Finn couldn't believe how easily the three of them gelled. Already, they'd made huge strides.

Of course, part of it was the binding spell. All three had bound themselves to each other at the start. A pang of uneasiness had rattled Finn when Wendy had placed the card against her skin and uttered the spell, but it wasn't like she was a Soulkeeper. She had less to lose and none of them planned to have her incorporate more than the one spell into her skin anyway. Plus, she knew what she was getting into.

The bond had done more than mark them as a coven. It had bolstered all of their magic. When one of them performed a spell, Finn could sense it like a dull hum in his bones. And he knew the others could draw on him as well.

Wendy lowered the card in her right hand until it slapped the palm of her left and the container landed, skidding across the wooden floor. "Hot wings must agree with me. I think this was easier than before dinner."

"Try starting it on fire," Finn said.

Wendy switched the cards in her deck and whispered, "Ignite." The cardboard container smoldered but didn't catch.

"Try again. This one took me a long time to master as well. You are creating fire from energy in the air. It takes practice."

Wendy raised her cards again but paused when her phone's ringtone cut through the flat. "That's my parents," she said. Her brows knitting. "They wouldn't call if it wasn't an emergency."

Theodor gestured for her to answer it. He looked tired suddenly, and Finn couldn't miss that his skin seemed thin and his eyes held a tinge of yellow. "I need a moment of rest anyway." He smiled at Finn as Wendy moved for her phone. "When you are as ancient as I am, you will understand." He stood from his chair and stretched his back and neck, which made a disconcertingly loud crack.

Finn glanced at Wendy and then at the clock on the wall. It was only 8:00 p.m. He didn't feel tired at all. "We can start again when she's finished."

The magician placed a hand on Finn's shoulder. "You go ahead. I need to stretch my legs. It might be good for Wendy to practice without the help of the coven's circle." He headed toward the door.

"Are you sure you're all right?" Finn stood. "Do you need some company?"

Waving his hand, Theodor flashed a yellowing smile, his cheek tight as if he were hiding something in a secret pocket behind his teeth. "I'm fine, fine. I simply need a moment and some fresh air." He slipped out the door and closed it behind him.

Wendy finished her call and plunked her phone back on the counter. "Get this. Someone broke into my parents' house."

"Oh shit."

"Yeah. But nothing was stolen."

"What?"

"They trashed my room. Nothing else."

Finn stiffened.

"What's wrong?"

"What if he knows you're back? Lucifer."

"How could he?"

Finn could think of several possibilities. Lucifer knew he'd brought back Theodor. He'd seen him in the cemetery trying to undo the damage. It wouldn't be a leap for him to guess Finn would try for Wendy and Mike. "I need to talk to Theodor. I'll be back."

"About the break-in? Finn, do you think it was him?"

"I don't know, but you're safe here. Keep practicing." Finn squeezed her shoulder. "I'll be right back." He disseminated to the base of the stairs, then noticed a neighbor smoking in the shared garden. The woman gave him a little wave through the window. Not a good idea to disappear if she was watching. He walked out the door the old-fashioned way and looked both ways for Theodor.

Movement in Dr. Beauvoir's window caught his eye. Behind the voodoo dolls and the shrunken head, the books and dried herbs, Finn saw the white of a shirt cuff. A candle flickered to life. He glimpsed two familiar faces.

With a twist of his shoulders, Finn turned into a column of silver smoke and passed through the door back into the hall.

Silently, he came back together with his back to the wall next to the inner door to the Voodoo Emporium.

"It's getting worse," he heard Theodor say.

"I told you it would." Dr. Beauvoir's double bass thrummed through the room. "This potion can slow things down, but it can't stop it. You're aging. It's natural."

"There's nothing natural about living as long as I have," Theodor said. "But I need more time. My protégé isn't ready for my departure."

"Here. It's ready. Drink."

Finn heard swallowing and then the hollow thunk of an empty cup hitting a table. "It tasted bitter this time."

"I increased the amount of snake bile. I believe it is the ingredient working the best for you."

Theodor cleared his throat, a stifled gag. "Thank you. Your payment is in the envelope."

There was shuffling and a few footsteps.

"About the coven..." Theodor's voice drifted.

More shuffling. "The candle burns. I've been feeding it, day and night. Have you noticed a change?" Dr. Beauvoir asked.

"She grows stronger. What you have promised, you have delivered. Thank you."

"Then what seems to be the problem?"

"The boy isn't healing. Not a hair on his head."

The scrape of a chair being pulled across the floor ended with the groan of its legs. Finn could picture Dr. Beauvoir sitting down, threading his fingers. Clearly they were talking about him, about the state of his physical body, which had not changed since he'd opened the portal.

"Your boy holds a power the likes of which I've never seen. A body, a human body, cannot contain that kind of power without consequences. His blood has accelerated. His heart is beating faster. His temperature is raised. He's burning years, aging almost as fast as you, I suspect."

"How do I fix him?" Theodor asked.

"You presume I know how to temper your magic? This isn't voodoo. The magic you perform is a type of spirituality I've never practiced before."

"Agreed. But you must have an idea."

"Do you know how I was blinded?"

There was a long, weighty pause. "No." Theodor's voice sounded uncomfortable, like perhaps he had his theories about the blindness, but he wouldn't dream of sharing them.

"When I was learning voodoo, there was a time when my power was increasing exponentially. My mentor, she warned me to slow down. I didn't listen. I practiced magic day and night. When my eyesight started to fade, I thought I was tired. I wasn't eating enough or getting enough sleep. So I did those things, but still, my vision faded. And the stronger my magic became the closer to blind I became until I couldn't see anything at all."

"I don't think I'm following you."

"Nature demands a price. If you want to save your boy, you need to drain off his power. He can't both keep the power and his health. One or the other."

"We need to remove the symbols from his flesh," Theodor said softly. "But that takes power—power only I can provide."

"Power that if you use will shorten your life. It would be convenient if I could reroute his extra power to you, to help with your condition, but my magic is incapable of such a transaction. Voodoo cannot take magic from one and turn it into life in another. Life to life, yes. Magic to magic, yes. But nothing more. I'm already siphoning as much magic as possible into the girl. Even if I give you more power, your use of it will burn years off this body."

"But if I don't do this, the boy will die too?"

"Not as fast as you, but yes, if you do not remove the magic in his skin, it will eventually kill him."

"How long does he have?"

"I couldn't begin to guess. A year. Three years."

"And me? How long do I have?"

"Months. Less if you help him."

Silence.

"I'm sorry," Dr. Beauvoir said. "I wish I had better news. I'm not the only brand of magic in this city. We could try someone else. Something... darker."

"No. No..." Theodor gave a little sob. "I have cheated death long enough. I will not defer the price that time demands any longer."

"And what about the boy?"

"Tell him nothing. I will attempt to convince him to allow me to remove the symbols, but he must never know the effect the cure will have on me. He might refuse if he realizes I'm trading my days for his."

"My lips are sealed."

"Thank you."

Finn flattened against the wall as footsteps moved toward the open door to the voodoo shop. He should go. Although a part of him was tempted to confront Theodor, another part, a greater part, wasn't ready. What would he say? Would he agree to allow Theodor to remove the symbols in his skin? He hated the idea. Even if the magic was killing him, he wouldn't let it go. No way. If Theodor was dying, he needed his power more than ever.

"Theodor," Dr. Beauvoir called. Finn cast his gaze toward

the threshold and saw Theodor's shadow. He stopped breathing. "Would you like to stay for a drink? I have an old bottle of bourbon I've been waiting to share with a friend."

The shadow receded, along with Theodor's footsteps. "What kind of man do you think I am?" he said lightly. "Of course I will relieve you of your bourbon. Out of friendship, mind you."

Finn released the breath he was holding to the sound of glasses clinking together and the gurgle of poured liquor. "To friendship," Theodor said.

"Friendship." The toast ended with a satisfied swallow.

Finn did not waste another moment. He twisted into smoke and formed again inside the apartment, where Wendy was standing on a chair, fanning the smoke alarm.

"What took you so long?" she asked.

He shrugged.

"Did you find Theodor?"

"What happened here?"

"I needed your help. I almost set the place on fire."

He chuckled. "Really?"

"Yes. After you left, the takeout container burst into flames. That made the smoke alarm go off."

"I didn't hear it."

"Of course you didn't. Theodor has a charm on the place, remember? No one can hear us or see what we're doing through the window."

"Oh, right."

"Anyway, I extinguished the container, but I've been fanning this alarm ever since. I can't open the window to let out the smoke."

For the first time, Finn noticed the haze in the apartment. He waved a hand in a wide arc. "Eliminate." The smoke swirled into a cyclone that absorbed into Finn's palm. He closed and opened his hand twice, then tipped a tablespoon of soot into the garbage can from his palm.

Wendy stopped fanning and jumped down from the chair. "Really? Do you know how long I've been up there? And it was that easy?"

He gave her a half-hearted grin. "I only make it look easy. You'll get it eventually, grasshopper."

"Yeah? Well, since you're the expert, would you mind fixing the scorch mark on the floor before Theodor gets back?" She glanced toward the door. "Where is he anyway?"

Pretending he didn't hear her, Finn walked over to where the floor was burned and passed his hand over the mark. "Construct." The wood filled itself in.

"Thanks," she said.

"Looks like you've got ignite down." Finn winked at her. "Good job."

"Yeah." She stared pointedly at the symbol for ignite scored into the back of his hand. She could see his tattoos now, couldn't she? Did she understand what they meant?

"Finn... why did you do it? I mean, thank you for what you did. You saved me. But why... do that?"

He turned to her, his shoulders slumping. Wendy had always been a force of sweetness and goodness in his life. Her splattering of freckles and doe-eyed good looks gave her the wholesome appearance of the stereotypical Girl Scout. He couldn't lie to her. And for some reason, at that moment, he couldn't help himself. He shared the real reason. The reason he'd never admitted to anyone.

"My mother died when I was five."

"I remember."

"I was helpless. It was cancer and there was nothing I could do."

Wendy nodded.

"This time, there was something I could do. This…" He held out his arms, the symbols dancing and spinning over his skin. "This ensured that I'd be strong enough to succeed. I've lived through failure, through being too weak to do anything. Believe me, losing a part of my soul was a small price to pay to have you standing here." *And dying now is a small price to pay to keep you here.*

"Oh, Finn." She crossed the room and pulled him into a hug.

And just like that, Theodor was forgotten. She talked about the magic, how fast she was learning and how much fun she was having. It was easy to get caught up in Wendy's joy when she was like this. He twirled her around and danced with her in the wide-open space of the loft. And then he kissed her, and it was like before, familiar and comfortable.

"Wendy, if I tell you something, do you promise to keep it a secret?"

"Who am I going to tell?"

"Theodor. You can't even tell Theodor."

"Wow, serious then."

"Yeah."

She tucked her head into his shoulder. "Okay. Tell me. I won't tell anyone."

He tucked her hair behind her ear and kissed her temple. "I think I know where the obsidian dagger is hidden, and I think I'm strong enough to get it back."

OUR GREATEST FEAR

Michael's mouth was dry as a stone. He'd been walking for more than an hour toward a forest barely visible on the edge of the desert that surrounded Time's realm, but the longer he walked, the farther away the woods seemed to get. If he stayed in this heat much longer, he was doomed. What was the point of killing him before he even reached the first challenge?

What was the first challenge again? Mara had listed three things. Face his deepest fear. Release what he desired most. Choose his course based on his wish to serve. Vague guidance at best. Except for the first one. He knew what he feared most.

In the blink of an eye, he'd reached the trees, the sand underfoot giving way to fallen leaves, the shade of the branches blocking the heat. That was strange. The forest had seemed so far away. But hadn't Mara suggested this place was both truth and illusion? The rules of physical space and time were different here; he had to remember that.

As he traveled deeper into the woods and the trees grew closer together, he licked his cracking lips. Water was a priority. But which way? He kept walking, following the path. He couldn't see it any longer, but he could *feel* it. Under the layers of pine needles, moss, and leaves, there was a force drawing him forward. Miles passed before the whoosh of rushing water met his ears. He ran toward the sound and fell on his knees next to a river, scooping the liquid in his hands. He drank greedily.

The light had dimmed overhead by the time he'd had his fill. There was no sun here, only an ambient light that had no discernable source. He checked the pocket watch: halfway through the first day. His feet were sore and he was exhausted. Was this the challenge? All he had to do was find the water?

"Is that it?" he asked the sky. There was no answer. Strangely, the path he'd been following seemed to go directly through the river, but there was no way he was doing that. After what he'd experienced at Revelations, Michael hated water. He remembered what it felt like to drown. He had no plans of doing it again.

Instead of following the path through the water, he kept walking along the bank. He'd wait for a bridge or a log to cross to the other side and pick up the path beyond. Pulling his jacket around him, he hugged himself against a sudden drop in temperature. Darkness had settled in and a light flurry of snow drifted around him. From desert to snowstorm. He'd reached the end of the first day. He'd have to camp for the night soon if he could find a place where he wouldn't freeze to death.

As soon as the thought had passed through his brain, the river ended at a small lake, covered in a thick layer of ice. It was much colder now and Michael shivered. Across the ice was a dilapidated cabin, smoke pouring from the chimney and the glow of a fire welcoming him through the window. There was a woman inside. "Aunt Millie?"

He started across the ice, his dress shoes quickly filling with snow. The frigid wind seeped through him, straight to his bones. Every step drew him closer to the cabin, to warmth. *Crack.* The ice under his feet shifted.

"No," he muttered and tried to run for shore. The lake opened its gaping maw, and he dropped into the frigid darkness beneath him. Numbing cold consumed him, made it hard to move, but he tried his best to swim for the surface, his fear of drowning filling him with adrenaline. But the harder he swam, the heavier his clothing became, until with one last gasping breath, he was swept under the ice.

All Michael could think about was his act at Revelations, how he'd been trapped and left for dead, locked inside to drown while the audience watched, unsuspecting of the horrors he was experiencing within. And he had drowned. He'd been dead when Ms. D fished him out of that pool. If it weren't for Hope and her healing powers, he would still be dead. He sank toward the bottom, too exhausted to swim any longer. His lungs ached. So this was how it ended? Death by his greatest fear? Drowned again, this time in a place between places.

No. There had to be a way. The rules of physics operated differently here. He couldn't give up. Quickly, he started stripping out of his suit, hoping to make himself lighter, so he could kick to the surface. But once the pinstriped jacket was in his hands, his fingers caught on the inside pocket. There was something in there, something that hadn't been there before.

Mara had said his clothing was supposed to be part of his guidance. A gift from her. He reached into the pocket and wrapped his hand around what felt like the hilt of a weapon. But when he drew it out of the pocket, it wasn't a dagger but an elephant's tusk that glowed in the dark water like a phosphorescent fish.

What the hell? Lungs spasming, Michael tried to swallow the air remaining in his mouth. There was nothing left. He needed oxygen. His body begged him to breathe, but if he opened his mouth now, his lungs would fill with water. Black spots circled in his vision. Soon, his fate would be beyond his control. He had to do something.

He raised the tusk toward the moonlit white sheet above him and kicked as hard as he could. When he reached the surface, it was all for nothing. He was trapped under a thick layer of ice, the current having carried him far from the opening he'd fallen through. Desperately, he kept kicking, drew the tusk back and thrust it above his head. The ivory sliced through the frozen sheet above him as if it were the sharpest of blades and the ice as soft as butter.

His head broke the surface and he gasped, sputtering, slapping the ridge of the opening and finding purchase with his free hand. Somehow, he wiggled his way out of the water, using the tusk as an ice pick to drag his body toward the cabin. Rhythmically, he dug it in and pulled, sliding on his stomach inch by painful inch, the jacket that had saved his life still gripped in his hand. He was wet and freezing, but he wasn't dead. If he could just make it to the cabin and the fire inside it.

Michael tried to stand and failed. The cabin was close, but he couldn't get his feet under him. His strength was gone. He looked at the tusk, pulled again, but wasn't strong enough to move even an inch more. The temptation to close his eyes and fall asleep was almost overwhelming. He rested his head on his arm. He'd close his eyes for one minute, and then he'd try again.

The blackness of his almost instant sleep was interrupted

when two hands dug under his shoulders and dragged him toward the cabin. He grunted as his back slapped the stoop. Limp as a rag doll, he didn't fight the hands, especially when they dragged him across the floor of the cabin and deposited him directly next to the fire. The warmth was almost painful. He shivered violently on the hard wooden floor.

"Excuse the rough handling," a woman's voice said, not unlike his Aunt Millie's but not the same. "That's gonna hurt in the morning. I'd lift you if I could, but I'm not strong enough. This should help."

Whoever it was dropped a thick, hand-sewn quilt over him that smelled of horses. He was too cold to move and shivered underneath it. His body burned as the heat warmed his limbs. Frostbite. He was sure of it. He moaned.

"I'll make you some tea. Tea with whiskey," she mumbled. "I have a little for emergencies, like you almost freezing to death." He caught sight of her then as she moved for the kettle over the fire, an older black woman wrapped in layers of clothing and a floor-length skirt. She ladled some water from the kettle into a cup and placed something into it he assumed held the tea. "Are there more coming?" she asked him, finally meeting his gaze.

More? He looked at her then, really looked at her. If steel were a woman, it would look like this. Black braids and a stare that had seen things he'd rather not know about. A dark suit with buttons running up the front of the jacket. A white neck scarf. She looked familiar. Could have been one of his aunt's friends. But her outfit, that was historical. It looked like a Harriet Tubman costume.

Michael's eyes widened.

"What's your name?"

"M-Michael."

"We'll call you Sam from now on. Don't use any name a master might know you by. You call me Moses."

Mike nodded. He squinted at a scar on the side of her head. He remembered reading somewhere that Harriet Tubman was struck on the side of the head as a child when a slave owner tried to throw something at another slave and she got in the way. He'd also read that she was called Moses. But, why would a historical figure be part of his initiation?

"Now, I know that you've been through something and it must be hard to speak, but you must tell me if there are more slaves with you. I have some rope. I can tie it off and send it down into the lake."

Michael shook his head. "Alone," he said.

She nodded. "Then, I am happy to tell you, you've made it to the safe house. We're not out of the woods yet. Got a ways to go to get to Canada, but you're close. Let's thaw you out, and I'll help you find your way tomorrow."

"Th-thank you," Mike said, still shivering. There was a thunk as the elephant tusk dropped from his hand and hit the floor.

"What have you got there?" She leaned down and picked up the tusk, rolling it between her fingers. It was etched with carvings of people and animals. "Oh my. I have heard tales of these. Never did see one with my own two eyes though."

"What is it?"

"When I was a child, there was an old woman who used to watch us while we were working. She told us a story about how her daddy had come from Africa and how, in his tribe, they would carve stories on elephant tusks. It's how they kept their important memories. Now, this tusk seems to be telling the story of a king who died without an heir to his kingdom. But it turned out he'd had a son. He'd thought the boy was dead, stillborn, and the wisest midwife in the tribe could not get the boy to breathe. The king tied a red string around the infant's wrist and left him in the jungle, where he prayed the gods would take him home. But a witch doctor found the infant and brought him back to life with magic and herbs. The witch doctor, thinking the king didn't want the infant, raised the boy himself into a healthy young man. But when the witch doctor became old and ill, he told the boy the truth. The boy returned to the tribe and presented the red string to his true father. He was welcomed as a prince." She smiled. "Do you think this is your family? Are you descended from a king?"

Mike blinked up at her and shook his head. He'd finally stopped shaking. "No." In truth, he didn't actually know. No one knew anything about his father. He didn't know his heritage or his true ethnicity. All he knew for sure was that his skin was dark. He was a black man. Beyond that, anything was possible.

She handed the tusk back to him. "Difficult times. Not many of us know where we came from no more." She passed him the cup of tea, and he watched a few loose leaves swirl in the water. "Don't mind me saying so, but it's easy once you've been owned to always feel like you aren't worth more than being owned. Maybe you having this is a sign that you should think of yourself as a descendant of a king. If you don't know where you came from, it seems like that's as good of a thing as any to believe." She handed the tusk back to him.

Mike inspected it, following the carvings that depicted the story. He stared at the last one the longest. It was of the boy king holding his hand above his head, rays of light shining down upon his people. It looked like... magic.

"There now, drink up." She pulled her shawl tighter around her shoulders. "I'll find you something to wear. You need to let those clothes dry." She rose and crossed the small cabin to a room in the back.

Mike looked down into the tea, the leaves swirling like they were caught in the wind. He would no longer fear drowning. After all, he'd already done it twice and survived. He ran his fingers along the tusk that had saved his life and for the slightest fraction of a moment, he wondered if he could be related to a king.

✻ 13 ✻

YOU SLAY ME

There were things Hope could control and things she couldn't. She could slay the demon they were hunting with the help of Jayden who was by her side and Jenny who was scoping out the bar where they were heading. She could not, however, change how distracted she was with Damien. No matter how hard she tried, she couldn't stop thinking about the angel. He was giving her space, walking along the rooftops, watching out for them from afar.

And every time she stole a peek to see where he was, he was looking back.

Why didn't he ascend to Heaven like other angels? It was infuriating.

"Jenny has visual confirmation," Jayden said. "The demon is in a bar called the Third Piglet."

They were in Atlanta today, hunting down a target that Jenny said should be easy. After the fiasco at the warehouse, they all agreed they needed a win. This demon was posing as a bar owner, preying on drunk customers. She'd been careful to keep most of them walking, although a few pints short of blood. Others had mysteriously gone missing.

Hope smoothed her hair. The neon sign for the Third Piglet glowed ahead of them. At least there was one less thing to worry about today. She wasn't a Healer anymore, which meant the demon wouldn't detect her. Damien, on the other hand, would have to keep his distance. He smelled like the world's best potpourri: citrus and cinnamon spice.

Which was why she was surprised when he landed next to her.

"Hey, you can't go in there. You're not exactly inconspicuous," she said to him.

"I can hide what I am."

She snorted. "No, you can't. I can smell you coming a mile away."

He gave her a hard look and shook himself like a dog. A ripple ran along his body, his hair taking on a tinge of gray, his nose widening, and his eyes darkening from gold to brown. Even his clothing degraded to a more wrinkled state. Hope sniffed. Nothing.

She crossed her arms over her chest and popped out a hip.

"You look more human than me," Jayden said to him. "And ignore Hope. We need you. With Finn gone, we're one short."

Hope nudged Jayden hard, but the guy ignored her. They entered the dark and dingy tavern without any trouble. Jenny had made them fake IDs, but there was no bouncer to ask for them. The place wasn't crowded. Aside from Jenny, who sat in a booth pretending to drink a beer, the only other patron was an elderly man, who looked like he'd fallen asleep on the bar. The bartender, a woman of about forty wearing mom jeans and a Braves T-shirt, greeted them with an unwelcoming scowl.

Hope slid onto a stool at the bar next to Jayden, disguising a sniff by rubbing her nose. Demon. The place was ripe with the saccharin-sweet stench. Out of the corner of her eye, she watched Damien slide in across from Jenny. The Helper reached across the table to squeeze the angel's hand. Hope flinched.

"Two drafts," Jayden said.

The bartender poured and slid the drinks across the bar. "Where you folks from?"

"All over. You?" Hope asked.

"None of your business."

Jenny stood, glanced at the sleeping patron, and raised an eyebrow in silent question. Could they do this without moving the old man? Hope nodded. It was a go. They'd keep him safe. Jenny strode out the door. As soon as she was safely on the other side, Hope hopped off the barstool and locked the front door, then whirled to face the demon.

"What do you think you're doing?" The bartender's hands disappeared under the bar.

"You've used that body long enough. It's over," Jayden said.

Eyes locked on Jayden, the bartender pulled a shotgun from under the counter and aimed it at Jayden's head. "Get out."

Fire exploded across the top of the bar, knocking the bartender back a step. As promised, the fire stopped before burning the old man, who didn't even flinch. Was he breathing?

The gun went off, but Jayden had already dropped beside his barstool. Damien stood, ready to help. But they had a plan, and it was Hope's turn to step up.

Clenching her gut, she focused on the wooden floor, on the weeds that were growing under the foundation, the roots of a tree that had split the concrete down below. With a stomp of her foot, Hope sent her Soulkeeper gift into that life, raw energy that made those living cells stretch and grow. Vines shot up around the bartender, snaking around her body and tearing the gun from her hands. She struggled, but Hope pulled her fists toward her stomach, tightening the vines and binding her to the shelves behind the bar.

In one slick move, Jayden sprang through the flames, drawing his dagger and bringing it to her neck. "Get ready, Damien. I'm opening this bitch up." He drew the blade across her throat. Hope was expecting the black ooze of a demon to explode from the cut, but instead, bright red blood gushed from the wound.

"No," Jayden yelled, pressing his hands over the cut. "She's human!"

Out of habit, Hope rounded the bar, ready to heal her. Then she remembered. She couldn't heal anyone anymore.

"Hope." Damien had moved to block the door. Over the flaming bar, Hope saw the old man, off his bar seat and pointing the gun at the angel's chest.

"Move out of my way, or I'll blow a hole in you big enough to fit through."

"The old man is the demon," she blurted.

"Hope? She's dying. What do I do?" Jayden asked, breathless.

She looked between Damien and the woman. He was the only one who could heal her, and the only one who could take a bullet like that and survive. She had to act fast. Thrusting both hands forward she sent her power into the earth again. Vines tangled around the old man's body as fast as she could grow them. The gun fired, but with a twist of her neck, she used the vines to turn the gun in time. The bullet blew a hole in the wall next to Damien's shoulder.

"Jayden, go." Hope pressed her hand over the woman's wound and pushed her friend into action. He leapt straight up, landing in the fire on top of the bar. His blade circled toward the old man's neck. Decapitation was the only way to kill both the clone's body and the demon residing in it. But the man jerked back at the last second. Jayden's strike connected with the demon's chest.

The explosion of black that broke from the old man's body was a buzzing mass of ill intention, a whirlwind of acid and fiendish mayhem. Hope screamed as the skin from the top of her cheek to her collarbone was torn away, the black wind sizzling through the bar, burning and tearing her flesh. It felt like she was being boiled alive. The worst was the sound. A million bees, each one stinging. On top of it all, the grating screams, Jayden's, the woman's, her own.

After a hellish eternity, the light came. Damien's hands connected and holy tongues of fire blazed through the bar, lapping up the black buzz and digesting it into ash. When every last wisp of darkness was gone, Hope toppled to the floor, her vines and roots going back the way they came. The bartender fell too. All Hope could think was that she was a ghostly white. Bleeding to death.

"Hope?" Damien was by her side, pressing his hands against her face. Warmth flowed through her.

"Heal the woman."

"No."

Jayden moaned, and Damien reached up to clasp his hand, which dangled bloody and torn over the side of the bar. Hope tried to protest, but couldn't deny Jayden needed healing. She watched his flesh stitch back together and his skin glow with Damien's healing light. Hope was glowing too. She pushed

Damien's hand away, trying her best not to enjoy the warmth of his touch.

"I'm fine. Help the woman," she said again, and it took all her strength to push him away. She was dying of thirst and turning away a glass of water.

But Damien fought her. "It's too late for her." He shook his head. "I can't help her anyway."

"No." A sob bubbled up from her throat. They'd never killed a human before. Never. This was wrong. How could they not have known she was human?

With a groan, Jayden sat up and dangled his feet over the side of the bar. His fire was gone, and he looked spent, like he could hardly hold his head up.

"What's happening to her?" he asked.

The bartender's body was shriveling, folding in on itself like a drying prune. Hope reached for her, some inherent part of herself overwhelmed with sadness over the woman's death. But Damien gripped her wrist.

"Don't."

He'd stopped her just in time. At that moment, the woman popped. There was no other way to describe it. Her shriveled body made a sound exactly like a popping balloon, and her flesh, like latex rubber, shrank and imploded until she was nothing more than shredded bits of leathery flesh. Her remains wouldn't have filled the empty whiskey bottle she'd left behind the bar.

"We killed her," Hope sobbed, the tears breaking through. "We killed an innocent human."

But Damien was shaking his head. "It appears she was his host. The reason she smelled of demon was that he was pulling her strings. I'm not sure this one even had a soul. It was a parasitic relationship. She would have died when you killed the demon no matter what."

"But…" She looked between Jayden and the woman.

Jayden scratched behind one ear. "Human women don't shrivel up when they die like that, Hope. And they don't stink like demon. I think Damien is onto something here."

Relief flooded through her and she couldn't help herself; she reached her arms around Damien's neck and squeezed.

"It's okay. You didn't do anything wrong. It's okay." He stroked the length of her hair. She pulled away, forcing distance between them, and collected herself.

Jayden cleared his throat and turned away, hopping down off the opposite side of the bar and unlocking the door. Jenny rushed in, pulling him into a hug.

"Everyone okay?" She flashed Hope a wide smile that wasn't returned.

"How could you not know it was the man and not the bartender?" Hope snapped. "This is your job, Jenny."

"What are you talking about?" Her platinum ponytail swung as her gaze darted between Jayden and Hope.

Jayden held up a hand. "Relax, Hope. I'm sure there's an explanation."

Jenny frowned and tapped the earpiece she was wearing. HORU appeared in all her kitty-cat splendor. "HORU, show Hope a picture of the student who attended Revelations."

"My pleasure, Jenny. Here she is and her contract."

A high school portrait of a girl that was unmistakably the bartender beamed against the paneled wall.

"That can't be right," Jayden said.

"She bled. She was human." Hope turned toward Damien. "What does this mean?"

The angel glowed brighter. "It means, the list we have has its limitations. It appears the demons have ways to jump bodies. This one was using its original clone as a protective puppet."

Jenny frowned. "Which means, this isn't going to be as easy as we thought. The demons could be anyone."

❧ 14 ☙

DEMIURGE

Dressed in a Greek gown with a crown of laurel leaves on her head, Victoria Duvall plucked the ancient-looking lyre in her hands. She'd used the instrument as a prop since they'd started production of Demiurge, and although they'd had to make some adjustments following the loss of Finn, the show must go on. Orelon had taken over the aerial act. It had been years since the instructor had performed, but he hadn't forgotten how to woo an audience. Their troupe might be dwindling, but the show was as good or better than the first time they'd performed it.

She played a short song, and a thousand dancing lights swirled around her like stars. In this production, she was a muse, a deity with power over the creative universe. She smiled broadly into the stage light and introduced the show.

"I am Euterpe," she began, explaining she was the daughter of Zeus and she was in trouble. She did this every night, framing up the story that would carry the production forward. Only, something felt different this night, like the audience watched from behind a window. She ignored the sensation and threw herself into her act, performing several feats of magic to open the show. From her pocket, she produced a lily-white dove that circled the audience before folding in on itself. Its feathers turning to paper, it floated to the stage transformed into a paper airplane. With a wave of her hand, she made lightning branch across the ceiling of the theater and thunder rattle the walls.

"Sit back, dear patrons," she continued, "and watch as we unveil a show worthy of the gods, where all the light in the universe will gather to dance in their praise. Please help me welcome our first act, Hephaestus and Hestia, the god and goddess of fire!" Her hand brushed the strings of the lyre as she exited stage left, replaced by Fuse and Jayden.

Fuse twirled to the center of the stage, graceful as a prima ballerina, while Jayden sauntered onto the stage, looking every bit a boy of sixteen. Beauty and the brute. The redhead fired up his hands and juggled tongues of fire, manipulating his creation around Fuse's dancing form. Flames flitted under her knee as she pirouetted across the stage and over her shoulder with every leap. A barrage of his fire assaulted her until she was backed into the corner of the stage. But then the tide shifted. Fuse's hands ignited, and to the delight of the audience, she attacked Jayden, turning the tables. Her feminine energy flicked and flitted around his masculine till they were both juggling flames as they cartwheeled and sparred across the stage.

As always, they were spectacular, but the audience reaction was weirdly tempered.

"It feels different tonight," she said to no one.

"I have a bad feeling."

Victoria whirled to find Damien in the shadows behind her.

"I didn't see you there. Do you sense it also? It's like half the audience isn't completely here."

"I smell demon."

"Demon?" The angel was almost always with Hope. Victoria worried he'd sought her out because this was beyond even Hope's abilities. Damien was worried for her. "Where do you smell demon?"

"The audience."

Victoria searched the rows of the small community theater in Mobile, Alabama. The place used to be a classroom and the cushioned seating still had foldaway desks. She took a deep breath. Beyond the scorched smell from pyro's act, she could make out a hint of acrid sweetness, a sick smell, like a fetid wound under a thick layer of perfume.

"I smell it too," she said, her hands balling into fists. "Which one is it?"

Damien moved toward her, into the light. "I'm not sure. I can't narrow it down without getting closer."

Pyro finished their act and bowed to rabid applause.

"Do you see that? That man in the front row isn't clapping." Victoria conjured the blessed dagger from her dressing room. Across the stage, Hope stood off curtain, holding her balance ball. Her act was about to begin.

"Tell her not to go on," Damien said. "It's too dangerous."

Victoria nodded in agreement, but it was too late. The audience applauded as Hope took the stage. Balanced on top of the ball, she walked it into position and started to flip.

"Victoria," Damien warned. "Front row."

The man who hadn't applauded reached into his coat. He had something in his hand, something dark. A gun. Hope was concentrating on her flip-flops with no idea the peril she was in. Victoria didn't hesitate. She hurled the dagger. Her aim was true, but its purpose was not. Although the blade impaled the man's wrist, there was a *pop, pop* from the gun. Victoria disseminated, moving in the blink of an eye between the bullets and Hope. She formed in time for the bullets to sear her shoulder.

"Oh!" Victoria yelled, grabbing the wound.

"Ms. D!" Hope was by her side, the red ball rolling off the stage. Vines shot up from the floor and contained the demon, forcing its arms to its sides. *Pop. Pop. Pop.* The gun fired harmlessly toward the floor, but it was enough to send the audience screaming for the exits. Victoria swayed on her feet.

"Help!" Hope yelled to Damien. Victoria cursed but allowed Hope to help her to the floor. Damien was trying to reach them, but as the crowd parted, pushing and shoving out the exits, it was clear the demon wasn't acting alone. At least five demons rushed the stage.

Damien clapped his hands together, producing the purple flaming sword he preferred to use. He lopped off the head of the second demon before it could burst its human skin. Jayden and Fuse bounded past them to take on demon number three. Fuse lit it on fire and Jayden split its skull like a watermelon. He finished the beast underneath with a second blow to its head.

As demons four and five attacked, Damien and Jayden met them head-on. Victoria cringed as people trampled each other in an effort to escape. "Orelon?" she yelled toward the rafters. Then she concentrated and threw her power toward the attendees. "Befuddle," she commanded.

The crowd settled. Orelon dropped from the rafters and helped usher the confused patrons out the door. "Remain calm. Single file. As quickly as possible."

At that moment, the first demon exploded. A black fog

rolled through the theater. Victoria choked and coughed on the foul air, her throat constricting. Hope couldn't breathe either. Her face was red and her eyes bulged. A bomb went off, light blazing through the place. Damien. The fog parted and Victoria and Hope gasped for breath.

The fourth demon retaliated, delivering a blow to the back of Damien's head that knocked him to the floor. "Help him," Victoria said to Hope.

But Paul and Amuke appeared and leapt into action the moment they saw what was going on. In the form of a bear and a panther, they landed on the fourth demon and tore it apart with their teeth and claws. With a slash of his mighty paws, Paul rendered the dark, oily demon inside into ash.

That left the fifth demon, still sparring with Jayden. This one wielded a dark scythe, meeting him blow for blow. Fuse was trying to light it on fire, but it was like the demon had learned. It refused to burn.

"More than one way to skin a demon." Hope leapt to her feet and cast her hands toward the creature. Branches covered in thorns, wrapped around the demon, tightened, and shredded it apart. The black beast inside didn't stand a chance. Jayden was there, stabbing into the split flesh until the demon popped like an ash-filled piñata.

Hope grunted as the roots and vines she'd summoned retracted through the cracks and crevices of the old classroom to recede into the earth.

"Is that all of them?" she yelled, scanning the theater.

"Yeah, I think so," Jayden said.

Orelon dropped down from above. "I've locked the doors. We're alone."

Black dots danced in Victoria's vision. She was still bleeding. All her limbs felt heavy and she'd broken a sweat.

"Damien!" Hope jumped off the stage out of Victoria's line of vision. But after a few minutes, she saw Hope and Paul carrying the angel toward her. A wound in his skull was leaking silver blood and he was barely conscious. They lay him down next to her.

"Put his hand on her wound," Hope said.

Victoria cried out as Jayden pressed the angel's hand over the gunshot.

"Come on, Damien. Heal her." Hope shook his shoulder violently.

The angel blinked rapidly and the hand started to glow. Victoria felt the warmth flow through her and the bullet move in sharp increments toward the entry point. With one last flash of pain, it exited her body with a jet of angry blood. Then the wound stitched itself up. There was more warmth and the wound ached, itched, and disappeared at last.

Damien's hand dropped and the angel passed out again.

Victoria sat up, alarmed. "Will he be all right?" She hovered over Damien's sleeping form.

Hope answered, "He's immortal. He has to be."

But Victoria thought she looked worried. Perhaps Hope cared more than she let on.

"How did they find us?" Victoria asked, Jenny who'd came out of hiding and was checking Jayden for wounds. She turned from Jayden's side and looked Victoria in the eye.

"It's worse than we expected," she said. "I think they know who we are and they know what we're doing."

Victoria frowned. "How?"

"When we took down the warehouse, we killed the demon we were after, but Lucifer went free. He must have spread the word. The demons know that Revelations Theater is our cover. Now they're using it to hunt us."

"Are you sure?" Victoria swallowed hard. She did not want it to be true.

"HORU saw chatter online. This isn't like the island. The show isn't a secret anymore. People have posted pictures of our act. It's everywhere. And now the demons know."

Victoria allowed Jayden to help her up. The Greek toga she was wearing was ruined, stained with blood. Paul and Amuke had shifted back, and along with the others, they circled her. She frowned at the blood and black filth that covered them all.

"There's only one thing we can do," she said. "We cancel the show. Revelations is officially out of business."

❧ 15 ❧

THE SECOND TEST

W hen Mike woke, the fire had died and Moses was gone. He sat up. Had he actually met Harriet Tubman? He rubbed the back of his neck. Of course it hadn't been the real Harriet, only an illusion, a mental construct, part of this In-Between world's magic. But oh, how he wished he could tell his aunt about this. A real-life hero had saved his life last night. Harriet... and the tusk. He picked it up and rolled it between his fingers, admiring the carvings. First challenge down. On to the second.

He was naked aside from some thin white shorts Harriet had given him to sleep in. Thankfully his clothes had dried overnight. He reached into the pocket of his vest and retrieved the pocket watch.

"Oh no!" He scrambled to his feet. He'd slept late. Half the second day was over. He leaped up and dressed as fast as he could, tucking the tusk back into the inner pocket of his jacket. It promptly disappeared. He patted the pocket from the outside, but there was nothing between his hand and chest aside from the material. Cursing, he reached into the empty inner pocket. Was this some kind of magic? Yes. His fingers met the base of the tusk as they had the night before and he drew it out again. When he replaced it in the pocket and removed his hand, both the tusk's weight and mass were gone.

He repeated the process twice, experimenting with the empty cup he'd drank tea from the night before. Anything he placed into the pocket both wondrously fit and disappeared until he chose to retrieve it. But had the tusk been in his pocket the entire time or did Michael's need for it cause it to appear? There was only one way to find out. Michael concentrated on his growing hunger and reached into the pocket. His hand met the smooth skin of an apple. He bit into it. Delicious.

"Cool," he whispered.

His head shot up at a scuffle outside the front window; a dark blur whizzed past. Was it Harriet returning from a morning forage? The door flew open, and a disheveled man rushed in along with a blast of freezing air. He grabbed Michael with one shackled wrist. "You gotta run. They're coming. They're coming for us." The man retreated through the open door, his wild eyes searching the snowy woods outside the cabin.

"Who's coming?" Mike wondered. The sound of dogs barking in the distance met his ears.

He cursed. Clearly, the man was one of the *others* who Harriet had expected, a slave looking for safe passage to freedom. And the dogs? That meant this safe house wasn't safe any longer.

Mike rushed out the door in time to see the man disappear into the snowy woods to his right along the mountainous terrain. When he looked left, he saw who the man was running from. A group of heavily garbed men on horseback were crossing the lake where he'd fallen through the night before.

They had torches in their hands and guns hanging from their hips. When they saw him, they pointed and started to yell, spurring their horses forward.

Why couldn't the lake swallow them too? Mike thought bitterly. He bolted for the woods, following the snowy footprints of the slave who'd gone before him. Driving deeper into the forest, he weaved between trees and shivered in the winter wind. He was fast. Always had been. But the dogs were faster. He could hear them panting and huffing behind him. Following his scent. Closing in.

Up ahead and several yards to his right, the man who had warned him picked his way through the snow. Mike changed course to catch up with him. Maybe they could help each other. But it was not to be. Mike stifled a scream as one of the Confederate soldiers on horseback bound forward and swept the man roughly from the ground, throwing him across his horse's shoulders. More were coming. Mike couldn't outrun them; he had no choice but to hide. To his left, he saw a crack in the mountain, barely wider than his profile. He wedged himself sideways into it… and got stuck. The barking dogs and stomping hooves closed in. Panicked, he let all the air out of his lungs and pushed. It felt like being born. He squeezed through the stone, scraping his skin until it hurt, and burst through into the mountain.

His heart pounded and his breath shook. As his eyes adjusted, he realized the inside of the crack was bigger than the outside. This was a cave. The rhythmic pounding of the horse's hooves approached. He held his breath and backed deeper into his hiding space. He could hear the mob curse and mumble about losing him. A dog sniffed at the crack he'd squeezed through but eventually moved on, as did the others. *Find a tree,* he heard them say.

He gasped. They were going to kill that man. If only he were stronger and could make a difference. But he didn't even have his triquetra. And even though he thought he might be able to draw a weapon from inside the pocket of his coat, he wouldn't know how to use it. He'd never finished his training with Hope. It had stayed behind when he'd come to the In-Between. There was nothing he could do. He was only one person, after all, and they had guns.

"*Michael.*"

He pivoted. The whisper had come from the back of the cave.

"*Michael.*" It was a woman's whisper, familiar but strange.

One step, then two. The darkness was absolute.

"Who are you?" he said quietly. His voice echoed through the cavern.

"*Michael.*"

Unable to see, he dug in the inner pocket of his jacket for the tusk. Last night, it had glowed. Perhaps he could use it to find whoever was back here. His fingers seized the round base and he pulled it forth. At the same time it was revealed, torches flamed to life. Their light flooded the cave. He was standing in an antechamber before an ornately carved stone door. At the center of the door was a groove the exact size and shape of the tusk.

Mike looked at the curved length of carved ivory in his hand and placed it carefully in the groove. Grinding gears, stone on stone, rattled the walls. The door opened.

What he saw inside struck him mute with fear. Beyond the door was a spider the size of a small bear, and all eight of her eyes were staring at him. She was close, hanging above the door in a silver web, a web that stretched tightly from one side of the cave to the other. One leap and she could sink her fangs into him. He'd be wrapped in her web like a fly in a heartbeat.

Slowly, he took a step back. Only a few more steps to the opening of the cave. He could escape if he ran.

"Wait," the spider said. "You've opened my door. Don't you want to see what I have to show you?" Her voice was equal parts sinister and sweet.

Paralyzed with fear, Mike froze. The last thing he expected to find in this cave was a talking spider roughly the size of a pony, or a web that was glowing to life with the reflective nature of a computer screen. As he watched, the spider repositioned herself in the corner of the web, resting her head on her furry front legs. A picture appeared across the silver filament beneath her, a woman's face forming larger than life as if it were projected on the web.

"That's... that's my mother," Mike said. She was exactly how he'd pictured her, partly from dusty memory and partly from the photo albums his aunt had shared with him. Her brown eyes twinkled and her hair shone with dark copper highlights in the light from the window. The image panned down to show she was holding a baby.

"And you," the spider said.

This, Mike had never seen. He didn't have any baby pictures where his mother was holding him.

"And your father."

Mike stopped breathing. Behind his mother was a handsome, distinguished dark-skinned man, smiling brighter than the sun. He kissed the side of his mother's head and whispered, "Michael is a perfect name."

"What is this?" Heat rose through Mike's torso, tightening the muscles of his jaw.

"This is the day you were born," the spider said.

"No. My father abandoned my mother. He wasn't there." He'd been told as much by his aunt since he was old enough to understand.

"Your father never abandoned your mother. It was a sad misunderstanding that resulted when the world changed after the Great Battle. Do you want to see what happened to your father?"

Mike didn't answer, but he didn't move either. He continued to watch the web.

The scene changed. His father was smiling, pedaling a bike down a city street on a cold winter's day. On the corner of Michigan and Wacker, he pulled his bike into a parking space and dismounted. Chicago. That's where Michael was born. There were two homeless men huddled against the building with a cardboard sign that read *Please Help.*

His father delivered a package to the owner of a hot dog cart. The owner gave him a similar package, which his father accepted and stored in the wagon behind his bike. He could see his father hesitating, thinking about something, and then after a quick transaction, he handed two hot dogs to the homeless men.

"You gotta keep movin', you two," he said. "You stay in one place too long, and they find you."

"You have a kind and generous heart," the older homeless man said, tilting his face up. He removed his glove and offered his right hand to Michael's father.

Shaking the man's hand, his father whispered, "You better keep those gloves on. There are only a few of us left. We've got to be careful."

"Generosity is more contagious than you might think," the homeless man said. "Perhaps all you need to expand your operation is a leader."

Michael watched as their coupled hands started to glow and his father's dark eyes lit from within. With his free hand, the homeless man reached into his coat and presented Michael's father with a copy of *Tom Sawyer*, an original by the looks of it. The illumination of their touch passed to the book.

"I don't understand," Michael said to the spider. "What happened here?"

"In the days before the Great Battle, no human could buy or sell goods without the mark of the Devil. Your father was part of the resistance. His generosity earned him favor with God. He became Tom Sawyer, the code name for the mastermind behind the black market that allowed resistance fighters to buy goods without the mark. He helped the Soulkeepers survive during the Great Battle," she said. "Those were hard times. Your father created a means of survival that saved the Soulkeepers from starving. He was the embodiment of God's gift of generosity. Sadly, fallen angels killed him in the last days of the war. But he was a hero, and he was loyal to your mother up until the very end." The spider dropped from the ceiling and turned into a lanky Indian woman in a red dress.

Michael trembled as four hair-covered limbs disappeared into her abdomen.

"You come from a long heritage of leaders, Michael," she said.

"How would you know?"

"I am Fate, the weaver of lives. Call me Fatima."

He shook his head. "Why are you showing me this?"

"Every choice you've ever made thus far in your life was based on a belief you've held deeply inside yourself, so deep you didn't even know it was there. The assumption that you come from nothing, that you were abandoned as a baby, that you were somehow not wanted, an unfortunate victim of your parents' poor choices… this thinking has followed you everywhere. But it's a lie. The thing you desire most is to be normal. But you are not normal, Michael Carson. You are the descendant of kings. You are the son of a gift from God. And now it is time for you to release this belief."

"My mother told my aunt my father abandoned her."

"He didn't. She believed he did. Your aunt wasn't lying to you. But she was wrong. All memories of the Great Battle were wiped from humans living during the time. Because your father had died during the war, your mother and aunt couldn't remember things clearly after the world changed. But your father loved you. He always loved you, and he died doing God's will."

Michael shook his head. "I…" He couldn't believe it. But why would Fate lie?

"Your mother loved you too. You come from love, Michael. You come from a father who risked his life to do what's right."

They sounded like happy words, but they didn't make Mike happy. He had a weird feeling deep within his chest. If this was true, it changed everything. The entire reason he'd refused to go back to Revelations in the first place, and the reason he didn't think he'd make a good Healer. If this was true, he was like Hope. His father was important to the cause, and so was he. But if this was true, it also meant he had no excuse. His failures were his own. And that was a thought he wasn't quite ready for.

"Thanks for letting me know," he said. Wasn't he supposed to be completing a test? "I should go. I'm supposed to follow the path."

Fatima laughed. "Oh, I see. I wouldn't want to delay you from the *test*."

He turned to leave. "Before you go…"

Michael turned back around and let out a scream. The woman was a giant spider again, and this time, she attacked. Her pinchers dug into his left biceps. He fumbled for the torch on the wall and swung it at her head. The spider reared, then flew to the ceiling, scampering back to her web.

Without a moment's hesitation, Mike ran for the exit, ignoring the pain in his shoulder as he squeezed through the crack in the mountain. Confederate posses and man-eating spiders. Mike hated this place. He paused to pull his jacket tighter around him. He was back in the woods, the ice and blowing snow chilling him to the bone.

His shoulder throbbed and he looked down at the spot where Fate had bitten him. Although the fabric of his suit jacket was intact, the flesh beneath ached. He wrestled off the jacket and rolled his sleeve. The flesh was torn but healing, dark scars striping his upper arm in a pattern not unlike a tribal tattoo. Great. The spot tingled with the spider's poison. He rolled his shoulder, then rotated his wrist in an attempt to stretch the ache from the muscle.

A silver shimmer fanned across his palm. "Huh?" He turned his hand over, palm down and the shimmer went away. Palm up and it was back. He raised his hand. The projection from his palm was not unlike the silver web the spider had shown him. He looked through it, toward a nearby tree.

He cursed. Where the tree once was, a series of cords branched off in all directions, each one with a different story to tell. Michael saw the tree as an acorn, then as a sapling, then in various stages of growth, bending in a storm's gusts and singed in a forest fire. He lowered his hand, and the cords blurred together, becoming the adult tree. As he tried to digest what the vision meant, he heard a scream.

The man, the escaped slave, they were hurting him, maybe

killing him. Michael ran toward the sound. He had to help the man. He may be only one person, but his father's story had inspired him. One man could make a world of difference.

He reached a clearing where his worst fears came to life. They'd strung a noose over the branch of a tree and placed it around the man's neck. He was seated on a horse whose reins were in the hand of one of the posse. On instinct, Mike reached for the triquetra around his neck but it wasn't there. He'd have to do this the hard way. Flying from the woods, he grabbed the dagger straight from the hip of the closest man and hurled himself into the air. The horse spooked, but Mike was already there, slicing through the rope as the man dropped. He landed on his feet and ran into the woods. Mike pivoted, raising the blade toward the men, and placing his body between them and the escaping slave.

The posse raised their guns.

He could throw his weapon and take out one of them, but he'd be shot before he could make his next move.

"Use the gift I gave you." He heard on the wind. His eyes panned up to a spider hanging from a web in a nearby tree. He lowered the dagger.

The men cursed and called him names, closing in. He ignored them. Flipping his hand over, he stared at them through the silver threads that appeared above his palm. As the threads fanned out, he saw the first man as a baby and then as a ruby-faced youth.

"What do I do?" he asked the spider.

"Pluck the string," she said, and it sounded like she was smiling.

Mike reached across his arm and plucked the string that showed the man as a baby. The guy collapsed, rolling onto his back and kicking his legs in the air.

"What did you do to him?" the second man yelled.

Michael focused on him and plucked a string that showed him sick in bed. He dropped like a fly, his skin turning red with fever.

The third man fired his weapon. Mike dodged the bullet, then focused his gift. With a pluck of the string, he heard a snap, the man reliving a past break of his leg. He crumbled to the ground, screaming.

"Voodoo," the fourth man yelled. He tried to run, but Mike focused on his back and plucked a string. He called out as a swarm of invisible bees began to sting him.

"None of this is real," Mike murmured.

"No. But it will seem real to them," the spider said. "Don't get smug. It only lasts a few minutes. I suggest you take the horse and get out of here."

He hoisted himself into the saddle and nodded at the spider. "Thank you."

She bowed in her web.

Mike clucked his tongue and took off down the path.

❧ 16 ❧

HERO

It was late when Finn heard Theodor stumble into the apartment, mumbling what Finn assumed was an old British drinking song. With a flick of his wrist, Finn cast a noise-blocking spell around the loft, the same one they'd cast on the apartment. Wendy needed her sleep. She didn't need to be woken by Theodor's raucous drunkenness or what Finn planned to say to him.

A heavy thud preceded Theodor's laugh. Finn climbed out of bed to find his mentor sprawled on the floor, laughing at the ceiling. Confronting him in this condition, clearly drunk and barely sentient, wasn't optimal, but it had to be done. Who knew when they'd be alone again?

"Why didn't you tell me?" Finn marched to Theodor's side and looked down his nose at him.

Theodor waved the long tapered fingers of his right hand. "Finn, my boy, come lie next to me and look at the stars."

"You're not looking at the stars. You're looking at the ceiling."

The older man snorted, his lips peeling back into a grin and his stomach vibrating with his laughter. "*I* see stars." He shrugged.

Finn didn't find it funny at all. "Why didn't you tell me you were dying?"

Filling his cheeks with air, Theodor blew out a breath that reeked of bourbon. "You're not supposed to know about that."

"Yeah? Well, I do. And I want to know why."

"Why? Because I left the island. It was the star that was keeping me young, and if I was a Soulkeeper at some point, I am no longer. I should be one hundred and eighteen years old. Without magic, I'd already be dead. Even with, no one can hold back the tide of time forever."

"Not why you are aging," Finn snapped. "I *know* why you are aging. I want to know why you never told me."

Bringing his hand to his mouth, he snorted, then held a finger in front of his lips. "Shhh. You're too loud."

"Tell me." Finn did not lower his voice.

"I know you, Finn. You'd try to save me. You're always trying to save people at your own expense. It's practically habit."

"You need to go back to the island. If you can get through the gate, the magic will stop you from aging."

"If I could get through the gate, I wouldn't be aging. I'd be a Soulkeeper. And judging by your old instructor, Soulkeepers don't age like everyone else."

"What do you mean?"

"Orelon, your old aerial instructor, he should be... eighty by now, but he hasn't aged a day since they left the island. Neither has Amuke, but to be sure, I can't remember how old he actually is."

"Soulkeepers don't age."

Theodor shrugged. "I'm sure they age eventually, but it

appears being a Soulkeeper mitigated the side effect of accelerated aging caused by the island's magic."

Considering this, Finn sat down in the leather chair. "How old is Kirsa supposed to be?"

With a surprised arch of his eyebrows, Theodor gave him a quizzical expression. "Older than she looks."

"Why do you think that is?"

"The Devil's magic, I suppose. She gave him her soul. He keeps her young." Theodor circled his hand in the air.

At first thought the explanation made sense, but Finn didn't fully accept that answer. "But how did he do it? He's cut off from the source of his power, which means he's using sorcery available here on Earth. Sorcery like *we* use. If the Devil can stop Kirsa from aging, why can't we stop you?"

Theodor's smile faded and a great sigh parted his lips. "I don't want to stop it."

"What?"

"I'm old. I've lived my life. I've loved and lost. It's time for me to die."

"No. That's stupid. If we work together, we can fix this. I know we can."

"Maybe you could. You are more powerful than any magician I've ever known. But what you'd have to do would be dark, deadly magic. Magic I would not want associated with me. The Devil's magic is ancient and evil. You don't come back from it unchanged. You can't dip a toe into magic like that. You have to dive in deep, over your head. It's not worth it." Stretching, he nested his fingers and cradled the back of his head in them.

"So... That's it? You're going to give up and die?"

With a sharp inhale, Theodor smiled broadly. He laughed at Finn until tears formed in his eyes. "I'm not giving up. I'm moving on. Death is but a doorway, after all. It is time for me to see what's on the other side." He went back to staring at the ceiling as if he could honestly see the stars. "Don't worry, Finn. I'll fix you before I go."

"Fix me? Fix. Me. I'm not going to be what kills you. You may be looking forward to your journey through the doorway, but I'll be stuck here trying to train Wendy, figure out how we can help the Soulkeepers, and wondering if I've completely lost my soul as well as my power. Not going to happen, you selfish—"

"Don't say something you'll regret." Theodor shot him a disarming look that didn't match his inebriated state.

"Then I guess I can't say anything at all." Fury brewing, Finn stormed out of the apartment and slammed the door behind him.

* * *

THE STREETS OF NEW ORLEANS WERE LACED WITH A DARK energy at night, as if an ancient power stretched under the surface of the city, latent but real. It coated the back of Finn's throat like a metallic aftertaste. This was a city of secrets, a city of magic, and he was now part of it. He'd never been more powerful than he was right now, and there'd never been more of a need for him to use that power.

"Extinguish," he whispered, and his body disappeared. He reached Saint Louis Cemetery and stood before the gate. His mind kept telling him to turn back, and he fought the pressing desire to forget the graveyard was there. That was what the spell on this place did.

"Finn?" HORU appeared in his peripheral vision, beamed from his earpiece.

"What is it?"

"Whatever is around this place is scrambling my signals. If you get much closer, I won't be able to come with you."

Finn frowned but screwed up his courage. "It's okay, HORU. You wait here. I'll do this alone."

"Fi—" He removed his earpiece, and she blinked out of existence. He set it down by the corner of the gate.

Placing his hand on the lock, he whispered, "Unbind." To his surprise, there was a click and the gate swung open. He waited, expecting Ravenguard to rush him and take him by the throat. Surely Lucifer had done more to secure the boundary.

Then again, maybe Lucifer did have a spell in place and he was being watched. Invisible as he was, he wasn't taking any chances. With a twist of his shoulders, he disseminated directly to the place he'd come for, a mausoleum on the fringes of the graveyard. He re-formed alone between the walls of two graves. It was here, not so long ago, that he'd argued with Ms. D about his tattoos. He understood now that she only wanted the best for him. She'd known the trouble he was getting himself into, even if he didn't know the exact price he would pay for his choices. He hadn't listened, and now he was here, standing in the dense fog that surrounded the cemetery, listening for the Devil.

When he was sure he was alone, he turned to the crack in the tomb wall. This was where he'd told Ms. D to hide the dagger. Did she take his advice? Hope had said she'd hidden it in the cemetery. That didn't mean it was here, where he'd suggested she hide it.

He squatted down and reached his hand into the crack. The spicy tingle of magic raced up his hand toward his shoulder. It was here all right, but it was protected, cloaked in a spell that made it practically undetectable. Now that he knew where it was though...

The symbols on his arms came alive. He ran the tips of his fingers along the spell, feeling its contours and rough edges, finding its weak points. With a grunt, he plowed his own magic into that enchantment, cracking it at its seams. His grip tightened and he withdrew the obsidian dagger. With the polished, symbol-engraved hilt in hand, he rotated the rough-hewn blade in the moonlight. He'd done it! Now, to get it back to the apartment where he could keep it safe until he saw Hope again.

Concentrating on the apartment, Finn twisted his shoulders and disseminated again. He re-formed still clutching the blade. Only, he wasn't where he'd told his body to go. This was not his apartment. Instead, he was in a living room with a plaid sofa and a roaring fire. He noticed Ravenguard first, sitting in an armchair sipping a cup of tea. He felt cold suddenly, despite the sweltering heat of the small room.

Lucifer oozed from the shadows, his dark eyes burning with hellish fire.

"Finn Wager, so we meet again."

❦ 17 ❦

THE INITIATE

It was possible that Michael had never in his life been this tired. He trotted away from the spider and the Confederate posse feeling heavy with what he'd learned from Fate. Not who his father was, per se. He was getting a handle on that. Deep inside, he'd always held on to the hope that his father would return someday and in his wildest dreams, he'd pictured living with him and his aunt, the day to day of being a family. Normalcy. Love.

That dream was gone now. His father wasn't missing; he was dead. He was never coming home. All he had was Aunt Millie, as it had always been. He was thankful for her, but seeing his mother and his father in the web made him long for the family that was stolen from him.

Deep in thought, at first he didn't notice the weather change. The snow stopped, the ice melted. Eventually though, he grew hot in his jacket. It was almost as if he'd passed from winter into spring over a few miles.

Tugging the reins, he stopped the horse in a grove of oak trees. Time had said he'd have to release what he desired most.

Fate had said he desired to be normal, but that was only part of it. He now realized what he'd wanted most was a normal family. Sure, he might someday have a wife and children, but he'd never have a mother and a father, never be tucked in at night by the people who'd brought him into this world. Somehow that was okay though. Now that he knew who his father was and what he'd done for the world, Mike couldn't help but feel proud.

He found two sticks and tied them together in the shape of a cross with a decorative leather tie he stripped from the saddle of his stolen horse. Once he plunged it into the ground, he folded his hands and prayed for his father and mother. He'd never attended a proper funeral for either of his parents. So, he gave them one himself.

Then he decided to let them both go.

When he turned back around, the horse was gone. He was standing on an English moor, and he was alone. It was impossible to tell what time it was based on the sky or position of the sun. There was no sun. He pulled out the pocket watch Time had given him and felt a knot tighten in his stomach. Day three. No wonder he was so tired. When had he lost so much time?

"It works differently here."

Michael looked up from the watch to find a boy about his age staring at him. Distinctly British, the boy's dark suit and stiff demeanor belied his otherwise friendly features. He was dressed for a funeral.

"Hello," Mike said because he wasn't sure what else to say. "Um. What works differently here?"

"Time. It conforms to the situation. The In-Between does not revolve around the sun as your Earth does."

"Oh." Mike remained silent, but when the other boy didn't

speak for a long stretch, the awkwardness factor went through the roof. "Uh, who are you?"

"Henry." Mike sensed there was a reason the boy didn't elaborate.

"Henry, do you know where I'm supposed to go next?"

A door appeared beside him, a familiar door. White wood with scuff marks at the bottom where he and his aunt had to kick it open. The door always stuck.

"Why is the door to my aunt's room next to you?"

"She's dying, Michael, and only you can Heal her."

"That's why I'm here, to become the Healer and then heal her."

"What if she doesn't wish to be healed?"

Mike raised his chin and made a sound like a growl. "What are you talking about? My aunt wants to live. She's only in her fifties. She's got a full life ahead of her."

"Does she? Or is this her time? Your aunt is a religious woman. Perhaps she's ready to go home."

One shake of his head and Mike dismissed the notion. "No. She would never choose to give up. She's all the family I have. She knows how much I need her."

"So, her living is about you and your needs?"

"Who are you?" Mike marched to the boy, his fists curling tighter.

"Henry."

"Why are you here? What do you know about my aunt?"

"I am Death. I am the immortal who will usher your aunt's soul on to Heaven when she goes. She has a good soul. A pristine soul. She'll be welcomed there with open arms."

Mike paced in front of the door. "Why... why are you asking me if my aunt wants to die?"

"I wondered if you'd considered it. You came here, ready to

die to save her. Now that you know what you know, would you become the Healer even if she chose to die anyway?"

"It isn't a fair question. She's unconscious. Neither you nor I could ever know what she wants because we can't ask her."

"*I* can ask her." Henry stepped forward between Mike and the door. "If we pass through this door, I can ask her soul what she'd prefer. The question is, are you willing to honor her wishes?"

Mike stared at the door, a hail of emotions pinging against his heart. "It's a moot point. I can't heal her. I haven't finished the third challenge."

"The third challenge is mine to give. So, I'm asking you, Michael, will you accept your role as Healer with or without saving your aunt's life? You came here to save her. Will you stay despite it?"

He scratched his jaw. Every part of him wanted to punch Henry in the face. How dare he suggest his aunt wanted to die? But the more he thought about it, the more he admitted to himself that he didn't know for sure what she wanted. Tears welled. He blinked them away.

"I'll do what she wants me to do."

"Will you choose to become the Healer regardless of her answer?"

Mike ground his teeth, forced himself to breathe. "Yes."

Death smiled, and the effect was truly frightening. "Good. Then find out the truth." One white-gloved hand reached for the doorknob. Mike flinched as Death gave the base a little kick to unstick it from the jam. And then they were in Aunt Millie's room, her tiny body stretched out on the bed as he'd left her. The place where the demon had sliced open her chest looked infected, with black veins running in all directions from the wound. Mike's body was there too, frozen next to her, staring at the triquetra. Gabriel hovered over both of them, a look of intensity in his blue eyes.

"Millie, I'm here to take you home," Henry said.

Mike's aunt sat up, or rather her soul did, popping out of her body and stretching her arms above her head as if she was waking up.

"Michael?" she asked. She turned toward Henry. "Who are you?"

"I am Death. I'm here to take you to Heaven."

"You don't have to go," Mike added quickly.

His aunt looked around her then, noticing her infected body on the bed. Her eyes widened. "I'm dead, honest and truly? That thing that was here… it killed me?"

"Yes," Henry said.

"No," Michael added. "Not yet. You can still be healed."

"Or you can move on to Heaven. That's where you're headed, Millie. There's no need to be afraid." Henry folded his hands in front of his hips.

This made her smile, and Mike's heart sank.

"Are you dead too?" she asked him.

"No. I'm fine," Michael said, and then he forced himself to add. "I'm… here to help you through this. Whatever you decide."

She smiled. "Oh, you must be an angel. You only look like Michael."

"You must choose, Millie," Henry said. "Whatever you want. It's up to you."

"It would be nice to see Momma and Pops again, and my sister. I miss them so. And to be done with the pain." She rubbed her wrists. Michael understood why. She never talked about it with him, but her arthritis had worsened over the years. And she refused to take medication.

It was all he could do to hold himself up. He nodded.

"But I couldn't leave Michael. I'm all he has in the world."

"He'd be okay," Mike said softly. "You've taught him how to survive and he's making plenty of money to support himself."

She nodded, her finger pressing into her lips.

"Anything you want is fine," he said, suppressing a sob. "Michael will be taken care of."

Henry held out a hand to her as if he were asking her to dance. Mike felt like he was being ripped apart. He closed his eyes. He had to do what was best for her. He'd become the Healer. He'd move forward, carry on the work his father had started, and he'd remember her always. She wasn't his. The choice she made had to be her own, but how it hurt him. As big as Mike was and as strong, the hold his aunt had over him was supreme. He loved her and wanted the best for her.

"If I have a choice, I choose to stay," she said. Mike opened his eyes. She had not taken Death's hand. "There are things I still want to do. Raising Michael is only one of them. That job is almost done. But there are more children out there, children who need an advocate. I can be that person. And my work at the library, it's more important than books. If you could see the folks who come in there looking for help... I can't abandon them. I can't. Heaven will have to wait."

Mike could barely contain his smile.

"Very well." Henry folded his hands at his hips again, looking mildly disappointed. "Lie back down, Millie." Her soul disappeared again. He turned to Mike. "Lay your hands on her, but know this, Soulkeeper, your ability to heal comes at a price that only you can pay. Good luck."

All at once, Death was gone. Mike felt himself drawn back into his body, sitting beside his aunt. Time started again. He dropped the triquetra. His aunt wasn't breathing.

"If you passed the initiation, I recommend you use your abilities quickly," Gabriel said. "She doesn't have much time."

He placed his hands over his aunt's heart, making sure his skin touched hers at the neck of her pajamas. He wasn't sure how he knew he needed to do this, but his gut told him the healing wouldn't work as well through material. For a moment, nothing seemed to happen, and then energy flowed. It rushed from somewhere deep inside him, flowing easily and unrestrained, straight to her heart. His light circulated through her body and the black wound started to heal.

But the more he gave her, the darker the room became. He blinked rapidly. "Gabriel? What's wrong with the lights?"

"Nothing's wrong with the lights. You're going blind. That's your price."

"What?" Mike almost pulled his hands away, but he could tell it was too soon. His aunt wouldn't live if he stopped now.

"Relax. It's temporary. You'll be blind for the length of time you healed someone. No biggie."

"No biggie? Are you kidding me?"

Completely blind, Mike heard rather than saw his aunt take a deep breath.

"Michael? Michael? What's wrong? Why are you in my room?" she said. He could no longer smell Gabriel.

He rubbed his useless eyes. "I'm sorry. I had a nightmare."

She pulled him into her arms. "Me too. I dreamt I was dead." She laughed. Thankfully the hug lasted long enough for his vision to return. Not fully, but enough so he could see vague outlines.

"Sorry to wake you. I'm fine now. I'll go back to bed."

"Okay."

He stood and exited his aunt's room... straight back onto the English moor. He blinked repeatedly until his vision returned, Henry and the door exactly where they were before. The door disappeared.

"Well done," Death said. With a snap of his fingers, they were on the veranda in front of his castle. Time... Mara was seated at a garden table sipping a cup of tea wearing a broad-brimmed hat the color of a dandelion. Beside her, the spider from the cave shifted into the dark-haired woman in the bright red dress. Fate, or Fatima as she'd called herself smiled at him.

Mara held out her white-gloved hand. "The pocket watch, please."

He pulled it from his vest pocket and handed it to her. She glanced at Henry. "One minute to spare."

"Imagine that. In the nick of time." Henry crossed to her and laid a passionate kiss on her mouth that made Mike blush.

"Don't mind them," Fate said. "Newly married."

He nodded awkwardly. "Is that it? Have I passed the initiation?"

Fate stood and formally raised her teacup. "Congratulations, Michael Carson. Soulkeeper, Healer, descendant of God's generous gift. You will heal with your right hand and command the strings of fate with your left. Lead wisely."

The three immortals raised their glasses to him, clinked them together, and each took a long drink. "Would you like to stay for tea?" Henry asked.

"I'd better get back. The Soulkeepers need me. They don't know."

"One thing before you go," Fate said.

Mike was inwardly amused. As if he had any control over this coming and going thing...

"Friends are a rare gift." Fate glanced at Mara and Henry. "All the power in the universe can't replace the magic of true friendship."

He waited. No one said another word. The three stared at him as if they had all the time in eternity to sip their tea.

"Okay," he finally said.

The three smiled, and it was as if a cannonball landed in his stomach. He flew backward, the silver scales shingling around him and spitting him out in his bed on the other side. Gabriel was there, hovering over him with an expression like he'd scored the winning lottery ticket.

❦ 18 ❦

REUNION

Was it just Hope or was the bus getting smaller? She tried to eat the slice of pizza in front of her, feeling like the walls were pressing in. There were too many bodies, too many murmuring voices in the cafeteria. Especially the one attached to a certain angel who insisted on sitting across from her.

"I was impressed with the way you handled the demon today," Damien said. "You may not be the Healer anymore, but your instincts are still sharp."

Hope gave him a curt nod but concentrated on her pizza, picking the pepperoni off before taking a bite.

"There's a place in the city that's supposed to have the best pecan pie in the world. Do you want to check it out when we're done here?"

"No." Short. Sweet. To the point.

He shifted in his seat. Jayden and Jenny were deep in conversation over the merits of Marvel vs. DC comics, completely oblivious to her pain. She stuffed more pizza in her mouth. The faster she could eat, the faster she could get away from him.

"You can't avoid me forever," Damien said.

She kept her eyes focused on the corner of the room. "I'm trying to eat."

"Come on, Hope. All I'm asking for is a second chance. Let's hash this out."

She dropped the pizza and glared at him. "You want to hash this out? There's nothing to hash, *Damien*." He balked at the way she said his name, like it was a curse. "You may be redeemed now, an angel, and we would be stupid not to use you for the greater good. But I don't have to forgive you, I don't have to like you, and I certainly don't have to date you." She stood up. "Look me in the eye so that there is no confusion."

"Confusion…" he mumbled, but he met her gaze.

"I don't want you here. I don't want to see you. I don't want to hear you. I don't want to eat with you. You may refuse to ascend to Heaven, but don't say you're here for me. I. Don't. Want. You." Wiping her hands on her napkin, she threw it onto her plate and stormed out of the cafeteria, trying not to notice that everyone else was staring.

Once she got beyond the door, she breathed a sigh of relief that he didn't follow her. What she'd said was true. She didn't have to like him or date him, but hell if she could control the attraction she felt for him. It was like living your life next to an unwrapped chocolate bar and never taking a bite. Sure, it would pass eventually. But sometimes, when she didn't have her guard up, she remembered how they'd laughed, how he'd spun her around on the dance floor and shared things that struck her deeply. Was any of it true? And the kiss. She touched her lips with two fingers and tried to forget the kiss.

It would be too easy to allow herself to fall for him again. And then what? He wasn't human.

A knock came from the front of the bus, and she strode up the aisle, grateful for the distraction. She wasn't sure who it could be. Everyone was in the cafeteria last time she checked. She approached the door slowly, ready to call upon her power if she needed it. When she saw who it was on the other side of the glass, she cursed.

"This can't be good," she said. Theodor and Wendy stared at her, faces grave. Not only did Theodor look thinner, his color gave her the impression he was ill. Wendy had her arm around him like she was holding him up. And Finn wasn't with them. She pulled the handle to let them in.

"What's wrong? Where's Finn?"

Wendy helped Theodor into a booth and shook her head. "Can you call Ms. D? Theodor had to disseminate with me to get here. He's not strong enough to explain this twice."

"Of course."

"Hope?" Wendy said, stopping her in her tracks. "Just Ms. D."

Hope frowned. "Okay."

A FEW MINUTES LATER, HOPE HAD SUCCESSFULLY CORRALLED Ms. D into the conference room without raising the suspicions of the other instructors or Soulkeepers. It was a hard thing to keep secret. The last time she'd seen Theodor, he was being dragged through a hole in the ground that led to Hell. And Wendy had been ejected from Revelations the day it became a new Eden. As gossip went, the fact they were both in the conference room was newsworthy. But Hope kept her mouth shut. Finn's life could be at stake.

"Tell me what has happened," Ms. D demanded. She'd initially been as surprised as Hope but was similarly focused when it came to getting to the bottom of the visit.

"It's Finn," Wendy began. "We think Lucifer is holding him captive."

Hope felt sick. "I talked to him a few days ago. He said you had protections on your place. How could this have happened?"

Theodor held up a hand. "Lucifer didn't take him from us. Finn walked into the cemetery on his own."

"What?" Ms. D shook her head.

Wendy held up Finn's earpiece. "We found this outside the gate. I think he intended to retrieve the obsidian dagger."

"Why would he do something so stupid?" Ms. D said through her teeth.

"Somehow he knew where you hid it. He's very powerful. He probably thought he could pop in, get it, and pop out before Lucifer noticed," Wendy said. "He told me he wanted to try to find it before Lucifer did."

"This can't be happening," Hope said, rubbing her temple. "The spell around that cemetery gave me a headache. How did Finn even get in there? We saw humans walk right past it. We all tried to get in. It was impenetrable."

Wendy cleared her throat. "But that's exactly what happened." She placed the earpiece in her ear and tapped. "HORU play the last time you saw Finn."

"Yes, Wendy." HORU appeared and projected a video on the conference room wall. Hope winced as the lock popped open for what she assumed was Finn. He was invisible.

"Why can't we see him?" Ms. D asked.

"He was using magic. Would you like me to enable thermal imaging?"

"Yes, HORU," Wendy said.

The recording started over, showing a silhouette of Finn's hand in shades of red releasing the lock. He pushed open the gate. When HORU warned him about the interference, he took his earpiece out and set it on the sidewalk. Hope watched the thermal image of his foot pass over the threshold and into the cemetery unimpeded. And then he completely disappeared, as if he'd dissolved into the night itself.

Hope shook her head. "How?" she asked Theodor. "We tried everything to get inside. What type of sorcery is this?"

Ms. D huffed loudly. "The real question we must ask is whether he was captured before or after he retrieved the blade." She laced her fingers together on the table. "We tried everything to get inside that cemetery. For Finn to walk right in, it's a little too convenient. I have a feeling he was let in. Lucifer wanted to follow him."

"Oh no," Hope said, as the truth dawned on her. "If it was after, that would mean Lucifer has the obsidian dagger." She turned to Theodor, pleading with her eyes for him to tell her it wasn't true.

"Finn was motivated to retrieve the dagger last night," Theodor said. "He most certainly would have disseminated directly to the place he knew it was hidden. Lucifer is extremely powerful and well fed. If the Devil let him in, I think you are right, Victoria. It was for the purpose of following him. If Finn wasn't able to come back out, I think it's fair to assume Lucifer has the dagger."

Hope's heart took off like a scared rabbit. "We've got to call Mike."

Wendy looked confused. "I think we have more pressing priorities than notifying Finn's ex-friend that he's missing."

"Mike is the Healer," Hope said, watching Wendy's eyes widen in response. "Well, *was* the Healer. Last we heard, he was planning to deny the call. Until he does, he's the last ingredient for Lucifer's spell. If Lucifer does have the dagger, Mike is the only thing standing between him and tearing down the veil between dimensions."

Ms. D placed a gnarly hand on hers. "We will go to him. We'll keep him safe."

Wendy leaned back in her seat. "Wow. Mike. I never thought he had it in him."

"There's something I don't understand," Hope said. "Theodor, you mentioned you thought Finn was motivated to get the dagger last night. Why? Why then? Why'd he go alone?"

Theodor glanced in Wendy's direction, then let out an exhausted sigh. "Because Finn learned last night that he is the most powerful he will ever be."

"I don't understand." Hope felt like she was missing something.

"Last night, Finn discovered that I am dying."

"Huh?" Wendy's usually perky disposition visibly darkened.

"The three of us, Wendy, Finn, and I, are linked." He held out his arm and a symbol danced across his skin. "We are bound together. The spell allows us to share power."

"They've been training me. It helps me to learn," Wendy said. It sounded like an excuse, like she was explaining why they'd done a bad thing. Hope supposed after what had happened with Finn, she wasn't keen to admit she'd taken a spell into her flesh.

"Finn found out that I am dying. Without Revelations and

the star beneath it, I am aging too quickly. If it weren't for magic, I'd already be dead."

"I am truly sorry, Theodor," Hope said. "But what does this have to do with the dagger?"

"Aside from Ms. D, Finn was the only one who knew exactly where the dagger was hidden, and he was the strongest he was ever going to be because he is linked to me. He has his power and access to my power too. And by the draw I'm feeling through our connection, I can tell you without a doubt that he is using it. Whatever Lucifer is doing to him hurts. It feels like… I'm keeping him alive. And I'm afraid, there's not much life left in me."

Wendy tugged at her hair and shivered. "Finn has been captured by Lucifer. Who knows what he's doing to him? We have to do something." Her voice cracked. "We have to get him back!"

Averting her eyes, Hope rubbed her chest to ease the heaviness that had formed there and cleared the thickness from her throat. She could think of no way to get Finn back that wouldn't endanger them all. As it was, Lucifer would probably try to use Finn to blackmail them to hand over the Healer. The Soulkeepers had to keep the Healer safe even if it meant losing Finn. It broke her heart to think that, but she knew it was true. The world as they knew it was at stake.

She turned to Ms. D and whispered, "We have to tell Mike."

Ms. D folded her hands, her mouth pulling into a tight line. "I need a few minutes with Theodor, alone."

❦ 19 ❦
THE DEAL

F inn hung from a pair of shackles in a dark room. He had no idea how long he'd been there, but it was long enough for him to wet himself multiple times and for his arms to feel like they'd never be the same. Whatever spell lined the chains that bound him, also stopped him from using his power, although he had the slightest sense that he still had his magic. Although he shivered, naked and alone in the darkness, something was feeding him, some tiny string of magic that Lucifer's chains could not cut off. His stomach panged with hunger and his head spun from lack of food or water, but he was still alive. He should be dead. By now he should be rotting.

Blink.

In the distance, a flicker of light cut the darkness. He must be hallucinating; the light was too far away to be real. Whatever it was, it was drawing closer. A candle and a girl. A familiar-looking girl. He couldn't quite place her. Could barely make her out.

Blink.

She was right in front of him. Her heart-shaped face

framed by perfectly shaped dark curls. Her clothes were strange. Dressed in a long skirt, blouse, and cardigan, something about her looked old-fashioned, like she'd walked off a movie set.

"You mustn't die," she whispered. "The monsters win if you die."

He laughed, longer and harder through his dry throat than he had intended. "They've already won," he mumbled.

"Shhh." She raised a small cup to his lips. "Here, drink this." Sweet water ran into his mouth and down his throat.

Blink.

"I know you. Of you. Your picture is on my dad's desk. I borrowed your trunk." His words slurred. Was he speaking out loud or was this all in his head? He remembered her. His great-grandma Mimi. She was a Soulkeeper during WWII, but her history was controversial. There were stories in his family, stories about her not doing the right thing. Stories about her potentially helping the enemy.

"Shhh." She looked over her shoulder. "You must listen to me. The most important thing is to survive. Dead men have no choices. Do not be the hero. There will be time for that, but not now. Now, you must do what he tells you to do. You must convince him to trust you."

"You want me to make a deal with the Devil?"

She brought her face closer to his and he could smell the wool of her sweater. "I want you to survive." She blew out the candle. Total darkness swallowed him again. Her voice came to him one last time. *"You have something he needs."*

He must have fallen asleep because the next time a light filled the room, he felt like his spine from his neck to his middle back had been wrenched out of alignment. His arm sockets were the source of so much pain, he couldn't breathe properly. This time, he wasn't so lucky as to have a visit from Great-grandma Mimi. It was Ravenguard and he was smiling.

"Still alive, Wager?" Ravenguard passed the candle under his bicep until it burned, but Finn was too weak to do much more than moan. The hunter snorted. "I don't know how you're still alive, but I'll finish you off if you beg me."

"Lu...ci...fer," Finn rasped.

"Excuse me? Are you asking for the Devil?"

Finn used all of his strength to nod.

Ravenguard moved in closer, sniffing a bit of blood that had dribbled from Finn's nose. "I think not. The Lord of Darkness has better things to do than kill the likes of you. I think I'll finish you off myself." He opened his mouth, and Finn had an extreme close-up of his fangs dropping.

"Leave us." Lucifer appeared beside them, his hand blocking Ravenguard's bite. The former admissions counselor gave Finn a bitter look before retreating from the room.

"You mentioned you wanted to see me?" Lucifer said. He raised a finger and poked Finn in the soft tissue on the inside of his arm. Pain like he'd never felt before instantly shot through his body.

Finn cried out. "D-deal."

The pain stopped. Lucifer's hand cupped Finn's chin and wrenched his head up. Finn's vision wavered as he tried to focus on the monster in front of him: dark hair, dark eyes, black Technothrob T-shirt. This close he could see all of his rock star tattoos. Oh...

"Symbols." Delirious, Finn wasn't sure he'd said it out loud.

"Do you think you're the only one who knows how to store magic in his skin? Now, what did you say about a deal?"

"H-elp you," Finn said.

Lucifer snapped his fingers and Finn's wrists were released.

His body slapped the floor, a new level of pain raging through him as blood flowed back into his shoulders.

"Do you know how I was able to capture you, Mr. Wager? You must have thought about it while you were languishing here."

Finn didn't answer. He was having enough trouble staying conscious.

"I knew eventually one of the Soulkeepers would come for the dagger. My enchantment would only allow a seeker through the gate if they were alone. Soulkeepers are predictable in that way, always trying to be the hero, always willing to sacrifice themselves. I waited for one to come alone and my plan was to follow, to kill, and to take. The obsidian dagger would be mine. But you, Finn, you sprang my trap in the strangest of ways. I could sense that someone had entered the gate, but I couldn't detect you anywhere. You were indistinguishable from one of us." He pointed at himself. "I admit that baffled me at first. After all, Kirsa, Ravenguard, and I were accounted for. I sent out Kirsa to search for the ghost who had opened the gate, and I did something else. I commanded the hellfire smoke to bring the dagger to me. As soon as you broke the spell protecting it, I sensed the obsidian. I didn't think it would work, of course. The smoke has no power over Soulkeepers. Imagine my surprise when it brought you here, still gripping it. Things have changed, haven't they? You're not a Soulkeeper anymore."

Footsteps passed in front of him, but he couldn't lift his cheek off the floor.

"When you disseminated, you came here, to this place, because the stuff you are made of is closer to us than to them. Like attracts like. I suspected the symbols in your flesh at first. Some of them are quite dark, but they aren't strong enough to do the damage that's been done to you. Far more likely that you injured your soul reopening the portal to Nod. I applaud you for that. It took power to undo the blessing around this place. You corrupted a tree growing on hallowed ground. You've gone dark, Wager. Far darker than you know."

Blood oozed from Finn's nose and dripped over his lip. He was dying. Probably going to Hell when he did. He closed his eyes.

"I can fix you, all of you. All you need to do is sign over your soul to me." Something cold and metallic was forced into his hand. He blinked. A pen. The *Love Kills Slowly* book slid in front of his hand. "Sign, Wager. Join me."

The Devil positioned the nib of the pen on the line. With the book so close to his nose, the lines on the page blurred as he mustered the strength to sign his name. Finn rolled his gaze up to see Lucifer grinning, his hand balling into a fist with his excitement. And then Finn's mind played a trick on him. He thought he saw Kirsa through the space between the Devil's feet, standing in the doorway. She was shaking her head. Her eyes were pleading, her mouth forming a silent *no*. Strange that his brain would produce such a thing. The real Kirsa would never discourage him from joining Lucifer. She'd signed her soul away months ago.

As Finn slowly scrawled his name on the line, he thought of his great-grandma Mimi, and then of his mother. He wasn't proud of what he'd become, but there was no turning back. Not from this.

The book slid out from under his hand. "You've made the right choice, Wager." He watched Lucifer's sneakers retreat toward the door. The last thing he heard before slipping into unconsciousness was, "Clean him up and find him a room."

🦋 20 🦋

THINGS LEFT UNSAID

"You've stepped in it this time, Theodor. You've ruined that boy's life." From the head of the conference table, Ms. D scowled at the magician.

"I know." Complexion ashen, Theodor slumped in his chair. "I didn't mean to. I told him to use the cards, but he felt he wouldn't be powerful enough without binding the spells to his flesh. I should have foreseen he would take things too far. I should have been more cautious with the spell we performed with the tree. I've made a terrible mistake, Victoria. Please, forgive me."

"It's not my forgiveness you need. It's Finn's. You have to get him back. You have to undo this mess you've made."

He circled one hand. "As they say, the spirit is willing but the flesh is weak. I'm dying, Victoria. I don't have much time."

"You're aging."

"Yes." His brow furrowed. "So is Finn."

"What?"

"He's taken on too much power too fast. He is dying too. Not as fast as me, but I believe he knew his time was short. Finn knew he'd either have to give up the symbols or give up his life using them. I believe he acted now because he understood that whether he allowed me to strip the symbols from his flesh or he allowed the symbols to kill him, he was at an impasse."

She chewed her lip. "Fuse, Orelon, and Amuke stopped growing older as soon as the island was transformed into the new Eden. We think being a Soulkeeper slows the aging process."

"You look beautiful. I'd forgotten before. At Revelations, before the incident, I should have known the clone wasn't you. I think I knew on some level."

"The others said they suspected as well. But what could any of you have done? We were duped for decades. None of us understood the true nature of the place, other than Ravenguard and Applegate."

"And Damien. Damien must have known before he was redeemed."

Victoria sighed. "Yes. The angel is an enigma. It is no wonder Hope is torn apart by her feelings for him."

"She has feelings… for the angel?"

"Not that she'll admit." Victoria laughed.

Theodor took a labored breath. "Now that I have you alone, I think it's well past time for me to make my own admission. I love you. I have always loved you. I think you are what I will miss most after I die."

Victoria stood and walked around the table, taking a seat in the chair beside him. "You always did have a flair for the dramatic." She rolled her eyes. Reaching around her neck, she removed the star amulet Damien had made for her, the one that had once saved her life.

"What is that?" he asked.

She took his hand in hers. "You've always thought you could control everything. I think it is part of your personality to want to predict the future and set your sails toward calm waters. For you, magic is a tool meant to prevent hardship for the people you love. You've tried to save everyone but yourself from the very beginning. But none of us can always be in control. Sometimes we have to have faith."

"I was never any good at believing in things I can't see."

"I know. For what it's worth, I forgive you, Teddy. But I won't let you off the hook. Death is too easy for you. I need you to fix what you've broken."

He laughed. "If only I had a choice."

She flashed him a lopsided grin and looped the amulet over his head, sliding the star down the neck of his shirt where it glowed amongst the soft curls of hair on his chest.

Theodor's eyes widened. "What is this?"

"It's a piece of the star. The only one in existence."

"But don't you need this?"

"No. I'm a Soulkeeper. I've been on the island, and like Fuse, Orelon, and Amuke, I don't need it anymore."

Theodor placed a hand over the bump in his shirt that was the star and closed his eyes. "I can feel it working. It feels warm, radiant. I remember this. I can remember when this was normal." He opened his eyes again and looked up at her with reverence.

She grinned. "That amulet doesn't come for free. From now on, you are on our team. You owe us your allegiance. If we're going to find Finn, we need your help and your power."

He leaned toward her until she could feel his breath on her face. "Thank you."

"I'm not ready for you to leave me," she said. A rush swept

through Victoria at the way he looked at her. She'd forgotten what it was like to be this close to Teddy.

"Victoria…" he said softly. She tipped her head, her gaze drifting to his mouth.

The door flew open, sending the two adults scrambling apart.

Hope appeared in the doorway, stopping short and narrowing her eyes on the two of them. "What's going on here?"

"Nothing," Victoria said quickly.

"Comparing notes," Theodor said.

Hope's brow furrowed before she seemed to remember something important. "Both of you need to come quickly. You'll never believe who is here."

Victoria glanced toward Theodor and then followed Hope toward the front of the bus. "Perhaps Wager has found his way back home after all," she whispered. But when they reached the booths where the other Soulkeepers had gathered, it wasn't Finn who was waiting for her.

"Hi Ms. D," Michael said. "How would you feel about adding a Healer to your team?"

MICHAEL SCANNED THE OTHER SOULKEEPERS, WONDERING WHAT they must be thinking. He hadn't expected a warm welcome, necessarily. He'd left on shaky terms. But the stunned silence that met him was hard to deal with. Were they angry? Did they hate him?

Hope spoke up first. "Does this mean you passed the initiation?"

"Like a boss." He smiled. "Gabriel flew me down here after I said goodbye to my aunt and packed a bag." He kicked the Samsonite behind him.

"But I thought you were abdicating? You said you hated this and were going to tell Gabriel to shove it," Hope said.

Mike shrugged. "That proved not as easy as it sounds." He ran his tongue along his teeth. "You bitches want to see what I can do? Turns out becoming the Healer comes with some dope perks."

The others nodded excitedly. Jayden folded his arms across his chest and gave Mike a smug grin. "Let's see it."

Mike flipped his hand and pointed the resulting fan of silver webbing at Jayden. The guy's life came into focus along more than a dozen interlocking strands. Mike focused in on one. Jayden was eight, screaming because his mom turned the lights out and he was afraid of the dark. A pang of guilt rippled through him. This was like reading his most personal diary entries. Mike almost abandoned the demonstration. Almost. Until he took another look at Jayden's smug expression.

He plucked the string.

Jayden's smile turned to horror, and his hands reached out to grab the booth behind him. "No. Nooo. Mommy!" he yelled. All the blood drained from his face.

Jenny grabbed his shoulders and shook. "Jayden, what's happening?"

Jayden started to sob.

Mike turned his wrist over, feeling genuinely bad for the dude now. "It should go away in a minute or two. That's how long it lasted before."

"What did you do to him?" Hope asked.

"I made him believe he was eight years old again and alone in a dark room."

Jenny shot him a disapproving look. But Ms. D looked fascinated. "How does it work?"

"It was a gift from Fate. The power she gave me allows me to see the fabric of a person's life, all of their major experiences. I saw Jayden was once afraid of the dark, so I plucked that string, sent him back to that experience. It's a very effective way to neutralize someone for a few minutes."

Jayden shook his head and gave Michael a dirty look. "You will never use that on me again."

Mike nodded. "Fair enough."

Theodor placed his hands on Victoria's shoulders. "That is a strange and powerful gift."

Mike had a moment to digest that both Theodor and Wendy were there. "Where's Finn?"

Victoria glanced at each of the others and then seemed to take it upon herself to break the news. "It gives me no pleasure to share this with you, but as the new Healer, you should know." She approached him, rubbing her hands together. "Of his own free will, Finn broke into the cemetery where Lucifer has taken up residence. He was trying to retrieve the obsidian dagger. He never came back out. We think he may have been captured."

"Lucifer has the dagger, doesn't he?"

"You are in grave danger, Michael," she said.

"And Finn?"

Victoria frowned. "Finn is missing."

❧ 21 ❧

FREE LUNCH

F inn came awake in a cozy cabin room with a fireplace and a handmade quilt. He was sore, but it didn't feel like anything was broken anymore. He felt surprisingly good for a guy who'd been tortured the last few days. A delicious smell filled his senses and he turned his head to find a club sandwich and a bowl of soup on his nightstand. Sitting up, he palmed the sandwich and shoved it into his mouth like an animal. He was so hungry, he didn't even stop to consider the food might be poisoned or could further bind him to the Devil. He just ate.

"Why did you do it?" Kirsa sat in a chair next to the fireplace. He hadn't even noticed her there, but by the book in her hands, she'd been there awhile. The novel she was reading had a woman with fairy wings on the cover, but Finn couldn't make out the title.

He swallowed before answering her. "Why did I do what?"

"Sign over your soul, shit-for-brains." She dropped the book and turned in her chair to face him.

"Is this a trick question? You of all people should know why I did it. If I hadn't, he would've killed me."

She looked down at her hands in her lap. "Have you ever considered you might be better off dead?"

Finn took another bite of his sandwich. "No. Death is never the answer."

"You've sold your soul to Hell, you know. However long he uses you, you end up there. Both of us do." Kirsa leaned back in her chair and crossed her feet at the ankles.

"I was going to Hell anyway." He shrugged. "Since when are you sentimental about your soul? You were the one who used to love stabbing a dagger into your students every chance you got."

She exposed her teeth to him. "Why did you come here? Why did you give yourself up?"

"I was after the dagger."

"And now Lucifer has it, and we are one step closer to our ultimate destination. All he needs is to find and capture the new Healer and he can perform the sacrifice to merge the realms and break God's spell over him."

Finn took another bite to disguise the nervous tick that had begun in his cheek. Hope had told him a new Healer had been called, but he had no idea who it was. It was possible the person called didn't know what they were yet. He hoped it stayed that way for a long time.

"Hopefully that happens sooner rather than later," Finn said.

The way she turned to him then, reminded him of an owl, eyes large and neck craning in surprise. Actually, the more he looked at her, the more the similarities came into focus. Her eyes hadn't widened, they protruded, larger than normal in her head. Her gracefully arching nose now extended beak-like from her face, accentuated by her sunken cheekbones. The island had made Kirsa indestructible, but she was no longer on the island. Was it possible she was aging? Were her powers waning?

"You want to get to the part where we spend eternity in Hell faster?" Kirsa asked as if the idea was ludicrous.

Finn chewed slowly. He needed to make this good. He was sure this was a trap. Kirsa was goading him, trying to get him to say something disloyal to the Devil. They were still in the cabin after all. No way was their conversation private. Lucifer was monitoring everything he said. He was sure of it.

"The whole world is going to go to Hell." He shrugged. "Lucifer is going to merge worlds." He pointed his pinkie finger at her. "But you and I will be rewarded for helping him. We'll be treated better than everyone else because we joined forces with him."

"What have you done to yourself?" she asked softly, her gaze drifting to his tattoos.

"I could ask you the same thing."

"I'm not the one covered in tattoos."

"Don't forget bald."

She snorted. "Not anymore. Lucifer took care of that."

Finn lowered the sandwich. A quick look around the room and he saw a mirror on the wall. He hopped out of bed, amazed he could hop after the torture he'd endured, and found his reflection. His hair *was* back. Perfectly trimmed, light blond, and spiked over the crown of his head exactly the way he liked it.

"Hot damn." He ran his fingers through it, smiling.

"Yeah. There are perks."

He snagged the plate from beside the bed and brought it to the fire, taking the seat across from her. "What kind of perk did he give you? I thought he'd stopped you from aging since you left the island, but you look a little worn out. No offense."

"No offense taken." She stared at him long and hard. "First tell me about the tattoos."

"I'm a sorcerer. Theodor taught me magic and I... kept going. I'm stronger than he is now."

She sighed heavily, her breath shaking a little as she exhaled.

"What's wrong with you?"

"You're the final piece." The uneven light from the fire sent shadows dancing across her face. "The Healer is something of Heaven's. She must be sacrificed with the obsidian dagger—something of Hell's. But Lucifer can't be the one to perform the sacrifice."

"What are you talking about? Why not?"

"He thought I could do it. I guess the person has to have a soul. But I've known for a while now I'm not his first choice for the job. He needs a sorcerer who has one foot in Heaven and one foot in Hell. It's ancient magic. If he does it, there's something about a loophole..." She shook her head. "The spell is unbalanced or something. Like I said, I could do it, because I have a human soul, originally from God but now the Devil's. Only, I'm not a sorcerer. The tear in the veil won't be as powerful. He's seen what you did with the tree. You're the perfect tool to merge the realms."

Soulkeeper and sorcerer. So, that's why Lucifer kept him alive. It was like his great-grandma Mimi said. *You have something he needs.*

Kirsa stared into the fire. "Once we find the new Healer, you'll be the one to drive the dagger into her heart. You'll be the one to thin the veil between realms so that Lucifer can tear the whole thing down." She brushed invisible dust from her pant legs.

Over the crackling fire, Finn listened to his heart pound.

The idea of plunging that dagger into a Soulkeeper's heart was horrifying. He wouldn't do it. No matter what happened. No matter how Lucifer tortured him, he simply would not sacrifice the Healer.

"You won't have a choice," Kirsa whispered as if she could hear what he was thinking. "He can force you to do things you don't want to do. Once you sign your name, you sign over your free will."

"I didn't say anything," Finn said defensively. "I'll do whatever he asks me to do. What do I care as long as I come out okay?"

She placed her hands on her knees and stood. "It's time to get ready. Technothrob has a show tonight. You're replacing the drummer."

"I can't play the drums."

"Doesn't matter. A little Lucifer mojo and you'll be Neal Peart before the first number. Trust me, Lucifer has me playing bass and singing back up, and I'm no good at either."

"What happened to the old drummer?" Finn remembered the band consisting of the original members of Technothrob at one point.

"Ravenguard ate him." She moved toward the door. "Your outfit is in the closet."

"Hey, Kirsa, you never told me what you did to yourself. You look like you're losing weight."

She paused with her back to him, her shoulders slumped. "Unlike Ravenguard, I can't eat a band member when I get hungry."

He parted his lips to ask her more, but she was already out the door. Once her words sank in, he returned to his food and ate every last bite.

22

TECHNOTHROB

Michael strode toward the Tilted Raven, twitchy and ready for a fight. A few days had passed since Ms. D had told him about Finn's abduction, a few days that Mike had stewed over what to do next. He and Finn might have had a falling out recently, but no one hurt one of his friends, past or present, without dealing with him. He was the Healer now, their leader. He would find Finn, and they would bring him home, one way or another.

"Are you sure about this, Mike?" Jayden said. "How do you even know he'll be with Technothrob? Lucifer could have him locked up somewhere while he plays this gig."

"I don't. I'm betting on the fact that the Devil won't want to leave Finn alone. He's too powerful. But if Wager isn't here, we can assume Lucifer is keeping him in the cabin in the cemetery."

"And then what?"

"We'll cross that bridge when we come to it."

"We should have run this one by Ms. D," Jayden said.

"He's got a point," Hope said, catching up to them.

"I'm the Healer, okay? I've got a feeling about this. Finn is our friend. We owe this to him."

Jayden and Hope gave each other a worried look, but they both nodded. They were in.

There was a line to get in. Mike stopped at the end of it, smiling down at a few girls who whispered and glanced in his direction. The three were grouped together like a school of miniskirt-clad fish. One, with amethyst hair and an animated tattoo of a poodle winking, gave Mike a smile and a wave.

"Have I mentioned I have a girlfriend? Her name is Jenny," Jayden squeaked. Mike made room for him to move behind him, to where Hope was brooding. She'd never admit it, but she was worried. Word was that Damien, the redeemed fallen angel who was helping the Soulkeepers, had disappeared for days. According to the others, he'd disappeared after a particularly humiliating reaming by Hope over dinner. She'd told him to go away, and he had. Only Hope seemed less than happy about it now. Mike tried to ask her about it, but she refused to say a word.

"Mike." She nudged past Jayden. "You'll need this." She tied an amulet around his wrist. "I should have given it to you a long time ago."

"I'm not much of a jewelry person."

"It's Soulwort. It will shield you from Lucifer's influence… and Juliette's. Believe me, you'll need it." Her green eyes became as hard as emeralds. She was serious.

"I just became a jewelry person."

"Smart choice." She glanced over her shoulder. The other people in line were absorbed in their own conversations, but she stepped in closer anyway. "Remember, he'll be able to smell you if you get too close. Soulkeepers smell like sunlight and fresh air. Try to lay low." She pulled away.

"Wait, Hope?"

"Huh?"

"I'm trying to lay low, but people are staring at me. Can they tell that I'm, uh, different? Did you have this happen when you were a…?"

She laughed, her eyebrows bobbing toward her hairline. "Oh, you're different all right. About 250 pounds of tall, dark, and different. They're interested in you because you're…" She trailed off and gestured in the general direction of his abs and shoulders. "It has nothing to do with what you are."

His ears grew hot. "Oh." He turned and smiled wider at the girls in front of him.

Hope smacked his arm. "Concentrate on the mission."

He rubbed the spot where she'd slugged him. "Hey, I could say the same to you."

"What are you talking about?" She looked positively offended.

Mike straightened to his full height. "Methinks the lady doth protest too much. I'm talking about the fact that you are spending a lot of effort to not talk about what happened with Damien."

"How do you know about that?"

Mike sent her a pitying look. "Everyone knows. Literally everyone is talking about it behind your back."

"Those disloyal asshats."

"I guess they liked having him around, so…"

"I don't want to talk about Damien. He means nothing to me. It's not my fault he decided to go back to Heaven or… whatever. I don't know where he is." Hope toyed with the ends of her red hair. She was wearing a leather halter top and flowing silk print pants with chunky silver shoes. Pretty. Although, she wasn't Mike's type. Wager's though. If Finn was in this bar, under Lucifer's control or not, he'd notice her. Mike was counting on it.

Mike tipped his head. "Okay then. It's settled. Damien is nothing to you. Funny how your face changes though when you hear his name."

A high-pitched sound came from her throat. "Shut up."

The bouncer, a massive, red-faced man with a skull tattoo, pointed a finger at Mike's face. "You two. You're in."

For a second, Mike froze, unsure what to do, but Hope grabbed his hand and pulled him toward the door. She tipped the bouncer on their way inside.

"What are you doing? We left Jayden by himself out there."

"It's better this way. It's dangerous for us to all be in the same place at the same time. It makes us conspicuous. He gets it. Believe me."

Mike allowed her to guide him into the shadows at the back of the dance floor. The club was arranged like a pit with a raised platform where the instruments were already set up. Technothrob was scheduled to go on at seven, but a DJ was spinning tunes for the crowd while they waited. This was a smaller venue for Technothrob but closer to New Orleans. They'd noticed this happening more and more lately. The Devil, it seemed, preferred to stay close to home.

"Dance with me," Mike said. "I want to get closer to the stage."

He started moving his body to the music, guiding Hope toward the center of the floor. Pulling her close, he found the rhythm and tried to blend into the crowd. They'd almost reached the base of the stage when Winking-poodle tattoo popped up beside him.

"Hey, line neighbor. Want to dance?" She moved closer, putting herself between him and Hope.

"No thanks," he said.

"He's all mine, ladies." Hope grabbed Mike by the waist and hauled him against her.

Mike chuckled as the girl made an obscene gesture and moved away. "Damn. Girls fighting over me." He ran a hand down the front of his shirt.

She rolled her eyes. "Get over yourself." Suddenly, Hope missed a beat and grabbed his elbow. "There she is." Her dark tone broke the mood. Mike followed her gaze to the place where a peacock-colored guitar rested in its stand, the name Juliette scrawled across the baseboard.

Mike pulled her closer. "We should take it."

"What? No, Mike. It has to be protected by a spell. Lucifer would never—"

"How will we know if we don't try? If we get the guitar, Lucifer can't use it to lure more souls. We can weaken him. Or we can trade it for Finn." Mike's hands were itching to lift the thing and get out of there.

Hope gripped his collar and yanked him down so she could whisper in his ear. "No, Mike. You'll call attention to yourself and what you are. It's too dangerous."

But his gut told him to do it. Wasn't he the Healer? Didn't he have magical intuition or something? He needed to trust himself, or he'd never be the leader he was meant to be.

"Mike. No. I don't think you should—"

In a few quick steps, Mike ducked behind the DJ booth and leapt onstage, sliding behind the stage-left curtain. He grabbed the guitar and smuggled it into the shadows. Directly into the chest of a security guard. The man brushed the side of his jacket back to reveal the gun on his hip.

"Give me the guitar," the man said quietly. He reeked of Hell, although Mike could sense his soul. He wasn't a demon.

It was all very quiet, refined. No one could see them behind the curtain.

"No," Mike said. He was bigger and faster and he couldn't die. He was leaving with Juliette.

"Have you lost your mind?" Finn Wager appeared beside security, dressed to kill in a silk shirt and leather pants. He placed a hand on the security guard's arm and whispered in his ear. The guy left without another word.

Mike faced his friend. It was like looking at a complete stranger. Symbols danced under his skin, and the look on his face was less than welcoming.

"Finn, we can get you out of here. Come with me now. We'll take you someplace safe."

"We?"

"Hope's here too."

As if he'd conjured her by saying her name, Hope appeared beside Mike. "Your hair grew back. How did your hair grow back?"

Finn didn't acknowledge her. He snatched the guitar from Mike's hands. "You two are idiots. Can't you see it's too late for this? You need to get out of here, fast." Finn looked over his shoulder toward the backstage area.

"No," Mike shook his head. "We're not leaving without you."

Finn stepped in closer. "I don't know how they talked you into this, Mike, but you are way out of your league here. You need to leave before you get hurt. We don't have much time and..." Finn rubbed his nose. "Why do you... stink?"

"I'm not going to get hurt. I can take care of myself." Mike held up both hands like he was calming a skittish animal. "Let's talk about this outside."

"How did your hair grow back?" Hope asked again. "And why do you look like you've been on vacation?"

Finn cast a look in Hope's direction that Mike could only define as tortured. "It wasn't a vacation."

All the air seemed to drain from Mike's lungs. The friend he'd once known as Finn wasn't there anymore, but something dark and tainted. A dark aura surrounded him, seemed to consume him. Hope had once told him that Healers could see people's souls. Was that what this was? Because if so, Finn's soul was sick. It might even be dying.

"What happened to you?" Mike asked.

Finn glanced between the two of them. "I'm going to say this one more time. You need to leave, now. Lucifer is... eating, but if he finds you here, he will torture you for the name of your Healer and once he has it, he will kill you. Go home to your aunt, Mike. Stay safe. Stay out of it."

"I can't stay out of it. I'm the—"

Hope's hand clamped over Mike's mouth, and she started pulling him toward the stairs. "Goodbye, Finn." The salutation was sad, like Hope said it with tears in her eyes.

Mike didn't get it. He had absolutely not come here to rescue his friend only to be sent away. "Wait," he said. He reached out and grabbed Finn's arm.

As soon as Mike touched him, he knew it had been a mistake. Power flowed from his hand into Finn's skin. Healing power. And in exchange everything darkened. He pulled his hand away before he went completely blind.

Hope dug her nails into his skin, looking frantically around them. "Run. Mike, run."

But he was locked in a staring contest with Finn. And his friend seemed as horrified as he felt.

"It's you," Finn said. And then he cursed. "You stupid prick."

✤ 23 ✤

THE FIRST TIME I DIED

Finn hadn't wanted to know. But now he did, and there was no forgetting the truth. When Mike had touched his arm, healing energy flooded his body, causing every symbol bound to his skin to burn like a brand. Thankfully, he'd pulled his hand away before doing any damage. Finn needed his powers, especially now.

He'd told Mike to go. Begged him. Hope had figured out what was happening right away, but not Mike. That numbskull stood there being a loyal friend, probably trying to reconcile the person Finn used to be with the one he'd become. The guy didn't get it. There were no similarities. Finn was an entirely different person from the boy who saved Mike from embarrassment in the third grade. He was the Devil's accomplice now. He had to be.

"Listen to Hope," he said to Mike. "Run, now. Don't turn back." Thankfully, the idiot finally obeyed. Finn replaced Juliette on her stand.

"What are you doing?" Ravenguard appeared backstage,

which meant Lucifer wasn't far behind. How did he explain being onstage?

"Soulkeepers!" Finn pointed at Mike's receding form. Almost to the door. Almost. *Run, you bastard.*

The hunter sniffed the air. Ravenguard drew his dagger from inside his jacket and leapt into the crowd. He cut through the throng of gyrating bodies, his gripped dagger concealed inside the breast of his red jacket. He'd never catch up to Mike in time. Not unless he started tearing the crowd apart to reach them, and that was a publicity no-no.

Lucifer appeared beside him, nostrils flaring and tracking Ravenguard in the crowd. His eyes widened when he saw Hope.

"I couldn't stop them," Finn said. The Devil seethed, but he was too late. Mike and Hope were at the door.

Ignoring Finn, Lucifer picked up Juliette. He slung the strap of the peacock-blue guitar across his shoulder and struck a chord with the extended talons of his hand. Everyone in the crowd froze, drawn in by the sound. Everyone but Mike, Hope, and Ravenguard. Lucifer leaned toward the microphone. "Get them."

The bouncer blocked the door. They were there. Finn could see the streetlights through the open door. But that human elephant was blocking their way. Fists flew. Although Mike and Hope were stronger, the crowd had closed in. He watched Mike reach for his triquetra, but a dozen humans grabbed his arms before he could and tackled him to the floor. Hope tried to use her power too. A vine or two succeeded in restraining her attackers. But there were fifty people behind them, swarming over each other to take her down.

Blood sprayed. Shreds of her clothing were thrown above the heads of the mob. He could no longer see either of them.

Finn glanced toward Lucifer. Some part of him writhed. He wanted to help, but if he did anything, it would be the end of him. He didn't dare. And the longer he waited and did nothing, the more that tiny piece of him that wanted to help decayed. *They were idiots anyway. They had it coming. Don't be the martyr. Survive,* he told himself.

He was frozen, helpless. Even when the sounds of Hope's screams met his ears, he did nothing.

And then, the crowd parted enough for Finn to see Ravenguard standing over Michael, his red coat visible in the shifting crowd. He raised his hands above his head and plunged his dagger into Michael's heart.

That tiny light inside of Finn screamed. They were killing him. They were killing her. Hope's screams came again, cutting over the music as the crowd swarmed her, trampling her underfoot.

Without thinking, Finn took a step in their direction.

"Don't you dare," Kirsa whispered. She was behind him, so close, he could feel the bones of her shoulders pressing into his back. "You'll ruin everything."

He stayed where he was, but that tiny light in his chest refused to go out. *Please God*, he prayed.

Finn was not the type of person who had ever believed in the power of prayer, but it was clear *someone* had heard him. Everything changed in a flash of light.

HOPE NEVER THOUGHT THIS WOULD BE HOW SHE DIED. SHE LAY at the bottom of a heap of feet and grabbing hands, unable to breathe. A woman's nails gouged the flesh of her arm, while a man kneeled on her chest, and someone's stilettos dug into her calf. She was bleeding and terrified and had no air left to scream. Out of the corner of her eye, she could see Michael. He'd taken a dagger to the chest and was sheet white. His eyes stared blankly at nothing. He was dead.

He'd tried to call Gabriel, but the crowd had overpowered him too quickly. He wasn't able to reach his triquetra. He was the Healer. He'd come back. She wouldn't. Where was Jayden? A knee landed on her nose and blood sprayed across her face and into her mouth. The pain threatened to knock her out and sent a wave of nausea through her.

But she didn't pass out. She was conscious when a wave of light lifted the crowd off her body and washed over in an explosion of fire. Ravenguard was thrown off Michael and plowed into a sea of people, knocking them into each other. Others, the bouncer, the girl with the poodle tattoo, they floated through the air like rag dolls.

The fire was beautiful, hot against her skin, but somehow comforting. It lapped the air over her broken body. Bright. Colorful. Warm.

Starved for air, Hope tried to breathe now that there weren't fifty people parked on her chest, but the air whistled into her pinched lungs. She could barely draw a trickle. Black dots swirled in her vision.

The fire swept her off the floor and against a broad chest. "I have you. Breathe. Just breathe," it said. It hurt to move her eyes, but she knew who it was. Damien. His face was close, and he smelled of freshly peeled oranges and a picnic near the ocean. His warmth seeped into her skin.

"Mike," she wheezed.

A blast of dark energy bombarded them from the direction of the stage, but with a circle of his arm, Damien shielded her and Mike from the worst of it. Unfortunately, the other patrons weren't as lucky. Hope watched dozens of concert-goers collapse, twitching like poisoned roaches. Lucifer jumped off the stage and strode toward them.

"You," he seethed. "How dare you challenge me, *Brother*. Crawl back to Heaven where you belong."

Behind Lucifer, Hope saw Finn. He and Kirsa were standing there, doing nothing while people died all around them. As Lucifer strode toward her, he tore through the crowd of human beings hell-bent on taking her life. She cried then, for the boy she used to know, for the friend she'd lost who now worshiped at the altar of self-interest.

Damien noticed her tears. "Hold on to me." He grabbed Mike around the chest and twisted. Lucifer's howls followed them into the light. It was a rough journey. Unlike the last time she'd traveled with the angel, this passage was turbulent and squeezed what remained of her breath out of her. It seemed like an eternity before they slammed into the pavement in the parking lot where the tour bus was parked. Hope grunted from the impact.

Framed by a circle of artificial light from the streetlamp above him, Damien looked down at her, his healing warmth still flowing into her body. "I'm sorry. It's more difficult with artificial light. I would have helped you sooner if it hadn't been so dark in there."

Hope was too weak to talk. Beside her, Mike lay dead on the pavement. Blood covered his torso, stemming from the wound in his heart. His eyes were glazed.

"He'll come back," Damien said. "Give him time." He cupped the back of her neck along her hairline, and the curl of energy that flowed into her made her moan. For a few moments, she forgot about everything, even about who Damien had once been to her. All she felt was love, warmth, peace. It flowed into her, through her. It healed her. Her breathing eased, and the bright red of her bruised and broken flesh faded and disappeared. Bones that might have been broken became whole again.

Hope looked into Damien's eyes and saw the angel. The one who existed before the fall. The one who looked at her like she was the center of his universe.

"You came for me," she said, tears welling.

"You're crying. Where does it hurt?" Damien ran his hands along her limbs, searching, she supposed, for wounds he hadn't healed yet.

She grabbed his hand and placed it over her heart. "You came for me," she said again. "I sent you away, but you came anyway."

He stopped and wiped under her eyes, then smoothed her hair back from her face. "Of course I came. I love you. I'll leave again if you wish, but I could not let you die. I could not bear it." His face contorted into something truly haunted, eyes dark, cheeks gaunt. He carefully set her down on the pavement and pulled away.

"Where are you going?"

"I thought you'd want me to go now that you're healed."

She reached up and looped her arms around his neck, her pulse quickening. God help her, she could not push him away anymore. "No."

"No?"

"I don't want you to go. Please don't go."

He pulled her into his arms again and she pressed her cheek to his, inhaling deeply. This close it was impossible to deny her feelings for him. She dug her fingers into the back of his hair, felt his wing curl around her like a cloud. Her nose traced the line of his jaw from his ear to his chin. Her eyes landed on his mouth, his full, parted lips. She couldn't help herself. She kissed him.

Hope remembered what it was like to kiss Liam. She'd felt excited, alive, like the world was spinning faster than a moment before. Kissing Damien was so much more. She knew what he was and what he had been. And she accepted all of it. She kissed the boy and the man. The one who had waited and watched over her for longer than she would have bothered with herself. The kiss was warm and wonderful, timeless but somehow grounding. There was a tug inside her heart and she finally understood. The kiss had healed the last thing broken inside her: her heart.

Damien pulled away. "Now, will you call me Liam?"

She shook her head. "No."

"You still don't forgive me?"

She placed her hands on either side of his face. "It's because I forgive you that I will always call you Damien. I know who you are. I know what you've done. I forgive you, Damien."

He let out a shaky breath. There was a sound behind them, and Damien rose with one flap of his wings, setting her on her feet. She whirled to find Mike's body bucking off the pavement. His heart glowed like a beacon, his back arched between head and heels. With his eyes rolled back in his skull, his lashes fluttered as the light in his heart spread to his fingers and toes.

Hope rushed to his side. "You're okay, Mike. Don't fight it." She remembered the first time she'd died and came back. It was even more painful than it looked. She spoke to him in soothing tones. And when his body collapsed back onto the pavement, she was there, her hands on his shoulders.

He blinked twice at her, then said one word. "Ow."

"I know. Breathe through it. You're okay."

"Did I…"

"Die? Yes. Ravenguard stabbed you in the heart."

Mike sat up and patted his chest, digging his fingers into the hole in his shirt. He looked down at himself. "Damn. I liked this shirt. Not even a scar though."

Hope nodded. "It's pretty amazing until—"

"Oh, crap." Mike rubbed his eyes.

"Is that your consequence?" Hope asked. "It affects your sight?"

Mike nodded. "Completely blind right now."

"It's okay. I'm here. I'll help you."

"Hope? Where's Jayden, is he already on the bus?"

She turned to Damien, her eyes going wide."

"I'll go. I'll find him," he said. With a twist of his shoulders, he dissolved into the streetlamp, the bulb flickering as he passed into the wiring above their heads.

Mike squeezed his arm. "Damien saved us?"

"Yeah, he did."

"You need to give that guy a break."

"I know." She helped him to his feet and wrapped his arm around her shoulders. Slowly, they headed toward the bus.

"We failed. We lost him, Hope." He was talking about Finn.

Hope didn't want to agree, but when she thought back to the way Finn had stared at her, knowing the crowd would kill her, she had no choice but to agree he was right. "Yeah, we did."

Mike shook his head. They reached the bus, but when Ms. D opened the doors for them, Mike attempted to board without her help. He missed the bottom step and Hope had to keep him from face-planting.

"You okay?" she asked.

"Yeah. Disoriented. I need to get better at this temporary blindness. If you weren't here, I'd be doomed."

Hope guided his foot to the bottom step. "Don't think twice about it. It's your first time."

He paused when they reached the top of the stairs. "Do you think this will happen again?"

She guided him deeper into the bus. "How do you feel about learning to read braille?"

❧ 24 ❧
MALICE

Fourteen people died in the skirmish between Lucifer and the Soulkeepers. Their bodies were disposed of along a highway in the desert in Arizona, compliments of Ravenguard, who drove all night to do the job. Lucifer compelled the others, some after taking their souls. Finn had locked the doors while each patron was cleaned up enough to pass as unhurt. It was all an illusion. Broken legs would remain broken to be discovered later when the person was far from the Tilted Raven.

At Lucifer's command, Finn used sorcery to clean the place, mend broken glasses, and patch bullet holes. Only after the guests were gone and all four of them were back in the cabin in the cemetery did Lucifer ask Finn and Kirsa about what happened.

"Why didn't you pursue them?" Lucifer asked through his teeth as he paced before the fire. The room was hot, at least a hundred degrees, and Finn hadn't had anything to eat or drink all day. His head swam.

"Ravenguard was taking care of it," he said, his gaze darting toward the hunter.

"You could have used magic. You could have stopped them."

"I didn't think I was allowed to use magic without your permission," Finn said.

Lucifer turned and gripped Finn's lower jaw. "I have not taken your power for a reason. I *expect* you to use it when it serves my needs." His breath was foul as death and lingered in the heavy air. Finn swallowed a gag.

The Devil turned his attention to Kirsa. "What about you? Why didn't you intercede, Kirsa?" Lucifer's voice was low and even, laden with malice.

"I was in the dressing room. I didn't know what was going on until it was already over."

Lucifer bared his teeth, his hand coming around to slap her across the face. The blow sent her flying out of her chair onto the floor. Resilient or not, it looked like it hurt.

Lucifer whirled on Finn. He was next, and what hurt Kirsa would kill him. "Admit it. You wanted them to get away." The Devil pressed a talon into Finn's chest.

Finn considered what to say. He could tell Lucifer that Mike was the Healer. The healing energy that had flowed into him when Mike had touched him felt the same as when Hope had healed him on the island. But if he told, Mike was as good as dead. Although the light inside of Finn was tiny at the moment, buried under heaps of self-protection, it still existed deep inside. He remembered playing with Mike as a child: video games and monkey bars and laughter at midnight during their sleepovers. His eight-year-old self stood over Mike's name, armed with a toy rifle and the last remnants of love Finn's soul was capable of producing.

He would not give him up.

"Hope is extremely powerful," Finn began. It was the truth. "Without backup, she would have popped my head off with a vine before I could lay a hand on her. Hope and Mike had come to rescue me. By staying where I was, I thought I was using myself as bait until you and Ravenguard could over-power her."

"You were stalling," Lucifer hissed. "You wanted them to survive. You think of them as *friends*." He said friends like it was a filthy curse.

Finn scoffed. "What do I care if they survive? I'm not one of them. If you want to blame someone, blame Ravenguard. After he stabbed Mike, he could have killed Hope. She was right there, next to him. Instead, he was getting off on watching Mike die. Newsflash, there's no coming back from multiple stab wounds directly to the heart."

Ravenguard growled, his fangs descending. "I could not get to her. The crowd had closed in."

"Bullshit. You're stronger than ten men. You could have brushed them aside with one arm and had your dagger in Hope's ticker in seconds. You were scared. You were afraid she'd do the same to you that she did to Applegate. You were afraid she'd reduce you to a pile of ash."

The hunter snapped. Ravenguard launched himself at Finn like a raging beast, fangs flashing as the two toppled onto the floor next to Kirsa. Everything came into sharp focus for Finn, and he caught the man's bottom jaw. "Incinerate," he whispered.

Fire engulfed Ravenguard's head and then his trademark red coat. Finn shielded his own body from the flames, although the heat licked his face. The hunter's screams filled the cabin.

Snap. With a quick connection of his fingers, Lucifer extinguished Finn's magic.

"Stop your bickering," the dark lord said. "Mr. Wager, you

still haven't answered my question. As you have now demonstrated, your power is intact. Why did you not use it to detain Hope and Michael until Ravenguard could end them?"

"The crowd did it for me." Finn spread his hands. "Look, the problem was not keeping Hope and Mike from the door. They were trampled. They weren't going anywhere. The problem was the damned angel. None of us could foresee Damien rescuing Hope when he did."

Face half-scorched, Ravenguard hissed in protest. But Kirsa, who'd been rubbing her jaw silently eased back into her seat next to a disturbingly empty bookshelf. "He's telling the truth."

They all turned to look at her.

"I saw what happened. Ravenguard had both of them. Whether Finn used his magic or not, the outcome would have been the same. The fault lies with Damien. The angel overpowered us."

Lips twisted as if he'd eaten something bitter, Lucifer paced uneasily in front of the fire, his gaze drifting from Kirsa, to Finn, to Ravenguard, whose coat was still smoking. Finn wondered if the guy would be able to heal the wounds he'd caused. Ravenguard had no hair on the left half of his head and his skin had melted off the muscle in his cheek and jaw. If he'd been human, he'd be completely incapacitated.

"At least one of them is dead. Ravenguard killed Michael," Kirsa said.

"Michael had no power," Lucifer said. "He was a tool."

"And now the Soulkeepers have one less tool." She pulled a cigarette from inside her jacket and lit up, leaning back in her chair. Finn had to hand it to her. She was an excellent actress. No way was anyone that cool and collected after having her head pounded by the Devil. Not when he was still as angry as he was. They were all in real danger.

Lucifer turned to the fire, seeming to take solace in its unrelenting heat. "Go to your rooms. Don't come out until I invite you."

Kirsa huffed. "But we haven't eaten all day! Humans have to eat, Lucifer. If you don't feed us, Finn and I will die."

The Devil raised an eyebrow. "Lucky for you, I can raise the dead. No matter how many times you starve to death, Kirsa, I promise I will bring you back to starve again."

Kirsa tossed her cigarette on the floor and stomped it out with her heel. She stormed out of the room, toward the bedrooms. Finn rose to follow.

"Mr. Wager," Lucifer said. The Devil pinned him with his black stare. "Next time, do not wait for Ravenguard. If I find out you are holding anything back from me, I will have your soul in a tourniquet for the rest of eternity."

Finn nodded once and headed for his room.

THERE WAS NO EXPLANATION FOR WHY FINN COULD FEEL THE sunrise. The cabin had no windows. It was always dark aside from the raging fires. But something deep within him, a part of himself he never knew existed, could feel daylight spread across the horizon like a silver flash. Instinctively, he knew Lucifer would be sleeping at that moment, as weak as he would be that day.

Finn used the opportunity to disseminate into Kirsa's room and conjure a brunch fit for a queen. There were croissants, bacon, eggs, beignets, and a large carafe of juice.

Kirsa woke with a deep inhale and widened her eyes when she saw the spread.

"Is that real or an illusion?"

"As real as it gets. Compliments of the Two Sisters. It's a common misconception that magicians conjure things out of thin air. Whatever we take comes from somewhere. This is hot and ready."

"Does Lucifer know?" she whispered, glancing at the door.

He gave her a pitying look. "Of course not."

"He won't like it."

"He can't take away what's already in your stomach." Actually, Finn wasn't entirely sure that was true, but he didn't want to think about it. He reached for a beignet and took a bite. Kirsa couldn't help herself. She leaped out of bed and snatched a piece of bacon in one hand and a croissant in the other.

"Delicious," she mumbled, her eyes closing.

"You should have mentioned he was starving you. I would have given you part of my sandwich that first day."

She talked around a mouthful of half-masticated breakfast. "Why? You hate me. I spent half a semester stabbing you. You've wanted to kill me for months." Her eyes narrowed as if she expected he'd done something to the food, poisoned it or spit in it, but she didn't stop eating.

"Thank you for standing up for me to Lucifer," he said.

The tension in her face relaxed. "You're welcome. It wasn't our fault. I'm sick of taking the rap for Ravenguard's failures. He could have stabbed Hope. What the hell were they thinking anyway, sending two of their best Soulkeepers directly to Lucifer's concert?"

He shook his head. "Who knows? Totally stupid. It's incredible they're alive."

"A miracle," she murmured. She stared at the wall and Finn

could guess she was thinking about the angel. He'd felt it too when the fire blew through the venue. Everything they were missing by staying with Lucifer was in that fire. It was a warmth that had nothing to do with heat. Finn had never appreciated it until it was gone.

They ate in silence until they couldn't fit another thing in their stomachs; then Finn sent the remaining food, the table, and the linens back where they came from.

"I should go back to my room." He stood and prepared to leave.

"Wager?"

"Yeah?"

"I'm not your enemy."

Finn's gaze slid sideways toward the door. "Ditto." With a twist, he disseminated back to his room.

25

LOST BOYS

Everyone attending the emergency meeting of the Soulkeepers Council looked like they were going to a funeral. Ms. D's frown had grown so pronounced, Mike thought the lines around her mouth might become permanent. In the main conference room back on the bus, he'd explained in detail what he was trying to do at the Tilted Raven and what had gone wrong.

"You should have run your plan by the council before you acted," Ms. D said, her voice biting as a whip. "That's what this council is for. This isn't the Wild West. You are not a cowboy. You need to work with us."

"I didn't think we'd have time," he said. "This was our one chance to save Finn!"

"And it almost got us both killed," Hope said.

"How did you get out of there alive?" Ms. D asked.

Jayden cleared his throat. Mike was relieved when Jayden had returned safely to the bus. But he sensed his friend had more to say about what happened last night, and he wasn't sure he wanted to hear it.

"I started the place on fire," Jayden said.

There was a collective gasp.

"Yeah, I know. You don't become a Pyro without understanding how fire can get out of hand. It was a small one and contained, but it put off enough light to allow Damien to come to our aid. He blasted back the crowd and Ravenguard and got Hope and Mike out of there."

"Thank the Lord," Ms. D said. She gave a little nod to Damien who was standing in the corner of the room behind Hope.

"I hid in the rafters until Damien came back for me," Jayden said.

Mike's head popped up. "You were in the rafters the entire time?"

He snorted. "Yeah. Almost peed my pants watching those slime-buckets at work. Finn helped Lucifer clean up the carnage as if the dead and wounded were broken toys," Jayden said. "Finn isn't Finn anymore, Mike. He's something else. Something evil."

Mike shook his head. "That's not true. I don't believe that. Finn is in there. When I looked into his eyes, he was there."

"He used his magic to cover up what happened. He compelled people who needed to go to the hospital to go home instead, without compassion. Think about it, Mike, he could have easily come with you. He didn't."

"He is lost, then. Completely turned to the side of Lucifer." Ms. D shook her head.

Orelon said in his low, smooth voice, "In all my time training Finn, I've never known him to give up easily. If he is doing the will of the evil one, it is not by choice."

Mike was thankful there was someone else on Finn's side. "I

agree with Orelon. All we can say for sure is that Finn wouldn't come with us when we asked. We don't know why. Maybe he's being forced. Maybe he's staying to gather information for us."

But Hope was shaking her head. "You saw his soul, Mike."

"No."

"I know you did. Your skills and abilities might be new to you, but I suspect you couldn't miss it. I could smell it on him like rotten eggs."

Mike scowled.

"What did you see when you looked at him, Michael?" Ms. D asked.

"Mmm. Okay. He did have this dark and tattered halo thing around him."

"You saw his aura," Damien said. "That was his damaged soul."

Hope rubbed her temples and sent Michael a pleading look. "Finn's hair had completely grown back, Mike. Open your eyes."

Jayden inhaled a shaky breath. "He didn't do that himself. Think about it. He watched you die Mike and he didn't even shed a tear."

"No, I'm sure he didn't," Hope said. "He couldn't cry because Lucifer controls his every thought, just like he controls Kirsa. Finn has sold his soul for power. He practically told us as much. He told us it was too late."

"We don't know that," Mike protested.

"Lucifer doesn't give anything for free," Damien said.

"Finn is a lot of things, but he isn't evil," Mike's voice was low and even. He couldn't believe what he was hearing. They were all giving up on Finn… on his best friend!

"Many people who are not evil do evil things," Damien said.

The angel paced at the back of the conference room, making Mike uneasy.

Mike took a deep breath and let it out slowly. As far as he was concerned, it didn't matter why Finn was the way he was or had done the things he did. The most important thing was getting him back and helping him become Finn again. "There's only one thing for us to do."

"What can we do?" Hope shook her head.

"We need to try again."

The room went quiet and then erupted into confused murmurs.

"You can't be serious," Hope said. "Lucifer can't see you alive, Mike, ever. He'll know you're the Healer. Once he knows, he'll never stop until you're on a slab of stone with the dagger pointed at your heart."

"I'll be careful. I know what to expect this time."

"Are you insane?" Jayden's fingers sparked as his hands slapped the table. "It's out of the question. You are exactly what Lucifer needs to complete the spell to merge the realms. The Tilted Raven was a bad enough idea. Facing Lucifer again would be suicide."

"When I touched Finn, I felt him start to heal. I saw one of the symbols on his wrist fade. I can bring him back. I know I can."

Ms. D brought her fingers to her chin. "He's too close to Lucifer and you are too important. We can send a team to Technothrob's next concert to try to capture Finn and bring him to you—"

"No. It has to be me." Mike shook his head. "I'm the Healer. I know this is what I'm supposed to do."

"Just like you were supposed to touch Juliette?" Hope rolled her eyes. "You said the same thing about Lucifer's guitar, and that didn't turn out too well, did it?"

"That was different."

"It was? Healer wisdom is different from intuition, Mike. You need to go to the other side and ask the immortals. We can't follow your every whim." She said the last through her teeth.

"As it so happens, I've recently visited with the Immortals, something you can't do anymore," Mike snapped. Hope recoiled. "And they emphasized the importance of friendship. Friends do not let friends sell their souls to the Devil."

Ms. D gave a heavy sigh and held up her hands. "You have friends in this room too, Michael. We can't do it. I won't do it. If Lucifer gets his hands on you, all is lost. I've told Fuse to take us back to Revelations where you'll be safe. We can discuss next steps there."

Mike played with the corner of the notebook he was using. "I thought this Healer gig came with the perk of being your leader."

"You were. You are," Ms. D said. "But that also means we need to protect you. With time, you'll grow into your role."

Mike reached for the triquetra around his neck, intending to call Gabriel to back him up. It was too late. There was a lurch, and Mike felt like he was putty being pressed through a cheese grater. He couldn't breathe or move. Everyone else seemed similarly incapacitated. Jayden's face was roughly the color of a beet.

And then Damien disappeared.

A series of bumps indicated they'd landed on Veil Island. Of course, that's why Theodor and Wendy weren't here. They'd returned home because they couldn't travel to the island. And Fuse, she was driving, likely with Amuke as copilot. Everyone else was here, keeping him busy while they trapped him on the island.

"You brought me here against my will?" He turned the full weight of his rage on Jayden. "You're supposed to be my friend! Finn's too."

"That's exactly why we're here, Mike. I risked my life to save your ass in that bar. I'm destroyed we couldn't save Finn. I won't lose you too. We need to take a beat. We need a plan that doesn't include you offering yourself up as a sacrifice." Jayden bared his teeth and leaned toward him across the table.

"You have no right," Mike said. His stomach pitched, and he shot Jayden and Hope a look of disgust.

He stayed behind as everyone stood and started filtering out of the room. As she walked by him toward the door, Hope said, "As the Soulkeepers Council, we do."

Long after everyone else had gone to bed, Mike sat in the dining hall alone, staring up at the antler chandelier as he had his first day at Revelations. So much had changed since then. He had changed. He sipped Mrs. Wilhelm's version of root beer, a concoction that was heavy on root flavor and nothing like the tasty soda drink. The others had tried to talk to him, especially Hope and Jayden, but he'd refused. They'd gone against his will, trapped and imprisoned him. That wasn't something he'd forgive anytime soon. Nor would he forgive them giving up on Finn.

"Would you like cookies to go with your drink, Soulkeeper?" a voice asked. Michael stood and peered over the table to find a little man staring up at him, wearing green lederhosen and a pointy hat. At least he thought it was a man. The face was more like a monkey's.

"Uh, no. I'm good thanks," he told the man.

"It is Archibald's pleasure to serve the new Healer."

"Archibald, nice to meet you. Do you work here?" He extended his hand.

"Oh yes, Archibald has served the Soulkeepers for hundreds of years. I am a garden gnome, from the Garden of Eden." The little guy sniffed Mike's hand then pumped it twice, as if the gesture was unfamiliar.

Mike snorted and sat back down. "I don't suppose in those hundreds of years you ever dealt with mutiny against the Healer."

"Oh yes, of course I have," Archibald said with a sharp-toothed grin. "But it never lasts long. A Healer's power is not easily caged."

Interesting. Mike gestured for the gnome to come to his side of the table and patted the empty chair next to him. Archibald climbed into the seat.

"Not easily caged, huh? They seem to have done a good job with me. I'm stuck on this island instead of saving my friend Finn."

"Could you take the bus off the island? That's how the others go." The gnome's eyes loomed large in the dim light.

Shrugging, Mike spoke gently, as if talking to a small child. "No keys. Plus, I don't know how to drive a magical bus."

"Oh." Archibald pressed a tiny finger to his lips.

"It was a good idea though, Archibald."

"The others call me Archie."

Mike bumped the little guy's fist with his own. "Okay, Archie. If you have any other ideas like that, you let me know. I need to get off this island, and you seem like the kind of gnome that gets things done. The kind of gnome that respects the position of Healer."

The compliment widened the gnome's eyes, and Mike could almost feel the little guy thinking. "There is one other way off this island," Archie said.

With his drink halfway to his mouth, Mike froze. He looked over his shoulder before leaning forward and lowering his voice. "Did you just say you know another way off this island, other than the bus?"

The gnome smiled and nodded vigorously. "There is one other way. The way Archibald arrived here. Archibald did not come by bus."

"If you didn't come by bus, how did you get here?"

"By portal," the gnome said wondrously. "In a cave at the back of the mountain, is a tree. It used to be a portal to Eden. Years ago, gnomes could travel through a network of trees. Archie used gnome magic to bring him here when Eden was destroyed. The vibrations that toppled Eden also injured the trees. Archie can no longer use it to travel. Can't go home to Eden." Archibald looked wistfully at his hands

"Oh," Mike said. "I'm sorry you lost your home. I know what it's like to lose people you love."

"Mmm. Yes, I fear you do."

Mike rubbed his hands together. "So, uh, the thing you said about another way off this island... there was another way, but not anymore. The portal tree is, uh, broken."

Archie nodded. "Unless you can convince her to fix it."

"Her who?" Mike wondered if it was something Ms. D had to do. Maybe something that was broken when the star was destroyed.

"Your friend Hope. She has the gift of Life. If she were to

use her new abilities to heal the tree, the portal could be opened once more."

Mike's thumb tapped nervously on the side of his glass. "Are you saying that the portal will work if the tree is... healed?"

Archibald's hat bobbed as he nodded. "If Hope heals the tree, Archie can navigate the portal. Archie could take you anywhere there is another portal. Archibald is certain. And then you could go there without the bus."

A chill ran the length of his spine. "Thank you, Archie. Do you think you could show me where this tree is tomorrow?"

"Of course! It would be my pleasure."

"Terrific. Can you do me one more favor?"

"Of course. Gnomes adore serving their Soulkeepers." The little guy grabbed the sides of his hat as if the thought was truly exciting.

Mike patted the air in front of him. "Let's keep this on the down low. Don't tell anyone else. I want to ask Hope when the time is right, when she's most likely to say yes. You understand?"

Archie nodded. "Oh yes. Tell no one."

"Cool. We'll go after breakfast."

The gnome grinned. "Excellent. Good night, Soulkeeper."

"Good night." As Michael watched the gnome go, he smiled. It would be a good night after all, and with any luck, an even better tomorrow.

26

THE BROKEN TREE

Hope came down to breakfast the next day feeling sorry for Mike. She remembered what it was like to stand in front of a group of Soulkeepers, feeling utterly incompetent and trying to be the leader you were destined to be. He was supposed to be in charge and he knew it. Only they couldn't let him risk himself. All that stood between the Devil and Hell was Mike. It was worth ten thousand Finns to keep him safe. She was sorry to admit that, but it was true.

"Hey, Hope," Mike said, waving her over. "Can I talk to you for a second?"

She sat down beside him and selected a scone from the tray. "Sure. Honestly, I'm relieved you want to talk to me at all after yesterday. I'm sorry things went down the way they did."

"I know you care," he said. "Now that we're here though, I'd like to get to know the island better. I never got to see it as a student. I was hoping you'd take me on a tour."

Her face became serious. "Sure. I can show you around. Is there something specific you'd like to see?"

He shrugged. "The river. The mountain. Archibald tells me there is a gorgeous beach on the back side of the island."

She nodded. "He would know. All right. We go after breakfast." So that was it. Archibald. The gnome had likely convinced Mike the Island wasn't such a bad place. She'd have to thank the little guy, later.

With a small bag of provisions, compliments of Mrs. Wilhelm, Hope gave Mike the grand tour. She told him stories of the Crimson Forest, Murder Mountain, and how a water dragon that lived in the Fever River had once eaten her. "My legs grew back while I was dead," she said.

Mike sat down on a rock and pulled off his pack, taking a long gulp of his water. "I didn't like being dead."

"Nobody likes being dead." Hope laughed. "At least you came back."

"When you were gone… I mean before you came back, did you sense anything?"

She took a seat beside him, turning her face toward the sun and closing her eyes. "I think so. I could never be sure because when I came back, it all seemed so far away. But I think I felt peace. There were times it was easier to be dead than alive."

"Me too. I wondered if it was all in my head."

"No."

He shifted on the rock, looking across Fever River. "About Finn…"

"Ah, I knew there was a reason you wanted to get me alone. Here it comes." She smiled at him, expecting him to ask her to help him leave the island. She would refuse of course. But she expected this.

"You know Finn is where he is because he was trying to help us. That's always been the thing with Finn. He sacrifices himself."

Her heart grew heavy and she looked down at the toes of her hiking boots, suddenly tired. "Yeah. Just like how he saved your soul. You'd think the idiot would have learned by now not to take it this far. He never knows when to give up."

"Yeah." Mike laughed. "Problem is, I love the guy. He's the best friend I ever had."

"Look at you being so emotional. What happened to that hard candy shell I bounced off of last time you were here? I'm already to your gooey center and I didn't even have to throw stuff at you."

"Well, uh, I've done some soul-searching lately. Going through the initiation will do that to you."

She nodded. Now it made sense. He wanted to bond with her because she was the only one who had been a Healer and had been to the In-Between.

"Didn't you and Finn find the holy water around here?"

"On the back side of the mountain, near the beach Archie told you about." Hope nodded.

"Can you show me? I think it would be wild to see actual water from Eden," Mike said. He stood and headed for the water.

"Uh, do we have to? This process holds bad memories for me." Hope hesitated. Logically she understood that the dragons no longer lived in these waters. Veil Island was a much safer place to be these days. But it was hard to put the memories behind her. She abhorred the cold and wet.

Michael had already reached the other side. "What are you waiting for?" he asked.

"You know, there isn't much to see. Holy water looks exactly like regular water."

"Come on, Diva. You're not afraid to get your hair wet are you?" Mike teased.

Maybe there was another way. Hope reached out with her power and sensed all the plants and animals around her. She latched on to one form of life in particular and funneled her energy into it. A massive lily pad opened on the edge of the water, growing six feet wide and a foot thick with a giant white bloom at the center. Hope stepped on. The pad squished beneath her shoes as she carefully moved to the center of the blossom. At her command, the entire thing grew toward the opposite shore, skimming the current, slowly, deliberately. It wasn't as fast as swimming, but when she stepped off the other side, she was still completely dry.

Mouth agape, Mike pulled his shirt over his head and wrung it out between his hands. About a gallon of water splashed toward his feet. "Might have been nice to know you could do that before I swam across," he said through a bright smile.

She laughed. "You never asked. Come on, it's this way."

They rounded the mountain to the ocean. Hope couldn't believe how the island had changed since the last time she was here. The forest was greener. The ocean was no longer gray but a magnificent shade of lapis. Even the mountain was more welcoming. They reached the cave in a fraction of the time it had taken her and Finn, but she hadn't known where she was going then. Panting from the climb, she flipped on the flashlight from her bag to lead Mike to the tree and the pool.

"Wow," he said, his eyes locking on the tree. She understood. Although the oak was almost split in two, with only a few twisted branches bearing evidence of life in the form of green leaves, being in its presence was unforgettable. The tree felt like it had a soul. And when she stopped to think about its history, along with the water in the pool beside it, she felt connected to everything, like she was a piece of a grand puzzle.

"This used to be a portal?" Mike asked.

"To Eden," Hope said, stepping into the circle of light that poured through the side of the mountain. "This is how Archie came to be here. When the portals to Eden collapsed, he was able to escape through this. All the rest of his kind were trapped there. My mom said when Lucifer tried to take Eden apart, he couldn't enter it directly, so he made the world around it come apart. When she left, the earthquakes had practically leveled the place."

She couldn't blame Mike for being fascinated. He ran his hands along the bark, then squatted next to the pool. Although his back was to her, she heard his hand splash in the water.

"That's the water we used to save the island. It's from Eden as well."

Mike stood again and looked over his shoulder at her. "I have an idea," he said.

"What kind of idea?" Hope found the look on Mike's face strange. Her gut told her he was lying, but why would he lie about having an idea?

"What if you tried to heal the tree?" Mike said.

Hope laughed. "What? Why?"

"I know it sounds crazy, but if you could use your power to mend this tree, we might be able to travel back to Eden. It's possible that some of Archie's family are still there, and if the school is standing, the resources inside might contain a clue about how to stop Lucifer."

Hope raised her eyebrows. "It's a good idea, Mike, but this is big. I can't do something like this without talking to the council first. I've never done anything like this before. What if something went wrong?"

Brushing water from his hands, he smiled and crossed to her. "You're right. This is big. Dangerous." He sighed. As he brushed the water from his hands, he turned over his left arm, exposing his wrist to her. She saw him make a plucking motion with his opposite hand.

In the blink of an eye, Hope was back in the In-Between standing on an island that was dead. "Bring life," Nephthys's voice came on the wind. Hope was holding the seed. She needed to make it grow. But then the memory changed. There was a tree in front of her, one that needed healing. She placed her hands on it. This wasn't so hard. All she had to do was mend what was broken, not grow a new tree. She poured herself into the task, knitting the bark, the wood, the cells beneath.

After several minutes, she realized she wasn't on the island at all, but in the cave where she'd found Archibald. Only, she wasn't standing in the same place she had been before. Neither was Mike. Worse, the tree was whole again.

"What have you done?"

"What I needed to do," Mike said.

"You used your power on me. You sent me back to my initiation."

"I'm sorry. I didn't know how else to get you to do what I needed you to do."

Hope was livid. "Yes, you did. You could have waited. I told you I'd do it, but I wanted to talk to the council first."

Mike frowned. "That would defeat the purpose, Hope."

There was a swirl of green light and Archibald appeared. His eyes darted at Hope guiltily.

"Do we still have a deal, Archie?" Mike asked.

"Archibald lives to serve the Soulkeepers." He waddled to Michael's side.

"What are you doing?" Hope asked sternly. "Whatever this

deal is, the Soulkeepers don't approve." She narrowed her eyes at the gnome.

But Archie scowled. "The Healer leads the Soulkeepers," he said in a harsh voice Hope had never heard come out of the gnome before. "So it has always been. So it will always be, Daughter of Angels."

"Archie…"

Mike's big, dark hand wrapped around Archie's green-stained fingers. The size difference gave Hope the impression of father and child, although Archie was the far older of the two.

Mike's dark eyes met hers. "I learned something about portals recently. Portals when attached to a living thing like a tree, can be used as bridges from one realm to another. But, if you have magic or sorcery in your blood, they can be used to take you almost anywhere. Trees are connected, spiritually."

Her spine tingled as she realized where he was planning to go. "No, no. Don't do this." She reached out to him.

But she was too late. Archibald touched the tree. The bark climbed the gnome's arm, then over his head, then swallowed Mike as well. The two became a knot of wood that was absorbed into the trunk of the oak. In another moment, both gnome and Healer were gone.

Hope lowered her hand and fell to her knees. She knew where Mike had gone, and it wasn't Eden. She had to tell the others. She'd made a terrible mistake, and Mike was in great danger.

❧ 27 ❧

THE DEAL

Mike emerged from the tree at the center of Saint Louis Cemetery still gripping Archibald's hand. After orienting himself among the mausoleums, he made a quick self-inspection to make certain he hadn't burst into flame. He'd made it, whole and unscathed. Silently, he congratulated himself on doing the impossible. He had slipped inside the Devil's safehouse through the backdoor.

Each of the Soulkeepers had attempted to thwart the boundary surrounding the cemetery but the protective bubble had proven ultimately Soulkeeper-resistant. After talking with Archibald though, Mike had developed a theory that the portal in the tree Finn had opened could be used to circumvent the protective magic. It was a loophole. And now he was here, walking straight into the enemy camp. It seemed stupid when he stopped to think about it. Only, his gut told him the way to stop Lucifer was to change Finn's heart. You couldn't change someone's heart at a safe distance.

"Are you sure you want to stay here, Healer? Archibald hates this place. It smells of evil and makes my heart heavy."

The gnome's voice came out a high and tight whisper. He was afraid. It would be wrong to keep him here.

"I need to stay, Archie. Thank you for your help. I want you to use the tree to go home to Eden. Find your family if you can. If not, return to the Soulkeepers. Above all else, stay safe. Take care of yourself."

The gnome's eyes widened. "Thank you. Thank you, Soulkeeper."

"Call me Michael."

"Michael."

"Go."

The gnome bowed slightly at the waist. Backing toward the tree, he reached out his small hand to touch the bark as a smile splayed across his lips. There was a swirl of sparkling green light, the bark swallowed him, and he was gone.

Mike shivered against the chill air. It was summer in New Orleans, the middle of the afternoon, easily ninety degrees anywhere else in the city, but the cemetery was cold, dark, and foggy, as if a permanent storm had moved in. There was no wind. In fact, the air hung stagnant. But the chill went through him anyway.

Among the crypts, the scenery was creepy enough, curls of ill-colored fog coiling against the brick and plaster graves. He had heard that it took only a year for a body to completely decompose into ash in the New Orleans heat. Each of these crypts could hold hundreds if not thousands of bodies. But the most horror-movie worthy thing here was not the houses of the dead, but the rustic cabin that rose above them to his left. It had no windows, only one door, and a chimney that billowed smoke with the green tinge of burning copper. It was this chimney that seemed to produce the fog the tangled around his ankles.

This was a bad idea. He swallowed. This was his only idea.

There was no turning back now. He toyed with the triquetra around his neck. On shaky legs, he navigated the maze of tombs until he'd reached the cabin. Slowly, he placed his fingers on the doorknob and turned. There was a soft click and it opened. Not that surprising really. Why would Lucifer want or need a lock? The blast of heat that met his face as he stepped inside made him nauseous. Not just the temperature, but the smell: a combination of rotten eggs and burned marshmallow.

As quietly as possible, he strolled through the main room with its roaring fire and into the back hallway. Should he call out for Finn? The idea here, after all, was to get caught. He didn't think for a second that he could slip in and slip out without facing Lucifer. This was not about winning. This was about saving. It was about Finn and a friendship Mike was unwilling to let die. A friendship Mike was willing to die for.

Alas, when he raised his voice, no one answered. "I guess no one's home," he said.

He opened the first door. There was no light switch but the stench that met his nostrils told him enough. The room smelled of blood and sewage. A torture chamber? He closed the door again, thankful for the lack of light.

Behind the next door was a normal bedroom, but the blouse spread across the bed told him it probably wasn't Finn's. He was guessing Kirsa's by the weapons lined up along the dresser. His gaze fell on her nightstand and he was unexpectedly bewildered by what he saw there. A romance novel lay open beside the lamp. All he knew of Kirsa was death. She'd stabbed him more times than he could count. It gave him an uneasy feeling that she was reading about love. He closed the door.

The next room he was sure was Finn's. The bed wasn't made and the closet door was hanging open. *Typical.* He entered and closed the door behind him. Flipping through the clothes in the closet, he found the shirt Finn had worn the night before at the Tilted Raven. Yep, this was his room. He flipped through the other shirts, then paused when he noticed writing carved into the back wall. The letters were small and tight. He brought his face close to the wood to read it.

What good is it for someone to gain the whole world, yet forfeit their soul?

Mike recognized the quote from the book of Matthew. So Finn was quoting the Bible in the back of his closet. If that wasn't a sign the guy could be redeemed, what was?

The sound of the door opening made Mike whirl around. Finn saw him but didn't say a word. He closed the door behind him, then pressed his hand to the wood. A purple shimmer cascaded around the room.

"What the hell are you doing here?" Finn asked through clenched teeth.

Mike took a step forward. "I came for you. You're my friend. I wasn't going to leave you to that monster."

"Are you insane?" Finn charged forward, stopping with his face inches from Mike's. "If Lucifer sees you, he will know what you are. He will kill you. And after he kills you, do you know what happens next? We all go to Hell, Mike, because Hell comes to us."

Mike shook his head. "The Soulkeepers need you, Finn. Come with me to the tree. I can help you get back to Revelations. There's a portal. We won't go through the dragons. I can get you in. You'll be safe there."

"Shhh." Finn brought his finger to his lips. "Don't tell me

how you got in here. I don't want to know. Whatever way you were planning to escape, use it... without me."

"Why? You don't want to be here. You're not evil. I know you. You're my best friend."

Finn's face morphed into something ugly. "It's been a long time since we've been besties, Mike. A long time. There are things about me you don't know. Things you don't want to know. It's too late for me."

"No."

"I'm here for a reason." Finn paced the floor. "I earned my place here. And as long as I am here, I can do what I can to help you and the others. But only if you play your part and stay the hell away." Finn rolled his eyes. "Honestly, are you sick or just stupid? Why couldn't you let it be? All you had to do is stay away. Now, everything I did is for nothing."

"That's it, isn't it? You sacrificed yourself for us... for me. You did what you did so they'd lock me up on that island and Lucifer would never be able to complete the spell."

Finn said nothing, but he swallowed hard.

"And then what?" Mike said. "I hide forever? No. I'm done hiding. I'm done letting Lucifer have his way. This all started with Deviant Joe, Finn. We all rode the bus together to Revelations, and do you remember what you said to me? You said, 'We can handle anything they throw at us. We're together. We have each other's backs.' Well, we're together again. We can handle this. All you have to do is get us to the tree, Finn. Either take me there now, or take me to Lucifer." It was an ultimatum, but he knew Finn would take it. No way would he hand him over to the Devil.

A muscle in Finn's jaw twitched. "You're serious."

"I've never been more serious." Mike reached for Finn's

hand. If he could heal him… But Finn pulled away before he could make contact.

"Don't touch me," he snapped. "Don't you get it? I don't want to be healed. I need the power. Without it, I'm helpless."

"With it, you're a pawn of the Devil." Their gazes locked and Finn's expression turned hard.

"Finn…" Mike took another step toward him and slammed into an invisible barrier. Finn was shielding. Not only shielding—holding Mike in his magical grip. He struggled, but it was no use.

"I want you to know, you did this to yourself. This is not on me." Finn snapped his fingers. The purple barrier he'd put in place disappeared as quickly as it had come. He raised an eyebrow at Mike, shook his head, and cracked the door.

"We have a guest," Finn said, opening the door wider. In an instant, the Devil was there in the doorway, having come from the direction of the main room.

Lucifer's black eyes locked onto Michael. "I watched you die." He stepped into the room, his eyes narrowing on the triquetra around Mike's neck. His eyes widened and then he laughed long, wicked, and loud.

❧ 28 ❧

INTRODUCTIONS

Nothing could prepare a person for the day they looked into the eyes of the Devil. Mike couldn't move, couldn't speak. Everything he believed about the inherent good in the world was lost in impending darkness. The Devil charged forward, fisted his triquetra, and tore it from his neck, then cast it into the corner of the room with a curse. Mike caught a glimpse of the Devil's palm, the symbol burned into the flesh there. Lucifer flexed and contracted his fingers, and the three overlapping ovals faded from his skin.

"So we meet again, Michael Carson," Lucifer said through his teeth. "It seems death agrees with you."

"Do I look dead to you?" Mike asked, the words holding more bravado than he felt.

"No, you do not. Which means, as your friend Finn suspected, you are the Healer."

In these types of situations, Mike had learned it was best to keep his mouth shut. There was no reason to give someone information they claimed to know already. No reason to admit his identity or further add to the pile of reasons Lucifer wanted him dead. So he stayed silent, his face impassive. But deep inside, his heart ached to know that Finn had told Lucifer his true identity. It was traitorous to their friendship.

Lucifer walked into the room and circled Mike, his feet falling slowly one after another. "Oh, Finn didn't give you up immediately. I'll have you know I had to work the knowledge out of him. A sorcerer's mind is a hard nut to crack, but crack he did. I couldn't have Finn changing his mind about the sacrifice. I control him now. It's far easier that way."

Mike glanced toward Finn. His eyes were glazed and stared directly at the wall. But he'd seemed clear enough a few minutes ago. Mike wondered how much was an act and how much was real. The last thing Fate had said to him before he left the In-Between was that all the power in the universe couldn't replace the magic of true friendship. His friendship with Finn had to be stronger than any spell Lucifer could dole out. He believed that.

"Why did you come here, Michael?" Lucifer asked.

Mike didn't hesitate. "To save Finn."

The Devil raised his face to the ceiling and cackled. "Honestly? After he refused to go with you the first time, I would have thought you would get the hint. He doesn't want to be saved, Michael. Finn is enjoying the power I gave him, and after I bury the obsidian dagger in your heart, he'll be rewarded with even more."

"I won't fight you. I'll go willingly... If you let him go," Mike said. It was the offer he always knew he was prepared to make. His life for Finn's. He was the one Lucifer wanted, after all. He was the sacrifice.

Lucifer paused, his eyes raking over Michael. "How noble of you. Unfortunately, your arrangement does not suit me. You see, Finn is a sorcerer. A powerful one at that. You Soulkeepers never appreciated him. But I digress. Finn, as a Soulkeeper turned sorcerer is in a unique position to serve my purposes. Ironically, the ancient magic I must use to tear the veil requires that it is he who plunge the obsidian dagger into your heart." Lucifer clapped his hands in front of his lips and shrugged his shoulders. "If I free him, I have no one to perform the sacrifice."

Mike shook his head, feeling undone. "Finn... has to..."

The smile that spread across Lucifer's face made Mike's stomach turn. "You didn't know?" He laughed. "Hadn't figured that one out yet, had you? With all your Healer wisdom and godly resources? Why did you think I was so interested in finding Damien? Before he was so rudely redeemed, he being a former angel turned evil was the perfect catalyst. Though thanks to Hope, now he is useless to me. But, as I always say, when one door closes, bulldoze the entire building to the ground. Finn turns out to be an equally valuable catalyst. And now that you've walked into our lives, we have all the parts we need to do what needs to be done."

Mike stared at Finn, but his friend continued to stare at the wall. He did not react to this news at all. Was he dreading the thought of stabbing him in the heart? Or had Lucifer fried his brain to the point he didn't care?

Lucifer tipped his head to the side. "As for you participating, you don't have a choice. Either you walk yourself to the stone altar, or we have Kirsa carry you. If you try to run or hide, Ravenguard will hunt you down. You can't leave the cemetery. I've already made sure of that. However you got in here, you will not get out. Everything else, Mr. Wager can handle with magic."

"Finn, this isn't what you want, is it?" Mike asked, keeping his eyes on Lucifer.

Finn didn't answer. Didn't even look at him.

Like something out of Mike's scariest nightmares, Kirsa swaggered into view in the doorway. She smiled when she saw him and retrieved a dagger from a sheath strapped to her thigh. "My old friend Michael," she said, stepping toward him and pressing the tip of the dagger to his chest. "You must've missed playing with me. Remember the fun we used to have?"

Mike did remember. He remembered every single time she'd sank a knife into his gut, and the memories made him want to knock her head off. He'd dreamed of giving Kirsa a dose of her own medicine. Now he cringed at the thought of being her pincushion again.

"Now that you're the Healer, there are no limits to the fun we can have," she said. "Why stop at a stab wound when I can gut you like a fish, then watch you slowly heal yourself, only to do it all over again." She gasped as if she'd thought of something wonderful. She circled a finger and pointed it at his chest. "No, no. I won't gut you. I'll drown you."

It took an iron will to keep his knees from buckling. His worst nightmare. Oddly, that was the end of it. To his surprise and confusion, Kirsa turned on a dime and completely changed the subject.

"Can we eat?" she asked Lucifer.

The Devil rolled his eyes.

"I'm hungry too," Finn said, seeming to wake up from the trance he was in at the mention of food. "If you want me strong enough to perform magic, I need food and clean water."

Mike was temporarily stunned at the strange turn of the conversation, but he remained silent. Food seemed vitally important to Kirsa and Finn. It didn't take a super sleuth to guess why. Both of them looked thinner, gaunt even. Lucifer wasn't feeding his pets.

With a sneer, Lucifer snapped his fingers. "Very well. You'll find the table set and the food prepared." He stepped closer to Michael. "I'm afraid I can't join you. I have preparations to make."

Kirsa gestured toward Mike. "What do you want us to do with him?"

Lucifer shrugged. "As you wish, Ms. Hildburg. Have your fun. As long as he's on the stone altar at midnight, you can do whatever you'd like to him."

Mike's face must have paled because Lucifer looked positively delighted as he left the room and called for Ravenguard. Kirsa walked around him, digging the tip of the dagger into his back. "First we eat, then we play." She nodded at Finn and the magic binding him loosened. Mike took a deep breath and cracked his neck.

Finn led him down the hallway to a room Mike could have sworn wasn't there a minute ago. A table was set worthy of a king. Goblets filled with what looked like water and wine sat next to silver serving pieces and bone china plates. Candles burned at the center, the fire harboring that same green tinge. Platters of beef, potatoes, and vegetables lay between them. The food proved too much for Finn and Kirsa to resist. They seemed to forget all about him. Kirsa sheathed her dagger and grabbed her plate with both hands. As fast as she could move she loaded it with food.

The smell wafting from the spread was heavenly, but Mike knew this dinner was straight from Hell. Although he hadn't eaten since breakfast, he had no appetite for any of it.

"Sit down," Kirsa said around her first bite, pointing at the chair across from her and beside Finn with her fork. He obeyed.

"Is it just us?" Mike asked.

"Ravenguard and Lucifer don't eat," Finn said, shoveling in a spoonful of potatoes.

"And they don't like to watch us eat. They find it disgusting," Kirsa added.

Mike scratched the side of his jaw, noticing he could move freely now. Aside from clearly being starved for food, he wondered if the absence of Lucifer and Ravenguard was another reason they were excited for the meal.

"It's dead," Finn said, by way of explanation. "Those two only eat the living."

"Aren't you hungry?" Kirsa asked Mike between bites. "This is your last meal. You might as well make the most of it."

"I think I prefer to die on an empty stomach." Mike folded his arms across his chest.

"Suit yourself." She took another bite.

Mike had to try again. They were alone. This was his only chance. "Finn, I know you don't want to kill me. Help me get out of here. Come with me."

Finn's fists hit the table on either side of his plate. "How do you know I don't want to kill you?" he said flatly. "Maybe I think the world would be a better place without you."

Mike recoiled. This was not Finn. This was not his friend. "You don't mean that." He reached over the glasses to touch Finn's hand, but his former friend leaped out of his chair to avoid his touch. All Mike managed to do was knock over Finn's glass of wine. The red soaked into the tablecloth and spread toward Finn.

"Sorry," Mike said, dabbing at the wine with his napkin and moving his own full glass in front of Finn.

"Don't try to touch me again," Finn warned before sitting back down. He snapped his fingers and the wine and stain were gone, all of the glasses back in their original positions.

Leaning forward, Mike lowered his voice. "I don't understand what you two think you're getting out of this. Why help him? Why not fight for your freedom?"

Finn sat back down and resumed eating while Kirsa glared at him.

"He's the father of lies," Mike said. "He's not going to reward you. Once he's used you, he's going to kill you."

More chewing. More vacant expressions.

Kirsa took a long drink and then set down her glass. She wiped her mouth with the back of her hand. "What you don't understand, Mike, is that Finn and I don't have a choice. Lucifer is pulling our strings. We are aware of it. We still have our souls and we can feel him controlling us. In theory, we have free will. But in practice… there's no choice."

"Stop, Kirsa. He won't like you talking about this," Finn whispered. "He'll punish you."

She snorted. "What does it matter if I tell *him*?" She gestured at Mike. "He's going to be dead in a few hours."

Finn looked at her and then down at his plate. "Yeah."

The word sent a chill through Mike. Finn only looked like Finn. His will was no longer his own. And if there was any fragment of his friend left inside the tattooed shell beside him, it was so deeply buried that it was likely beyond his reach.

Mike focused on Kirsa. "Did you know that you're a Soulkeeper too?"

The woman shuddered like she'd been struck by lightning. "What the hell are you talking about?"

"It's why you haven't aged and you've kept your power away from the island. It's not because of anything Lucifer has done for you. It's you. You have the Soulkeeper gene. We found your information in the scrolls. You inherited it from your great-grandmother on your father's side."

"No." Her eyebrows knit and she shook her head. "No. No one at that school liked me. I was nobody."

"That's the thing about being a Soulkeeper. God doesn't pick the most likable people, or the most talented, or even the purest of heart. It's not like a fairy tale where you drink the potion and gain Soulkeeper status. He picks you because he picks you, because there's something about you that you can give to the world, something that no one else can."

Kirsa's face paled. Mike thought she looked younger then, and thinner, like her eyes were too big for her face. But as he watched her, he had to admit that her soul had the faintest silver lining. Not a healthy soul by any means, but brighter than Finn's. It wasn't what he'd expected.

"Are... are you saying that God... picked me? You think I'm a Soulkeeper?" She'd stopped eating and her hand trembled next to her plate. It was a small twitch, barely noticeable, but there.

He nodded. "I don't think. I know. I'm the Healer. I can see it in you."

She looked at Finn, who ignored the conversation in favor of picking at his food, and then back at Mike. "But not now. Not after..." Her eyes shifted toward the door.

"Still," Mike said. He tried to appear sincere. "It's not something someone can take from you. It's a free gift. It's what you are. All you have to do is choose it."

The dishes rattled as Finn's glass hit the table. "Shut. Up." He turned on Kirsa. "He's lying to you. I used to be a Soulkeeper, but I'm not anymore. It *was* taken from me. And after the things we've done... for him..." He pointed his chin toward the door and Lucifer. "Kirsa, you are an idiot if you believe there's any chance of coming back from this."

Kirsa scowled, fisting her fork. She stabbed a piece of meat and gave Mike a deadly look. "Yeah. I didn't think so." She pointed at Mike. "Don't say another word to me or I'll make it so you can't. Healer or not, a gag works the same."

Mike leaned back in his chair, thinking he'd made a terrible mistake. He'd come to rescue Finn, but there was nothing left to bring home.

29

GONE

Hope was out of breath by the time she arrived back at Revelations. She'd run as fast and as hard as she'd ever run. Even Soulkeepers weren't machines, and unlike Finn, she couldn't fly. She burst through the doors to Revelations panting and nauseous from the exertion.

"Help," she called, but she was too breathless to put any real power behind it. "Ms. D! Someone! Please..." Now the tears came. Oh, how could she be so stupid? "Someone help!" she yelled even louder.

Ms. D appeared on the stairs and ran to her. "What is it? What has happened?"

"It's Mike... He... He tricked me. Confused me. I... I..."

"Slow down. Start from the beginning."

After a deep breath, Hope told her everything, ending with both Archibald and Mike disappearing through the tree. "They'd planned it together. The gnome was helping him. I never considered that Archibald is like... programmed to obey him. And Mike wanted off this island terribly."

"You don't think he..." Ms. D gave her a horrified look. "He wouldn't do something stupid like go after Finn on his own, would he?"

"Where else would he go?" She grabbed Ms. D's shoulders, as much to hold herself up as to comfort her.

"Help me find the others. We'll load the buses and get off the island. We need Damien."

"If Mike went to Lucifer, what can he do? None of us can get inside!" Hope desperately wished she was still the Healer. What was Mike thinking leaving them like this? It was one thing to resent the power. She could relate to that. But to misuse it? To deny the team the leadership they needed? It was wrong. It was a mistake. She wondered if Mike was figuring that out now.

"We will do what we have always done," Ms. D said. "We are performers in a circus of good and evil, delighting our audience with feats of strength and courage at the whim of the ringmaster. We are entertainers and warriors, Hope." She held Hope away from her by the shoulders. "The show must go on. We will go, and we will fight."

Paul limped from the dining hall with a plate of Mrs. Wilhelm's empanadas in his hand. He was always eating these days, a habit that had bolstered his weight to the point he almost looked like the old Paul, before he'd lived for weeks as a wild animal.

"What's wrong?" he asked. You two look like someone died. Did someone die?"

Ms. D took the plate from his hands. "We need your help. Round up the others as quickly as possible. Tell them it's an emergency. I'll explain everything once we are all on board. We leave as soon as we can get everyone on the bus." Paul nodded and transformed into a parrot, leaving his clothes where he stood. *Smart*, Hope thought. He wouldn't have to shift back to relay the message.

Hope's heart pounded. This was wrong. All wrong. It wasn't supposed to be like this.

Swiveling around, Ms. D gazed at Hope, her eyes piercing. "I don't think I need to tell you this, but as soon as we are on the other side, you need to call Damien. You are the only one who can do it. We are going to need his help."

Hands on hips, Hope said, "The same goes for Theodor. We need him too."

An unspoken admission passed between them. Victoria gave her a curt nod, raised her chin, and departed toward her office.

* * *

THE BUS BOUNCED INTO EXISTENCE ON A ROAD IN RURAL Louisiana and Hope reached out for Damien. It wasn't like the angel carried a cell phone. In the past, he'd simply shown up when she thought of him and sometimes when she hadn't.

"Damien?" she said, looking toward the ceiling. Nothing. Not even a cool breeze to suggest the angel was near.

A curse from across the aisle drew her attention. Jenny was hanging her head into the aisle, calling her name. Hope crossed to Jenny's booth and slid in across from her, next to Jayden. "What's wrong?"

Jenny pointed at her earpiece. "HORU says that all the known demons she's been tracking are on the move. Every single one of them is heading toward New Orleans."

It was Hope's turn to curse.

Next to her, Jayden shifted, his fingers sparking. "Didn't

you say before, when you were the Healer, the immortals thought the demons served a purpose?"

Hope nodded. "Yes. They thought they formed some kind of network to support Lucifer's power. It's why we've been trying to kill as many of them as possible. To weaken Lucifer."

Jenny snorted. "This isn't a good sign. If Mike did something stupid and went to Finn, then its very possible that Lucifer has all the pieces he needs to perform the sacrifice. Now he's calling in the demons to intensify his power. And Hope, they are moving fast."

With a tap of her finger, Jenny signaled to HORU to project the map for the others. Hope watched dozens of red dots from all over the world move steadily toward New Orleans.

Hope shook her head. "I prayed it wasn't true, but I think I knew it in my gut. The Devil has Mike. Lucifer has everything he needs to drop the veil and he isn't going to wait to use it. I think he plans to sacrifice Mike soon."

"How do we stop him?" Jayden asked.

"I don't know," Hope answered.

Jenny raised an eyebrow. "We need Damien."

Burying her face in her hands, Hope mumbled, "More than you know." All she could think about was the feel of his arms, his wings, the way she felt safe in his arms. She longed for him intensely enough that she thought she could smell the citrus and cinnamon scent that followed him everywhere.

"Did you miss me?" She dropped her hands. Damien stood in the aisle, a smug grin twisting his lips.

She leaped out of her seat and tossed her arms around his neck. "You heard me. Oh thank the Lord."

He kissed her lightly on the temple, his wings folding around her, cocooning her in his strength. For a moment, she was safe and all the problems of their world melted into oblivion. Then he backed away to address the others and it all came crashing home. She read too much in the tightness around his mouth. What he'd seen was bad. Really bad.

"I'm sorry I'm late. I've been watching the cemetery," he said.

"Then you know what's happened."

"I know. Lucifer has Michael." There was a collective gasp as their darkest suspicions were confirmed. "There's something else. Jenny, do you still have HORU's drones?"

Jenny nodded.

"Can you release them and send them to the cemetery? There's something I think you all should see."

Jenny reached into her bag and pulled out the marble sized drones. "Meet me in the conference room. This will only take a minute."

While Jenny released HORU's drones, the others gathered around the table. When she joined them again, HORU was by her side, tail twitching and face as worried as an AI unit could be. She passed right through Hope on her way to the center of the room.

"Show them, HORU," Jenny said.

Hope planted her hands on the table as HORU projected the video feed. An aerial shot of the cemetery spread across the wall. Around the barrier Lucifer had in place, rows of people stood like statues, staring toward the cabin. They were all different ethnicities, some dressed professionally, others in casual clothing. Some looked like they'd been homeless before they'd come. All were in some sort of trance, catatonic, swaying like grass in the wind.

"Those have to be demons," Jayden said. "The humans can't see the cemetery. They walk around it."

"There are more than a hundred of them. What are they waiting for?" Hope asked.

Damien spoke up. "They're not waiting for anything. They're doing what they were made to do, channeling power to Lucifer." The room grew quiet enough to hear a pin drop. "They are here for the sacrifice."

It was even worse than Hope expected. There was no time for a rescue mission. The Devil was sacrificing Mike... tonight.

❧ 30 ❧

THE SACRIFICE

As Kirsa and Finn led him into the graveyard at knifepoint, Mike shivered and not from the cold. When he'd gone through the tree with Archibald to come here, he'd been operating on adrenaline. He'd felt nothing but bravado and exhilaration over the possibility of rescuing Finn. Something else too. Part of his haste was in reaction to the Soulkeepers Draconian imprisonment of him on the island. He'd wanted to show them, to demand their respect through actions. Only, he hadn't considered how hard it would be to heal Finn or to convince his friend to save himself. Every part of him had believed he could change Finn.

He should have known better. Once Lucifer had his hooks in you, he didn't let go. Clearly, Finn was brainwashed. Or maybe the Devil had succeeded in collecting his soul and now controlled his every move. Either way, Hope and the others were right. It was stupid for him to come here. So then why had the immortals and every whisper of intuition in his body led him to believe that this was the way to stop Lucifer?

In a clearing beside the tree, Lucifer had set up a stone altar at the place where the ground dipped. Strange symbols were etched into the edge of the stone. Those weren't there for decoration. A thrum of power rippled around him when he studied them, and they seemed to dance in his vision although he could not read them. Crimson liquid pooled at the base, in the depression under the sacrificial table, as if the stone slab was the top of a twisted and morbid fountain. Blood, he was sure of it, although human or animal he couldn't say. He didn't want to know. The altar and blood were at the center of a symbol formed using stones, a five-pointed star.

"A pentagram? How cliché," Mike said sarcastically. If he were going to die anyway, he wanted to get a few jabs in before he did.

Lucifer turned slowly, his wicked smile falling lazily on Mike. "Ravenguard, since our friends Finn and Kirsa wisely wish to avoid touching our guest, could you do the honors? It seems young Michael would like a closer look at the ritual altar. We're almost ready to begin."

From the shadows, Ravenguard appeared like an apparition, glasses first, then face and fangs, then the red riding coat he always wore. "My pleasure," he said, closing in.

Mike flipped his arm over and looked at Ravenguard through Fate's web. All he saw was darkness. He cursed. Of course, he couldn't pluck Ravenguard's strings. The man had none. He'd long since lost his soul, lost his history. He was a killing machine. A demon. Mike reached for his triquetra. He cursed when he remembered it was gone, ripped from his neck by Lucifer himself.

As easily as if he were a child, Ravenguard tossed Mike over his shoulder; his gloved hands roughly gripped his legs. Mike struggled, slamming his elbow into Ravenguard's back with enough force to break a human's spine, but the man didn't even slow down. With unnecessary force, the hunter slammed Mike's back against the stone. The sickening crack and searing pain of his bones breaking left Mike unable to breathe, but that didn't stop Ravenguard from strapping him to the stone. He wrenched his arms and legs apart without mercy, growling through his distended fangs.

Healer or not, the pain was intense enough that when he did finally take a breath, it came in the form of tiny sips inside aching lungs. The heavy blanket of air over him stank of dirty copper and wood smoke, blood and burning. Lucifer snapped his fingers and a bonfire flamed to life in front of the altar. The fire held the same green tinge as the ones he'd seen inside the cabin. Hellfire.

On the other side of the fire, Finn waited, his blue eyes reflecting the flames, his pale hair seeming to glow in the light.

"Finn, help me," Mike pleaded.

But Finn ignored him. He kept his eyes locked on the fire. Kirsa, however, stared at him from outside the symbol, her expression unreadable. Oddly, Lucifer and Ravenguard hardly seemed to notice she was there. Mike wondered if she was invisible to them now that they didn't need her any longer.

It was strange—she'd inflicted what seemed like endless horror on him at Revelations. Now, she was his only relief. Her pale features were fixed in an expression of empathy, her blond eyebrows washed out by the light of the fire. He'd never seen Kirsa pity anyone before and he wondered what he'd done to earn that expression from her. Perhaps it was nothing more than disappointment that she couldn't be the one to wield the blade. Still, he locked eyes with her and breathed. Neither said a word, but there was an exchange in that stare. Two human beings saw each other for what they were. It was the only comfort Mike had to hold on to, the only part of this that seemed the least bit human. His heart pounded. His chest rose and fell quickly with his mounting panic.

Pain radiated through him. Half his body, the half next to the fire, was too hot, burning. His other side shivered from the eerie cold of the cemetery. It was a strange and subtle torture. No matter how he tried to shift, he could not relieve the burning. He closed his eyes for a second to say a prayer for God's help. When he opened them again, Kirsa was gone.

"You'll need this," Lucifer said, pulling the obsidian blade from the fire. Its surface blazed with symbols brought to life by the heat. The twisted, roughhewn stone blade corkscrewed toward the fire. This wasn't surgical steel. This dagger was designed to hurt as well as kill. Lucifer shoved the weapon into Finn's hands.

The hot stone must have burned. Lucifer had handed it to him straight from the fire. Hell, Mike could hear the sizzle and smell of burning flesh. But it didn't even faze Finn. He walked around the fire mechanically, stopping only when he was centered on Mike's cold side. Finn flipped the dagger over to point toward the ground, both hands gripping the hilt, his eyes vacant as some kind of robot. Was he even in there?

"Finn... Finn, listen to me. If you do this, you'll regret it. You'll never forgive yourself."

He didn't flinch. Was he breathing? The reflection of the fire licked in Finn's pupils. The full moon was in position and Mike could feel a change in the air, like the humidity had grown thicker with the fog. A gray wisp passed over his chest and Mike winced when it paused to look at him. Not fog but a soul. A damned soul. The veil was thinning.

Out of the corner of his eye, Mike saw three thick oily demons rise from the ground. Without hesitation, they began drumming instruments he supposed came straight from Hell. The eerie rhythm was anything but soothing, the music made even more disturbing as Lucifer started to chant. The Devil paced around the stone table as he sang. It occurred to Mike he was reading the symbols off the side, the ancient magic rising from its stone home as it had before and feeding the words to Lucifer.

At the center of the ritual, everything else seemed to melt away for Mike. It was Finn, him, and the dagger. His only hope was the boy standing beside him. The boy on the verge of becoming a man. The friend who had drifted from him, who he'd pushed away. They had so much history. If he could just make Finn see.

"Don't you know who I am, Finn? Do you remember the day I had an accident on the bus and you switched pants with me? We've been friends ever since."

Finn didn't show a twitch of recognition.

"Remember when those guys were bullying you after basketball? They poured ice down your back and threatened to beat you up after the game. I put a rest to that without saying a word." He flexed his fists remembering how he'd punched both boys defending Finn.

If Finn remembered the incident, he didn't react.

"Deviant Joe!" Mike yelled. "We started it together. You, me, Jayden, and Wyatt. Nobody could pull a prank like us, Finn. No one could do what we did because no one trusted each other like we did. Like I'm trusting you now. You *can't* do this. You gotta fight it. Don't listen to him. Don't do what he wants you to do!"

The corners of Finn's mouth twisted downward, and a bead of sweat drew a trail from his hairline to his chin. His lips parted. "Can't."

The word was nothing but an exhale, yet Mike heard it. It was true, then. Finn's will was not his own.

"Touch me. Touch my hand. I can heal you. I can break the curse."

As the chanting grew louder, stronger, Mike's head started spinning. The Devil's face passed in front of his, around and around to the rhythm of the music. With his eyes, he traced a path between the moon, the Devil, the dagger, Finn.

As he met Finn's widening eyes, he knew it was over. "I forgive you," he said, loud and clear.

The chanting stopped.

Finn raised the dagger above his head, aimed at Michael's heart.

✿ 31 ✿

THEODOR

Every magical barrier had a weakness. Theodor had created enough of them to know. If he understood Lucifer's magic better, he might be able to reach in with his own and pull the string that would unravel the entire thing like a ball of twine. But he did not understand this magic. It was ancient and it was strong. Strong enough to make the hair on his arms stand on end as he neared it.

As he stood outside the cemetery, behind two rows of demons entirely preoccupied with what was going on inside, Theodor examined the unseen force with Wendy at his side. They had to find a way in. If he was to atone for what he'd done to Finn and the tree, he must save Michael. His entire life had prepared him for this. He was a powerful magician and the piece of the star that glowed from the pendant around his neck had restored his strength, thanks to Victoria. He owed her.

A ripple traveled through the dome of power. "Interesting," he said. If he could get to the barrier, he could test a few spells, see how the magic reacted to the manipulation of various elements. Unfortunately, that would require battling the demons that blocked his path shoulder to shoulder around the graveyard. Right now, they were alligators sleeping in the sun. He had a feeling they wouldn't stay that way if he tried to get inside.

"Wendy, do you have your phone?" he asked.

"I'm sixteen years old. We don't leave home without it." She reached for her back pocket. Theodor glanced at the device in her hands and entertained the fleeting thought that if he survived this mess, he might need to learn to use one.

"Send a message to Victoria," he said. "I believe the barrier is weakening. The closer Lucifer gets to the sacrifice the weaker he becomes and therefore the weaker his wards become. With her help and a little luck, we might be able to take it down."

"No need for an email. I am here."

Theodor spun around. Victoria Duval, wild gray hair flying, stood like a force of nature behind him, her eyes reflecting the ripples in the boundary. She wore her favorite purple suit, the one she often wore at Revelations when she was playing the role of ringmaster. Her body put off a thrum of magic he could feel in his bones.

"How did you find us?" Wendy asked.

Victoria clasped her hands in front of her waist. "HORU. She's monitoring this place with her drones. We saw you on her recording." She pointed toward the shimmering barrier beyond the rows of demons. "Shall we?"

"Where are the others?" Theodor asked.

"Taking advantage of the fact that these demons are woefully distracted to clear us a path."

She took a step back as a head tumbled between them. Jayden arrived, his blazing sword connecting with the dark wave that emerged from the broken shell of a human body.

The thing was responsive but slow, and he had no problem reducing it to ash.

"They can still fight," Jayden said, "but they're lethargic." He ran a hand through his red hair and swiveled back toward the demons.

Before the next demon could react, two vines shot from the earth and tore its cloned human body in two. Jayden slayed the darkness within. Hope stepped out of the hole they'd created in the ring of demons, her vines holding the others back to give Theodor, Victoria, and Wendy access to the barrier. She grunted with the effort of holding the demons back.

"A little help here! Paul? Amuke?"

Two tigers bounded to Hope's side, tackling two more demons and shredding them. Hope tore another three apart, breaking a sweat now. Theodor raised his hands to help her, but Ms. D gestured for him to wait. "Save your strength," she whispered. "Look."

Out of nowhere, Damien appeared in the clearing and used his light to finish off the recently husked demons. Now the hole was larger, their path to the barrier fully accessible.

"Get to work, you three," Hope said. "We've cleared your way. Use your magic to take that thing down and let's save our Soulkeepers." She raised her clawed hands and new vines shot from the earth, corralling a fresh set of demons.

Theodor looked at Victoria, purple magic sparking from his fingers. Wendy followed his lead, her magic smaller, less powerful, but there nonetheless. Victoria nodded and ignited her own magic. He met her gaze. The buzz of her power was music to his ears. They'd accomplished a lot together over the last century. Beaten the odds again and again. Practiced the impossible on a regular basis. It was ironic really that Lucifer was responsible for making them what they were, yet the Devil truly didn't know what he was dealing with.

Victoria raised an eyebrow. "The first one inside wins bragging rights."

"You know how much I hate to lose." The corner of his mouth curled upward.

"Wendy?"

"I'm ready," the girl said.

Side by side, they waged war on Lucifer's shield.

"FINN, TOUCH MY HAND. DON'T DO THIS." STRAPPED TO THE stone table, Mike panicked, his heart pounding, his breath flailing in his lungs. He couldn't get through to Finn. The tip of the obsidian dagger was raised high, poised over his heart. Lucifer's chanting had ended, on a crescendo that he suspected was Finn's cue to drive the business end of that thing through his heart. There was no coming back from that. The obsidian blade didn't merely kill the body: it killed the soul.

Sweat beaded on Finn's upper lip. He was fighting it, but he wouldn't last long. Mike was going to die. Worse, Lucifer was going to use his death to merge the realms. The Soulkeepers wouldn't last long in Hell. Some, he supposed, would be corrupted, like Finn and Kirsa. Others, like Hope, would never bow down. She'd be lucky to meet a swift end.

He should have listened to her. What was he thinking trying to be the hero?

Thing was, he thought he had a foolproof plan. Before he'd gone through the tree, he'd filled a vial with holy water. Water from Eden should have been strong enough to break any curse or influence Lucifer had over Finn. He'd even managed to get some in both his water and wine glass at dinner. Actually he'd put it in his own, then switched the glasses when he purposely knocked over Finn's wine. Finn had been so afraid of Mike touching him, he hadn't even noticed.

Unfortunately, although Finn drank from his cup, Mike had observed no effects from the holy water. Which meant he had made a terrible mistake. Either Lucifer's influence was too strong or the water was too weak. It didn't matter anymore. He was in the wrong place at the wrong time.

He eyed the point of the blade. This was going to hurt. He was going to die, with pain. He forced himself to look away, straight up toward the full moon.

A flash of purple lightning cut across the night above him. Not across, around. Purple lightning followed the arc of Lucifer's protective enchantment leaving a fissure in its wake. For a moment, he got the distinct impression of being inside a fragile and cracking egg. Magic.

"Finn, look. They're coming! You don't have to do this!"

"Ravenguard, kill!" Lucifer ordered. Ravenguard took off toward the border at a run. "You." He pointed at Kirsa. "Shut him up!" Lucifer pushed Kirsa toward Michael. Lucifer strained, directing all his mental energy at Finn whose spinning tattoos told Mike he was doing everything in his power not to obey.

Kirsa reached Mike, positioning herself behind the top of his head, and placed her hand over his mouth. "Shhh," she said, her eyes meeting his. That's when it dawned on him; she was touching him skin to skin. He looked at Finn, then at her. His best friend focused on the space over his heart.

"Stay absolutely still," Kirsa whispered in his ear. "Whatever you do, do not move."

Mike felt the binding around his wrist give way, then his other wrist. He obeyed and did not move. What was she doing?

His mind flashed back to dinner. He'd knocked over the wine. Finn had leapt back and Mike had switched the water. "Sorry. Here, have mine," he'd said, putting his wine in front of Finn. He dabbed at the tablecloth, moving the glasses to reach the spill. Then Finn had snapped his fingers and the stain had cleaned itself up. It had cleaned itself up and the glasses had rearranged themselves on the table. The setting had become perfect again.

Mike had missed it. The glasses he'd placed in front of Finn, had moved in front of Kirsa. Finn never drank the holy water. It was her. It was Kirsa!

"Now, Finn! Do it. Do it!" Lucifer stepped into the fire, his body transforming into something monstrous with horns and hooves and talons that clacked toward the moon. He extended razor-sharp claws toward Finn.

"I'm sorry," Finn cried, plunging the dagger toward Mike's heart. Faster than Mike thought possible, his body was shoved across the stone. With power only the resilience instructor could have mustered, Kirsa thrust him off the table, away from the fire and Lucifer. Mike's shoulder hit Finn in the gut, and he ricocheted into the pool of blood at the base of the table, his ankles still bound.

With an oomph, Finn bent in half from the blow, but the dagger continued its descent. As Lucifer bellowed from the fire, the dagger hit its mark. Only, Mike's heart wasn't there anymore. Kirsa's was.

When she'd swept him off the table, she'd leaned forward for leverage. The dagger slid into her back, left side, under the shoulder bone. Mike cried out and reached for her hand. Their fingers tangled beside Finn whose eyes had gone red and glazed. Mike's gaze connected with Kirsa's. "No!"

"I feel it," she said to him, her expression genuinely astonished as blood gurgled over her bottom lip. To Mike, she seemed more surprised than anything else. After decades of being invincible, Kirsa's time had come. Her abilities had failed her. Mike watched the light fade from her eyes. Her last words were, "I'm sorry."

"I forgive you," he said. Her last breath blew cold across his face. She'd tortured him, even tried to kill him once. He felt no pleasure in watching her die. She'd saved his life. No matter what she'd done in the past, she didn't deserve this.

Finn blinked, his hands still gripping the dagger buried in her back.

Mike would not wait for a second blow. With Soulkeeper speed and strength, he tore the bindings from his ankles and scrambled to his feet. But Lucifer took no interest in him. All of his attention was on the swirling vortex of power hovering over Kirsa's body.

"Oh no," Mike mumbled. Kirsa drank the holy water. Something from Heaven. And her soul was the Devil's. She may not have been a Healer, but judging by the tear opening between the Devil and Finn, she was enough to complete the spell.

Lucifer gave a wicked laugh. He reached his hands into the swirling magic and pulled.

❦ 32 ❦

BATTLE

"It's cracking!" Hope yelled. Purple lightning branched across the sphere of power protecting the cemetery, and Hope was ready with an army of vines growing in and through the cracks. She flexed her muscles and tried to use the new growth to spread the fractures. She wasn't strong enough.

"Damien, help!" She turned her face to her angel, her love, teeth gritted.

The angel clapped his hands together, a sword forming between them out of heavenly energy. Flying to the top of the barrier, he came down hard, stabbing through the crack she'd created with the help of Theodor, Victoria, and Wendy. A few yards to her left, the three caught on quickly to what Damien was doing. They redirected their magic at the fracture point.

"Eviscerate!" Theodor dealt the deadly blow with the toss of a single card. A hole formed right under Damien's cut. The angel slid down the side of the barricade, slicing the magic as he went. By the time the card was back in Theodor's hand, a spiderweb of cracks had branched out from Damien's cut as if they'd shattered the ward like an egg. Hope heard the cracking.

It spread up, across, and around, painting the night sky with a series of branching forks. Damien landed beside her, sweeping her into his arms and out of the way just in time. From beneath the shelter of his wings, she watched the shield fall like broken glass, purple fragments washing out and over them.

They were sharp as glass too. She saw Theodor shield Wendy and Victoria from the debris. Paul and Amuke were able to race away in time, and Jayden and Fuse produced a wall of fire that absorbed the sharp energy. When it was over, Hope knew Damien was hurt. He'd shielded her at his own peril. Shards of the magic stuck out of his back and wings. Hurrying, she removed them, gasping as silver coated her fingers.

"You're bleeding," she said.

"It's nothing. I will heal."

Her stomach turned at the sight of his silver blood dripping near his feet. "No. You need to rest."

Ignoring her, he whirled on the cemetery. "There's no time."

A chill rocked Hope's body as she saw what Damien had seen. Near the center of the graveyard, a cyclone of magic had opened a hole in the night sky. Under the glow of the blood moon, a crimson circle was rimmed with electric yellow lightning. They'd killed most of the demons. They'd taken down the shield. But they hadn't been quick enough.

"Oh no, it's already happened! Mike. Oh dear Lord, Mike." Hope turned to Damien, tears flooding her vision.

With a look of determination, Damien lifted her into his arms, his silver blood soaking her shirt. He grunted in pain as he took to the sky and flew over the cemetery wall toward the expanding portal.

* * *

VICTORIA DUVALL WATCHED THE SHIELD CRUMBLE, HAND IN hand with the man she once loved and could easily love again. Theodor was changed. She could see that now. He was putting everything he had behind undoing the damage he'd caused— damage that began with the two of them the day they'd started Revelations.

With a revolution of his hand, he cast an arcing purple shield, protecting her and Wendy alike. A quick check told her the others were safe as well, although Damien had taken on substantial injuries protecting Hope. As soon as the barrier was completely gone, she watched the angel take to the sky with Hope in his arms.

A growl ripped through the night, as Paul and Amuke, in the form of two tigers, wasted no time taking down the last three demons to her left. The men's orange fur was blackened with the oily remains of the demons they'd killed that night. With the help of Jayden, Fuse, Hope, and Damien, they now had clear access to the cemetery.

"Jenny texted," Wendy said. "HORU's drones show there are no more demons around the periphery. She warns it is possible that some have survived by jumping bodies."

Victoria turned to the girl, noticing the dark circles under her eyes, the fatigue that came from overusing magic. She discreetly nudged Theodor.

"Wendy, I am afraid for Jenny and the others on the bus. They don't have anyone there with magical ability to protect them. Orelon can fly but he can't fight. Will you go?"

The girl nodded. "I won't let anything happen to them."

She was gone before Victoria could thank her.

Theodor grabbed her elbow hard. "She needed a break," Victoria began but soon realized Theodor was not looking at Wendy.

"Do you see what I see?" he asked.

She scanned the graveyard through the bars of the front gate. A streak of red darted from one mausoleum to another.

"Ravenguard," she said through her teeth.

"We are not the only two responsible for what happened at Revelations." He led her toward the gate, unlocking it with a simple touch of his hand.

"No, we are not." She followed Theodor across the threshold and into the graveyard.

"I think it's time we take care of Revelations' unfinished business," he said.

"I agree. I should have fired that bastard a long time ago." She raised her hands defensively and walked deeper into the graveyard. The streak of red appeared again, but like a true coward, Ravenguard ran for the gate.

"Bind," Theodor yelled. The gate slammed shut and locked before Ravenguard could sneak through. He slammed into the bars, then whirled around, hissing. He'd always dressed like a hunter: khaki pants, red riding coat, white shirt and ascot. A hunter of children. A killer. A demon. He and Applegate were the ones who'd enforced Lucifer's edict that they start the school. Everything about him made her feel ill.

"Not so tough without your dogs and Applegate to back you up," Victoria said. She took a step toward him.

Ravenguard drew his dagger and bared his fangs. He rushed Theodor. Victoria tried to blast him with a pulse of energy, but he dodged the purple mass that flew from her hand and leapt onto Theodor. Both men toppled to the ground and rolled along the pebble walkway. Sparks of magic flew between them as Theodor tried to block the attack. Ravenguard's fangs drew closer and closer to his neck.

Victoria's stomach twisted at the thought of losing Teddy

again. She'd watched him get stabbed and dragged to Hell by Ravenguard once before. It wouldn't happen again. She may not be able to deliver a direct hit with her magic without hurting Theodor, but she had other weapons at her disposal. She rushed the two and delivered a kick to Ravenguard's ribs with all her Soulkeeper strength. Pain shot through her foot, but the move worked. The hunter grunted. The distraction gave Theodor room to manage a repulsion spell, sending Ravenguard flying back a few feet.

Circling her arms, Victoria blasted Ravenguard with icy magic. It plowed into him, taking her breath away and turning the tips of her fingers blue. Ravenguard froze, icicles forming off the tip of his nose and the lobes of his ears. She raised her hands to finish him off, but Theodor did the honors.

"Eviscerate!" He tossed a card at the center of the hunter's red coat and Ravenguard, admissions counselor and disciplinarian of Revelations, shattered like glass. Red shards the color of blood sprinkled onto the pebbles between the mausoleums, turning to ash when they hit the stones before sinking into the earth.

"We are no longer in need of your services," Theodor said, kicking the stones to make sure nothing of Ravenguard remained. He brushed a hand over his dark jacket as if to ensure that none of Ravenguard's remains clung to the clothes.

"Are you hurt?" he asked her, rushing to steady her by the shoulders and look her in the eyes.

"My foot is sore, but I don't think it's broken," she said. But he didn't let go of her and his face... his expression was almost pleading. "What's wrong?"

"Before another thing happens, before something else tries to kill either one of us, I must tell you Victoria, I love you. I have always loved you. I will always love you. This ancient flesh will not take another step without making sure you know." She'd never seen him look as human, as fragile. When a man like Theodor trusted you with his heart, it was important not to take it for granted. She didn't leave him twisting in the wind.

"I know," she said. "I love you too. I have since the first time I met you. I should have left with you that night at the cabaret. I should have listened to you."

He kissed her then, in a way he hadn't kissed her in decades. *Magic*, Victoria thought. This thing between them was pure magic, larger than life and completely invincible.

Thunder rumbled behind them. Not thunder, the portal. Theodor pulled away as the red hole that had started as a slit in the night sky widened, crackling with power. "It's getting bigger. I don't think this is what Lucifer intended to happen. It's taking too long. Something has gone wrong. We may have a chance yet to change the outcome this night."

"How do we stop it?" she asked.

"I don't know." He turned his face to hers again.

She shrugged. "Not knowing has never stopped us from trying." He held out his hand to her in invitation. She smiled and took it. More determined than ever, they took off at a sprint, straight toward the Devil and the sacrifice.

❧ 33 ❧

FINN

F inn clutched the hilt of the dagger, the sticky warmth of Kirsa's blood oozing from her back over his hands, but he couldn't move. Every time he tried to let go and pull away from the nightmare in front of him or even think about doing so, hot pressure squeezed his brain. He blinked. Stared at the blood. At Kirsa. At the fire in front of him that still housed Lucifer. He should feel something, shouldn't he? But he didn't. It was hard to think at all.

On the bright side, whatever curse he was still under was an old one. The Devil was too busy trying to wrestle the portal open to worry about him now. The ritual's magic was weaker than he'd expected. But then, the sacrifice of the Healer was supposed to fuel this magic. That hadn't happened. Kirsa was an adequate substitute but far less powerful. It looked like Lucifer was trying to finish the job himself.

"Oh God, Finn," Mike said from beside him. Out of the corner of his eye, he saw Mike staring at the portal above their heads. It was the size of a beach ball and blazing like a small sun. Lucifer clawed and pulled, forcing it open. A rush of molten power wrapped around his head and Finn winced. He was not supposed to look at the portal. He looked back down at the blood.

"Sorry, buddy," Mike said. "This is going to hurt."

Cold hands touched the bare skin of his ankle, and a different kind of rush flooded Finn's body. It felt like cold water was being pumped up his leg and into his torso, enough that it clashed inside him with the hot magma that had coiled around his brain like a snake. The pain was instantaneous.

He released the dagger and clutched the sides of his head, a scream catching in his throat. Kirsa's blood matted sticky and warm in his hair. His brain couldn't grasp what was happening, but he moaned against the pain, his voice drowned out by the chugging mass of energy that was the portal above him. Mike did not let go of his ankle.

"Finn," Hope's voice came from somewhere near the crypt beside him. "Finn, look at me."

Finn tried but when he attempted to turn his head, the pain intensified. He glanced at the fire. Damn, the Devil was big. In his natural form with the horns and the teeth, he was truly terrifying. The tear between the realms was getting bigger, and Lucifer was too. He was drawing on the power from the other side. Finn could see that now.

"Hope, I'm totally blind, girl. I can't hold on," Mike said. The grip on Finn's ankle loosen and then slip away. The cool feeling abated and he doubled over from the loss.

"Finn," Hope said again. "He's using you. It's your sorcery fueling the tear. You opened it. You can close it. Pull your magic back inside." Her voice was calm, clear, and demanding.

He noticed Damien then, trying his best to distract Lucifer. But the Devil was too large, too powerful. He swatted the angel away like a pest. Silver blood fizzled as it dripped into the open flames below. The angel was hurt. He would not last long against the Devil.

Finn understood what Hope wanted him to do and why. It was impossible. Close it? Didn't she comprehend the amount of power chugging above their heads? Only something equally as powerful could stop it. Finn wasn't strong enough to do such a thing, even if he could choose to do it. It had been a long time since Finn had made his own decisions. He knew that now. The symbols he'd bound to his flesh had been making his decisions for him for months. It was strange how they'd taken control. It had started so innocently. A little power, a little more to save a friend. But the power was intoxicating. If he was honest with himself, and there was no better time to be honest than now, the hour of his probable death, he'd come here to this cemetery because the idea of possessing the obsidian dagger had made him drunk with the potential for power. The Soulkeepers couldn't reject him if he had such a thing. He'd be their hero.

It hadn't gone the way he'd planned.

Something large and black buzzed past his face and he swatted at it. A small bird? A large bug? It hovered in the corner of his vision and then *she* was there, projected from the onboard camera in her drone, tail twitching and anime eyes wide with wonder. HORU.

"Finn, finally. I've missed you so much. My system hasn't been the same. I'm in need of maintenance and recalibration."

"I can't help you anymore, HORU," Finn said. Every word cost him. Splitting pain cut through his head. But he had to tell her. She was his creation. He owed her an explanation. "Ask Jenny. Tell her how to do it. She'll help you."

The drone whirred as HORU's image shifted. "That is unacceptable, Finn. You programmed me to take care of you.

I've protected you and your data for the length of my existence."

"I'm not doing this on purpose. I have no choice."

More whirring. "The symbols in your skin are a virus, not unlike the one that infected my data index years ago. Do you remember?"

"Yeah. We fixed you." He groaned and squeezed his eyes closed. So tired. So much pain.

"My analysis shows that removing the symbols from your skin would undo the damage they've done and the hold Lucifer has over you."

"I can't just shed my skin," Finn said.

"No. You did not delete my data index to remove the virus."

"No. We copied the good stuff, extracted the bad stuff, and filled in the holes through the trapdoor I coded into your operating system." Finn frowned and looked up at Lucifer, who was now roughly the size of a house and doing a mighty fine job tearing the veil between realms. The hole was now big enough to drive a car through.

Finn blinked. She was right. HORU was a genius. The Devil was a virus and it was his responsibility to remove it. "HORU, record."

"Yes, Finn. Recording now."

Finn grabbed the hilt of the obsidian dagger and yanked it from Kirsa's back. Every symbol on his body swirled to life on his command. All the power he'd ever had or could ever draw on filled him at once. He backed up a few steps, gained momentum, and flew.

It had been a long time since Finn had flown, not because he couldn't fly, but because with his magic so readily available, he hadn't needed to fly in months. But now, there was no better way to do what he wanted to do, and flying was his original power, one that came as naturally as walking. He flew as fast as he could, straight into Lucifer. At the Devil's current size, Finn could only wrap himself around the beast's neck, but that's where he wanted to be anyway. He plunged the obsidian dagger into Lucifer's throat, right where the carotid would be on a human.

On the plus side, Lucifer couldn't both swat him and Damien away and hold the portal open, which meant he was safe for the moment. On the other hand, Lucifer didn't even flinch.

"Obsidian can't hurt me, boy," the Devil roared. Finn watched him swipe Damien out of the sky with his free hand to Hope's panicked cries below.

"I didn't want to *hurt* you," Finn said. "I wanted to distract you." Gripping the Devil's neck as tight as he could with all his limbs, Finn twisted his shoulders. He thought of hellfire and obsidian, of the spiraling hole that he had opened to Hell in the basement of the school. But mostly, he thought of the space on the other side of the portal.

It was slow breaking apart. Dissemination was hard enough on his own. Doing it while holding someone who was as large as a semitruck was nearly impossible. But Finn was the strongest he'd ever been, and he drew on his bond to Theodor and Wendy to become even stronger. Cell by cell, he came apart, and he took Lucifer with him. He didn't have to go far. A few inches. A few more. Into the heart of the portal to Hell.

Lucifer realized what was happening too late. He tried to sink his talons into the edges of the opening, tried to hold himself in the earthly realm. But even the Devil couldn't grip the night sky. The truth was, he was weak. Lucifer had used his power to perform the ritual and then struggled to expand the tear. And although his access to Hell had increased his size, that expanding girth was a detriment now. Finn had used that weight against him. All the forces of Hell now drew on Lucifer like gravity, helping to move the beast into the portal. Finn was relieved when his strength wasn't the primary force driving the Devil toward that place, toward the wicked green fire and the walls of obsidian.

When he and the Devil were entirely through the opening, he reached out a hand, tattoo spinning. "Bind," he yelled. After the incident at Revelations, Finn had learned one simple rule: anytime he opened a portal he must close it behind him. His failure to do that with the tree had been part of the trouble. This time, he wouldn't screw it up. The slit in the night sky stitch itself closed at his command as they tumbled toward Hell. With a sad smile, he watched the portal disappear, knowing he'd sealed his fate.

❦ 34 ❧

THE FALL

To the sounds of Lucifer's howls, Finn dodged shredding talons and slashing teeth, clinging to the back of Lucifer's neck as they plummeted through the fiery abyss. The obsidian dagger was still buried in Lucifer's thick cord of muscle and Finn used it as an anchor as they fell through time and space.

He'd channeled everything he had, every power he had left, to propel Lucifer through the portal. Now, there was nothing left to do but fall with him. God's curse was still in place. If Finn could return the beast to his dungeon in Hell, Lucifer would be a prisoner there. Finn's choice came at a price. He watched the spell for bind rise from his arm and burn off, the magic fueling his propulsion. Eviscerate dissolved next. That one hurt. When he arrived where he was going, he wouldn't be able to defend himself. Ignite, silence, portate. One by one, the spells he'd placed in his skin ignited, sparked like a firecracker, and dissolved in the atmosphere. Farther, faster, the magic propelled him forward until they reached their destination.

Through a barrier of green flames, Finn burst into Hell,

finally tumbling off Lucifer and rolling across the hard black stone of Hell's terrain. He grunted, his body feeling raw, like his skin had been flayed from his body. He had no spells left. No tattoos. No weapons either, aside from the dagger in his hand.

The Devil landed on his feet, still howling like a wounded beast. Although Finn raised the dagger between them, he was powerless against the Devil here. When he'd thrown himself through the tear in the veil, he'd known he was going to Lucifer's domain and that here the Devil would have the ultimate power over him. All of his sorcery, any power he'd had before, would be lost in the fall. He knew, yet he accepted his fate. He may be trapped here, but so was Lucifer.

It was worth it to Finn to save his friends.

Still seething, the Devil transformed from the beast into something that looked like a man. Not the lead singer of Technothrob this time, but more like the man Finn had raised in the basement of Revelations. With platinum hair and blue eyes, a straight back and a proud jaw, the Devil paced toward Finn, unblinking, irate. A flick of his finger and the obsidian dagger flew from Finn's grip, skidding across the stone and out of his reach. A pack of oily black hounds fought over it like a bone, dragging it away.

Lucifer bared his teeth. "Do you know what you have done?" Fire rose in a circle around Finn, the heat like sticking his head in a hot oven. "I would have given you power beyond your wildest dreams. I would have brought the humans what they wanted, ruled them with hate, greed, lust, anger, and fear. You could have been rich, my minion, my honored slave. Instead, you do this!" The fire blazed closer, singeing Finn's already raw flesh.

"I did it for my friends," Finn said. "I did it for the people I love and most of all because I love myself. Because letting you rule humanity would have meant the end of everything dear to me. If you'd ever known love or friendship, you'd understand that no amount of money or power could ever replace those things."

Lucifer growled and the flames contracted, close enough that Finn cried out from the pain. He folded his shoulders in to try to avoid the heat and felt a tingle in his torso. He concentrated on the feeling, trying to sort it out.

"You are a worm, Finn Wager. Nothing more than excrement. I will roast you. I will allow the demons and tormented souls of Hell to rip you apart and eat you. And when you are nothing more than vomit from the stomach of the wretched, I will slowly and painfully put you back together only to rip you apart again."

It was no idle threat. Finn watched the shadows move in. Dark souls clawed closer, hellhounds at their sides, oily and sharp. Demons with claws to tear and teeth to bite licked their jowls.

The Devil growled through flashing fangs as the flames licked Finn's shoulders. He was burning alive. But inside, he felt a tingle, a part of him the Devil couldn't touch.

"I wasn't sure if it was true," Finn said.

Lucifer rolled his eyes. "If what were true?"

"Theodor told me that being a Soulkeeper was in my genes, and that the real problem, the reason I was rejected was that I'd polluted my skin with spells."

"Hmm. A lot of good this knowledge has done you."

His skin blistered. He focused on the tingle. "Being a Soulkeeper was always inside me. It was always a part of me. It's why I could fly and why magic came easily to me. It's why I was able to open the bridge with Theodor. For the longest time, I didn't understand. Theodor never suspected either. He thought his spell had gone wrong. He never supposed that the variable was me. That something about me was different, stronger than he expected. I didn't know it at first. I'd put a piece of my soul into that tree. That was my price and why I couldn't enter Veil Island."

"How sad. A damaged soul. Let's find out if we can damage it some more." He hissed.

But Finn wasn't done. "Hope told me that I couldn't grow as a Soulkeeper because I was distracted by sorcery. She was right too. Now that the symbols are gone, I know what I can do, what I've always been able to do. I can feel it under my skin begging to be used. It should have been obvious based on what I was good at. At Revelations, I could fly. I've always been fast and light and nearly invisible in my human life. Flying under the radar was the talent that made Deviant Joe possible"

"You bore me with your stories."

"I was able to open the portal that brought you back and able to disseminate faster than any magician before me. I could do these things because I didn't need a card or a symbol to do them. Those things were just training wheels. The power to open a portal, to tear the veil, to fold space and move between places, that had been my God-given power all along. The thing I was searching for with the spells and the magic, the power I thought I needed to keep my friends safe, the way I was never able to keep my mother safe… All this time, I was searching for something I already had."

He placed his palms together in front of his heart, prayer position. His flesh burned. He closed his eyes and prayed.

"Thank you, Lord for my Soulkeeper gift. I accept." When he opened his eyes again, he twisted his shoulders. The last thing he heard before he broke apart was Lucifer's howl of rage.

There were no symbols left in Finn's skin. They'd all been burned away when he'd descended into Hell. And he was weak and exhausted, starved by Lucifer these last weeks, and used as part of the ritual. But the talent God had given him was enough. Not enough to carry him all the way home, but enough to take him to safety. He didn't have to go far. He focused on the tree, on the part of his soul he'd left inside it. And as he had anticipated, he was strong enough to make the leap from Hell to the place Hope and Theodor had called Nod. Hell and Nod were close, which was why Theodor had been able to slide here, as injured as he was, during his descent to Hell.

Finn became whole again in a garden of thorns at the base of a fountain that was dry as a bone. Sand blew across the marble, and the sculpture of an angel loomed over him from its center, wings outstretched. There was nothing living here. Nothing good. But he was not burning. He was not in Hell.

And beside the fountain was the tree. Well, a skeleton of a tree. It looked dead. And when he touched it, nothing happened. He slid down its trunk, to its roots, and closed his eyes. He was too exhausted to do more.

If what Hope had told him was true, Lucifer was bound to Hell now, returned to the curse that Finn and Hope had freed him from. Even if Finn spent the rest of his days in this barren wasteland, it would be worth it. This was a good thing. What-ever happened next, it was a good thing.

With peace in his heart, he slept.

🐉 35 🐉

THE SOULKEEPERS

"Finn, no!" Hope ran toward the altar and the closing portal. With all the strength she could muster, she shot a vine toward the closing hole, her intention to lasso Finn. But the hole in the night sky collapsed on all chance of rescue.

"What happened?" Mike was on his feet. He steadied himself with one hand on the sacrificial stone, staring blindly in her direction.

"Don't move," she said. "The fire is still smoldering. Damn, you're covered in blood."

"Is Finn okay?" he demanded.

"Are we too late?" Victoria and Theodor arrived at a run, staring at the place in the sky that had once been a revolving ball of fire.

Mike stomped his foot. "Is Finn okay, Hope?"

"He's gone. He... dragged the Devil through the tear in the veil."

"Kirsa?" Victoria released Theodor's hand and stepped to the sacrificial table where Kirsa was facedown on the stone in a pool of her own blood.

"It's her. She sacrificed herself to save Mike. I think she assumed the obsidian dagger wouldn't pierce her flesh. No weapon ever had before. But somehow it did."

"It was my fault," Mike said.

Hope's forehead furrowed. "How could Kirsa's sacrifice possibly be your fault?"

"I brought holy water from the pool on Veil Island."

There was a collective gasp. Hope couldn't find the words to berate him for the risk he had taken. A vial of that water had changed an entire island and made it inhabitable only by Soulkeepers. Using it on Earth could wreak havoc.

Mike couldn't see their faces, but by the silence that followed he must have known they were deeply disappointed with his actions. "I meant to have Finn drink it," he explained, "to break whatever hold Lucifer had over him. But Kirsa and Finn switched glasses. She drank it instead. I told her she was a Soulkeeper. Once the water broke Lucifer's influence, her instinct was to protect me."

"You had no choice, Mike. You had to use the resources available to you. Her death is not your fault. Accountability for this horror falls fully and completely on Lucifer." Victoria crossed to him and led him away from the bloody stone.

Damien hobbled out from between two crypts and Hope rushed into his arms. "Thank God you're okay. I was about to come look for you." She kissed him fully on the lips.

"I'm sorry. I could not stop him," the angel said.

"What happened to Finn?" Theodor asked, his voice cracking with concern.

"He disseminated with Lucifer in his grip," Hope said. "He carried the devil into the portal."

"Impossible," Theodor said. "Even Victoria and I couldn't disseminate with a beast that large in tow."

"I saw it. All of his tattoos came to life. Lucifer had his hands in the portal—he was trying to make it bigger, pull it open. Finn only had to move him a few inches. He did it. I don't know how but he did it."

"I can help." HORU appeared between them, her drone hovering nearby.

"HORU…" Hope had seen the AI unit talking to Finn, but from the place where she was hiding, with the chugging of the magic above his head, she couldn't make out what was said.

"Finn gave me specific instructions to record what happened. Would you like me to play it back for you?"

They all said yes at once. Mike cursed. "You'll have to tell me what you see," he said. "I'm still blind." Ms. D put her arm around Mike and assured him she would relay what happened.

HORU broadcast the video. It was as horrific as the first time Hope had seen it. Finn leapt onto Lucifer's neck, plunging the dagger into the beast's flesh. Then he disseminated, slowly taking the Devil with him through the opening in the night sky. All of Finn's tattoos were raised from his skin, spinning and swirling. He lifted his hand and the portal closed behind him.

"Finn is truly a prodigy. A gifted magician," Victoria said. "I have never seen anyone that strong."

"Yes, he is," Theodor said softly, stroking his chin. "HORU, rewind the video and zoom in on Finn. Slow motion please."

HORU blinked twice and did as he requested.

Hope would never have noticed it at regular speed, but in slow motion and zoomed in, it was clear Finn's tattoos weren't just spinning; they were burning.

"He used them as fuel," Theodor said. "Look, they're coming apart."

"Did you know he could do that?" Victoria asked.

"No. I didn't know it was possible," Theodor said. He narrowed his eyes. "He's saying something toward the camera."

Hope leaned forward, concentrating on Finn's lips. At the moment he cast the spell to close the tear, he looked directly at HORU's camera and said, "Trapdoor."

"Trapdoor?" Hope repeated. "What does that mean?"

Theodor laughed and kept on laughing. He shook his head.

"Somebody tell the blind man what's going on," Mike said.

"Finn sent me a message to retrieve him, the same way I retrieved you, Michael," Theodor said. The magician became serious again. "Although, he will be lucky if it is possible. Risky is an understatement. Lucifer wasn't in Hell watching Mike and Wendy. He's there now and I'd venture his interest in Finn has not waned yet." Theodor walked quickly to the tree and reached for the trunk.

"Whoa, isn't that how this all started? " Hope shifted nervously. "Is it safe for you to travel through that thing?"

"Absolutely not," Theodor said. He winked at her, touched the bark, and was gone.

* * *

FINN COULDN'T MOVE. HE WASN'T SURE HOW LONG HE'D BEEN lying there next to the tree, but it was long enough to feel like a shriveled prune. His tongue was stuck to the roof of his mouth, his eyes would no longer open, and his breathing had become uneven. He'd gone through stages of increasing hunger, but there was nothing to eat here and he dared not leave the tree. What if Theodor got his message and came back for him, only to not be able to find him?

One thing Finn had learned about Nod from helping Theodor was that time was different here than on Earth. He needed to wait a little longer. Theodor would come. Unless he was dead. Or HORU's drone had been destroyed. In that case, Finn was doomed. He didn't think Hope or any of the other Soulkeepers would know where to look for him or even to look at all.

"Isn't this a sorry sight?" Theodor said.

Was Finn hearing things? Feeling things? It felt like a man's arm was beneath his neck and shoulders and that the edge of something wet was pressed against his lips.

"I conjured this. It's drinkable but, I will warn you, it isn't Aquafina." Liquid poured into Finn's mouth and he coughed up as much as he swallowed. The water tasted of sulfur, but at that point, anything was welcome.

"Keep your eyes closed. Don't struggle. We'll be home soon."

Finn was lifted into his mentor's arms and then he became the tree again and his body was stretched like taffy into the next world. He didn't have the strength to fight it. But when he heard the crunch of pebbles beneath Theodor's feet and felt himself being lowered to the ground, he knew he was home.

"Dear Lord," he heard Mike say. "What happened to him?"

"Time functions differently where he was, Michael. He is very ill. He needs food, water, and rest, and if I may make a suggestion, healing."

"Yeah, of course. Hey, I've only been able to see for like ten minutes anyway. What's the bother?"

"I'd do it but I need my strength for..." Damien said.

Finn had no idea what Damien needed to conserve his energy for but Mike responded, "Yeah, yeah."

Finn felt two hands come to rest on either side of his neck.

"Here. Give him this," he heard Ms. D say.

Cool, wet liquid coursed down his throat. Sweet. Sweet tea,

he realized. Warmth spread from Mike's hands, through his body. More tea. And then slowly, as if they were dragging two boulders, his eyelids cracked open. Hope and Damien were leaning over him, as were Ms. D, Theodor, and Mike. And there, between them all, was HORU and her drone.

"Welcome back, Finn," she said, wiggling her ears. "I did what you told me to do."

"Thanks, HORU," he rasped. "Good job."

"All right, all right," Ms. D said. "Let's get you back to the bus. The others must be beside themselves with worry."

"You go," Hope said. "We have unfinished business." She looked toward the tree and gestured for Damien. Of course, they were going to close the portal. For a moment, Finn felt nothing but gratitude that everything had turned out as it did. He deserved death for what he'd done. Even though he knew God had already forgiven him, it would take time to forgive himself. Exhausted, he closed his eyes, and let his friends carry him home.

FINN WOKE WITH NO IDEA HOW LONG HE'D BEEN ASLEEP. WHAT he did know was that he was in his room on the bus and it was dark outside his window. He remembered bathing and eating until he couldn't eat another bite. But that was hours ago and he was hungry again. He got up, got dressed and headed for the galley.

All was quiet and dark in the hallway. Everyone must be sleeping. He checked the clock on the wall of the galley. 3:30 am.

"You're looking better," Mike said. The big guy was sitting at one of the long tables, sipping a glass of milk.

"What are you doing up?" Finn asked.

"Couldn't sleep. I keep having nightmares that Lucifer is back."

"Well, he's gone and so are the demons."

Finn grabbed a roll from the basket leftover from dinner and sat down across from Mike. "Can I ask you something?"

"Yeah."

"Why did you do it?" Finn examined his fingers. "You could have stayed on the island where you were safe. Why risk everything to try to save me? You must have known popping up at the center of Lucifer's lair was a bad idea.

"Why did you sacrifice yourself to carry Lucifer through that portal? You must have known the odds were against you. You might still be trapped in Hell if you weren't the luckiest bastard who ever walked the Earth."

"I did it because I couldn't bear living in a world where I was responsible for your death. You and the others." He rubbed his eyes and tried to hide the way his voice cracked. "I feel so damn guilty thinking this, but I'm so glad Kirsa did what she did. I wouldn't have been able to stop myself—"

"Don't waste your time on guilt," Mike said. " I forgave you... I forgive you. I knew you had no control."

Finn felt a wave of relief.

Mike cleared his throat. "I knew I'd probably get caught. I came because... I always felt our friendship was stronger than evil."

With a snort Finn started to laugh and Mike joined in. "Stronger than evil," Finn repeated, finding it funny once again.

"Hilarious. Sappy. But true," Mike said. "Friends like us, we stick together. I wasn't going to let no Devil take my homeboy."

He reached across the table and pounded Finn's hand with his fist.

A lump formed in Finn's throat. "So, uh, we're okay, right?"

Mike smiled and started laughing again. "Yeah. We're okay." They sat for a moment in silence before Mike stood. "Eat your damn roll. I'm not healing you again."

Finn did.

❧ 36 ❧

EVER AFTER

Weeks later, Finn sat in a pew at the back of a church, thankful that it was comfortably padded. He'd mostly recovered from his ordeal with Lucifer and Nod, but he was still underweight and lacking in energy. Every day was better than the last though, and now that he was living with his father at home again, he was eating more and moving less. He'd picked up where he'd left off, playing video games with Wyatt and attending Beaverton High School with Mike and Jayden. One thing was different though. Deviant Joe was dead. They'd deleted all the videos. The four of them agreed that pranks weren't where they wanted to spend their time and energy anymore.

As strange as it seemed, Kirsa's death hadn't been easy for any of the Soulkeepers. They'd all hated her. She'd tortured Hope and contributed to Mike's near drowning at Revelations. But in the end, she'd been a hero. And while it was true that her change had been due to Mike's intervention with the blessed water, she'd still had free will. Finn remembered how she'd looked the day he'd signed over his soul to Lucifer. She wasn't a monster. She was human. And he realized that what the water had done for her was make her feel part of something. It was sad she had to die to make that connection.

They'd given her a Soulkeeper's funeral and buried her in a cemetery in Virginia near the house where she'd grown up before moving to Revelations. Every single one of them had cried. Lucifer had said the obsidian blade didn't just kill the body; it killed the soul. A lie, he hoped. Like the Soulkeeper gene, Finn didn't believe the soul was something that could be taken from you. He liked to think that Kirsa was in a better place. He'd probably never know for sure, but he refused to imagine otherwise.

"Theodor changed his suit," Wendy said from beside him, squeezing his hand. He squeezed back.

"I told him he had to. That uniform of his was starting to give me the creeps." Finn smiled toward the front of the church where Theodor waited in a marvelous purple three-piece with an orchid pinned to the lapel.

The organ started to play and everyone stood. Finn looked toward the doors at the top of the aisle.

"Oh, she's beautiful," Wendy said.

Finn had to agree. Ms. D was wearing a dress Finn thought belonged somewhere in the past. It was white lace with long sleeves that ended in a bell shape at her wrists. The material was form fitting and stretched all the way to the floor. This was not a Cinderella ball gown. It was sleek and sophisticated with a flair true to her eccentric personality. A purple top hat crowned her gray curls, and as she passed them, making her way to the front of the church with a bouquet of wildflowers in hand, Finn noticed a row of amethyst buttons that ran the length of her back.

Everyone sat back down when the ceremony started. "I

can't believe they waited this long to get married," Wendy whispered. "They've been dating for like sixty years."

"Ms. D says no one was allowed to get married on the island and they were never able to leave at the same time. Revelations owned them."

"Damien owned them. He owned the place and was pulling the strings." Wendy frowned. "Back when he was… evil."

"Ravenguard and Applegate too."

"Hmm." Wendy nudged him and pointed with her chin. "Do you think he's truly in love with her?"

Finn followed Wendy's gaze to where Hope and Damien sat across the aisle and a few rows up. "Damien? It seems like it. He can leave anytime he wants to. He's an angel. He could be in Heaven. He doesn't go because he wants to be with her."

"She doesn't seem to fully reciprocate. I mean, obviously they're together. They're always together," Wendy whispered. "But it's like she holds him at a distance. She's holding something back."

"It's none of your business."

"I only thought, you know, because you guys are such good friends…"

"That I'd give you the 411 on her relationship status?"

Wendy did a double take. "Well… yes."

He snorted. "Sorry. I don't know. And I don't blame her for taking things slow. Those two have a long history. He may have changed, but she hasn't and she remembers everything."

The elderly woman in front of them turned around and gave them the stink-eye. "Shhh!"

"Sorry," Finn said.

Who is that? Wendy mouthed, pointing at the woman's back. Finn shrugged.

A woman at the front of the church broke into a traditional

wedding ballad. Her voice was pristine and reminded Finn of Juliette. Once Lucifer was vanquished to Hell, his guitar became a normal guitar again. He wondered what happened to Juliette's soul. He supposed he'd never know.

"It was nice of Ms. D to pick Fuse to be her maid of honor, but I thought for sure Theodor would choose you for his best man."

"Orelon doesn't have any living family left. They're old friends. It makes more sense than you think."

"What about Amuke? I didn't even see him when I came in. Is he here?"

Finn shook his head. "He and Paul moved to Kenya."

"Kenya?"

"Amuke has a great-granddaughter who lives there. They went so they could have a safe place to shift. Paul didn't want to go home. I guess his home life wasn't the best."

Wendy chewed her lip. "That's too bad. I know how that goes." She'd moved back home with her parents, but the relationship was strained. She'd mentioned she was looking forward to college.

"Thanks for bringing me. This is beautiful." She smiled sweetly. "I'm glad I could be here with you."

"Uh, Wendy," he whispered.

"Yeah?"

"Will you go to prom with me?"

She squeezed his hand again and flashed him a broad smile. "Yeah. I'll go."

He smiled back. "Good."

The woman in front of them turned around again. "Shhhh!"

"Sorry," Finn and Wendy said at the same time. When she turned back around, they raised their eyebrows at each other.

The rings were exchanged and the kiss was shared. Finn

stood and clapped as the two walked hand in hand down the aisle and exited the chapel.

"So, Victoria Duvall is now Victoria Florea. That's unfortunate." Wendy sighed.

Finn chuckled.

"Where are they going to live now?" Wendy asked.

"Santa Fe. They're considering opening a school for gifted children."

"They have plenty of experience. I suppose they can't use Revelations anymore. None of the kids could make it through the gate. What will happen to the island?"

"It's still there. Mrs. Wilhelm and Orelon have decided to stay there as caretakers. I guess it will remain as is for as long as any Soulkeepers need it. But Hope says our powers will likely wane over time now that Lucifer is gone."

"Then, I should thank you for bringing me here. Airfare is expensive." She grinned.

Finn had traveled to Cincinnati using his Soulkeeper power and traveled back with her. He didn't have a single symbol left in his skin and he'd destroyed his deck of cards. The ability to fold space and move from point A to point B was his own. It had always been his. And he planned to appreciate it for as long as he had it.

He kissed her cheek. "You're welcome."

❧ 37 ❧

PARIS HIGH SCHOOL

Hope Laudner leaned against the wall of the gymnasium in a regrettable dress with a regrettable attitude. She hadn't wanted to come to prom. In fact, she found the entire idea of a high school dance laughable after what had occurred only months ago. But her parents Jacob and Malini had insisted. They said she'd regret missing it. So she'd donned a strapless, puffy-pink princess dress she'd found at a vintage shop and thrown her hair into a bun. A few pictures and a glass or two of punch and she'd be home in her jammies with a book in no time at all, time served.

"Can I have this dance?" a velvet smooth voice said from beside her.

"I should have known you'd come." Damien was never far away and was the closest thing to a boyfriend she'd ever had. He looked dapper tonight in a dark suit with his hair slicked back and her stomach did a funny little flip when she looked at him, as it always did. Before she could say another word, he produced a corsage and strapped it to her wrist.

"I heard you were coming alone," he said.

"You heard that from me."

"I thought we agreed we were... together?"

She smiled up at him, his golden stare doing wicked things to her. "We are. As I said before, I cannot think of a more torturous way for someone who has been around for thousands of years to spend an evening, than at my prom. I was thinking of you." She gestured around herself at the sad display of tables and decorations. The theme was Virtual Reality, and hologram discs at the center of each table worked with special glasses to change the décor for the viewer. One viewer could have an Old West theme while the next celebrated the age of grunge music. Participants could change their table's choice on a whim. Without the glasses on, all Hope could see were the receptors, hanging silver discs that dangled from the ceiling all over the gym.

He shrugged. "Doesn't seem so terrible to me."

"I don't want to dance."

As he opened his mouth to say something else, Melissa Winthrop, class gossip, inserted herself between them like the room was on fire and Damien was the only one with a fire extinguisher. "Hope, who's your friend?"

"None of your damn business—"

"Damien." He held out his hand to her, too formal for a senior in high school. Melissa took it, giggling like the idiot she was.

Hope stepped in front of him. "He's my boyfriend, and we were about to dance." She took his hand and led him toward the dance floor.

"I thought you didn't want to dance," he said through a smug grin.

"I changed my mind."

She positioned herself at the center of the dance floor and

looped her arms around his neck. "It isn't that I don't want you here. I was honestly being considerate. This can't be fun for you."

He spread his fingers along the curve of her back. "Hope, being where you are is always fun for me. It doesn't matter what we are doing."

"So, you're just, like, going to hang around me until I send you away again?"

He nodded. "Yes. I've decided you are the only one for me. I'll be with you until you tire of me."

"What if you change your mind?"

He chuckled. "I won't. When an angel bonds with a human or another angel, it's forever."

"Like my mother and father," she said softly.

He nodded. "You have a choice. I would never force you to keep me in your life. You can send me away at any time. I'll go back to Heaven."

She narrowed her eyes. "But you're happiest with me?"

"Yes."

"Hmm."

He stroked the hair over her ear and she breathed in his cinnamon and citrus scent. Having him around was like being followed by a freshly baked apple pie. He smelled warm and homey. This close, she caught herself smiling up at him despite her desire to be anywhere but at the prom.

"So…" She clung to him as he turned her among the crowd of dancers. "What if I never get tired of you? What if I grow old and never tell you to go away?"

"Then I'll be with you, always."

"Always?"

"Always."

"Marriage and family and all of that stuff? I mean, hypothetically."

He raised an eyebrow. "If that's what you want. I'm very rich you know."

"So I've heard." She grinned.

"I only have one requirement."

"Requirements? What was all that about never leaving me? That's hardly a true promise if there are requirements."

"It's not a requirement about staying. It's a requirement about the other things... making a life together. Hypothetically."

"Oh. Okay. Hypothetically then, what is this requirement?"

"You go to school to become a kindergarten teacher."

She'd been swaying to the music but stopped, feeling like the wind had been knocked out of her. "How do you know I want to be a kindergarten teacher?"

"You told me, that night we went dancing in New Orleans."

"But, that was before."

"Before I was redeemed, yes. But I remember. There are many things about my past life that I don't remember, but this one I do. How could I ever forget that night? It was transcendent."

"I thought so too." She felt a little dizzy. Maybe, even back then, some part of Damien had experienced authentic feelings for her. She hoped so. Because when she remembered that night, and she thought about it a lot, she didn't want to think she'd been conned. She wanted to believe it was real.

"So, do you agree to my terms, hypothetically?"

"Yes." She nodded. "I have some terms of my own."

"Oh?" He lifted a corner of his mouth.

"Take me back there someday, to the place we danced. I want to live it again, as who we are now."

"Deal."

She allowed him to pull her in close and she laid her head on his shoulder.

He kissed her temple. "Are you tired? Do you want me to take you home?"

"No. Let's stay for a while longer," she said. "This is just getting good."

She tipped her head back to smile up at him and he didn't waste the opportunity. He kissed her. It was a kiss between equals, of promises that meant something and mutual understanding. It was electric, lighting her up from within. But it was also grounding. Damien had wings to fly, but he was also her anchor. She was way too young to know for sure what would happen between them. But if she had to decide today, she'd never let him go.

EPILOGUE

"Jenny, can you get us all in the shot?" Mike threw an arm around Finn's shoulders while Wyatt squeezed in next to Jayden.

"Yeah. Mike, move your dangly thing out of the way," Jenny said, backing up as she peered through the camera.

Mike adjusted his tassel. He never expected all four of them to be wearing the purple cap and gown of Beaverton High School. When they'd been accused of burning down the school and sentenced to Revelations Institute, he'd hoped that somehow they'd earn their way back here. But after learning about Lucifer and the demons, the most he could wish for was to stay alive. It seemed too much to ask to graduate too.

But here they all were. He'd walked across the stage and accepted his diploma moments ago. Such a simple everyday thing, but it seemed surreal after what they'd been through.

"Got it," Jenny said, sliding her thumb over the screen. "Oh, these are cute."

"Welcome to Wager Manor, everyone," Finn said to the crowd of graduates approaching the house from the street. As always, Wendy was by his side. She'd graduated last week from her school in Cincinnati but was here for Finn, just like Jenny was here for Jayden. "Drinks are in the kitchen. The pool is out back."

Mike wasn't surprised that Finn had thrown the biggest graduation party Beaverton had ever seen. The guy was rich and his dad wasn't exactly strict. He was happy to see Finn happy. The shy, nerdy kid Finn once was had disappeared. He couldn't take three steps these days without someone wanting to talk to him.

Jayden smacked Jenny on the shoulder. "Join me in the pool?"

She smiled and hooked her pinkie into his. "Yeah. I'll catch up with you. I want to talk to Mike."

Jayden started up the hill toward the front door where Wyatt was already waiting.

"I know I'm ready for a drink. See you guys inside." Finn threaded his fingers into Wendy's and led her up the hill after Jayden, leaving Jenny and Mike standing in the yard alone.

"What did you want to talk to me about?"

"Your plans. What did you decide to do next?" Jenny asked.

"I think I'm going to go back to my construction job. They need people. Half their crew is leaving for college."

"What about you? Don't you want to go to college?"

Mike groaned. "Yeah, maybe someday. Not this year. You know, there's my aunt, and I didn't get my applications in on time." Mike had missed a ton of school with everything that had happened. His aunt had saved most of the money Revelations sent her, that wasn't the issue anymore. There had been so much to do when he'd finally returned home. He'd been completely invested in catching up with his schoolwork and helping her with the house repairs. He hadn't had time to think about colleges or scholarships. He hadn't even applied.

"Finn was accepted to UI to study artificial intelligence."

"Good for him. I bet HORU's excited to go with him."

Jenny nodded. "Wendy's going too. Pre-law."

"I'm happy for her. I can picture her as a lawyer." He placed his hands on his hips. "I guess it wasn't in the cards for me this semester."

"I disagree." She pulled out an envelope and handed it to him. "You're wrong. It is in the cards, if you want to go."

"What's this?" Mike tore open the seal and unfolded the letter inside. "What *is* this?"

"You've been accepted at Tulane University, which happens to be where Jayden and I are going. Oh, and you have a full four-year scholarship, room and board included, compliments of Revelations Institute."

"What?" Mike stared at the paper as if he were looking right through it.

"I'm a Helper, you know. I can get shit done. I forged your signature so well even your aunt didn't know." She flipped her platinum hair off her shoulder. "You actually wrote your own admissions essay. I used the one Ms. Edwards required you to write for English class."

"I don't know what to say."

"Say that you're going to Tulane with us."

"I..." He thought of his aunt. Could he leave her? She'd want him to. And the house was fixed up now. She was safe.

A flash of light in his peripheral vision signaled the arrival of Gabriel, dressed in a Tommy Bahama-style shirt and shorts. He looked like he needed a shave. "Don't even think about staying back because of your aunt. I'll take care of her. You have my word. You saved the world. It's time you looked after yourself for a change."

Mike couldn't help himself. He pulled first Jenny and then Gabriel into a hug.

"Is that a yes?" Jenny asked.

"Yes," Mike said, tipping his head back and smiling up at the sun. "Oh, yes."

"What will you study?" Gabriel asked.

Mike thought about it for a minute. "Ever since I found out I had the Soulkeeper gene, I've been interested in cells, in DNA, in what makes us different. I think I want to study biology, maybe medicine eventually."

Gabriel smiled. "Interesting choice. Never forget that while what makes you different is important, it's far more important what makes you the same." He patted Mike on the shoulder. "Good luck, Michael." With a soft smile and a quick check over each shoulder, he blended into a shaft of sunlight and disappeared.

"He's weird," Jenny whispered.

"I hate it when he does that," Mike said.

Jenny started for the house and Mike followed. "Jayden is going to be so excited."

"Jenny…" Mike stopped. He didn't know what to say. He simply stared at her feeling like his heart might burst with gratitude.

Eventually, she smiled and hooked her arm into his elbow. "I know. And you're welcome."

* * *

ARCHIBALD ALWAYS THOUGHT OF HIMSELF AS A GOOD GNOME. HE did what he was told. He served the Soulkeepers selflessly. But if he were honest with himself, he hadn't strictly followed the rules when it came to Michael.

Simply put, he was lonely. He'd been lonely for a very long time, since the day Eden fell. Garden gnomes were meant to live in communities and his community had been destroyed. Or rather, he'd thought it had. While he was able to escape, he wasn't able to go back and check on the others. No one knew what happened to the gnomes. It was possible that one or more of his family members was still alive, cut off from him when the portal collapsed but living in Eden. He'd long wished for a way to find out.

When he learned of Hope's gifts, he knew it would be possible to heal the portal, but a garden gnome could not suggest such a thing. It was unheard of for a gnome to ask a favor of a Soulkeeper, let alone ask for something for himself or herself. It was a lucky break that the Soulkeepers had gone against the Healer's wisdom. Archibald's first duty was to the Healer, so it wasn't much of a leap to suggest to Michael that the tree could be repaired. And when Michael ordered Archibald to go home to Eden and to take care of himself, it was the gnome's dream come true.

Of course, Archibald didn't have to be in the dining hall at the same time as Michael or say the things he said that led the Healer to his plan. If he thought too hard about it, he might conclude that he wasn't following but leading in some ways, and leading was not something a gnome was supposed to do. Not ever.

It was best he didn't think too much about what happened but instead celebrate that it did happen. Because, although he suspected Michael knew on some level what Archibald wanted when he suggested healing the tree, the Healer didn't have to free him to pursue his greatest desire. That was a kindness he would never forget.

He popped out of the tree deep inside the forest in Eden and was relieved to find things much as he'd left them. Aside from a few stumps where trees had once been, the woods were alive. It smelled the same. He took off toward the Eden School for Soulkeepers at a run, not daring to hope. Not daring to think.

But when he passed the trail to the dock where the boat used to be, his heart sank. Both the dock and the boat were gone. And when he followed the trail to the school, he found the east wing was flattened to a layer of rubble. At first, the sight of this destruction made a lump form in his throat. If gnomes could cry, Archibald surely would have. But the longer he stared at the ruined school, the more he focused on one peculiar detail. The garden surrounding the school was meticulously groomed. Only one thing in Eden ever maintained the gardens here.

"Archibald?" The sweet, high-pitched voice behind him was at once familiar and strange. He hadn't heard it in over a decade. Sage emerged from between the trees, her green dress and pointy hat the same as always.

"Bless us all," he mumbled.

"You're alive!" she yelled, and ran to him, claiming him with an intense hug. "We thought you were crushed when the portal collapsed."

"I thought you died with the island!" Archie said.

She shook her head. "The island isn't dead, Archie. We're all still here."

"All?"

He saw them then, his family, his community. They

emerged from the trees, smiling narrow-toothed smiles and beaming with health and vitality.

"I've been with the Healer," Archibald said to all of them.

A collective gasp rang through the crowd.

"What did she say?" Sage asked.

"He," Archie corrected. "The Healer is a boy now. He says to take care of ourselves until we are needed again."

Sage smiled. "The same as before, then."

"The same as before." He nodded. She took his hand and led him to the collection of cottages deep within the garden that served as the gnomes' homes. They were all in perfect condition. But then, of course, they would be. Gnomes held powerful magic and could fix almost anything.

They welcomed him home with feasting and singing. He danced and laughed late into the night. When the festivities finally came to an end, Archie lay in his hammock looking up at the stars, wondering if the Healer was okay and hoping he'd been a good gnome. He thought so. The stars seemed to say he'd done the right thing.

It had been centuries since the Garden of Eden had known this kind of peace. Helpers, Healers, and Horseman throughout the ages had trained here to battle the ultimate evil. The Devil was far from this place now, far from Earth. To his bones, Archie knew the Soulkeepers had been successful, which meant it would be a long time before he or this place was needed again.

With the heavens smiling on him from above, he closed his eyes, his heart and the garden finally at peace.

ABOUT THE AUTHOR

G.P. Ching is a USA Today bestselling author of science fiction and fantasy novels for young adults and not-so-young adults. She bakes wicked cookies, is commonly believed to be raised by wolves, and thinks both the ocean and the North Woods hold magical healing powers. G.P.'s idea of the perfect day involves several cups of coffee and a heavy dose of nature. She splits her time between central Illinois and Hilton Head Island with her husband, two children, and a Brittany spaniel named Jack, who is always ready for the next adventure.

www.gpching.com
genevieve@gpching.com

f facebook.com/450457555307350

🐦 twitter.com/gpching

📷 instagram.com/authorgpching

BB bookbub.com/authors/g-p-ching

BOOKS BY G.P. CHING

Soulkeepers Reborn

Wager's Price, Book 1

Hope's Promise, Book 2

Lucifer's Pride, Book 3

The Soulkeepers Series

The Soulkeepers, Book 1

Weaving Destiny, Book 2

Return to Eden, Book 3

Soul Catcher, Book 4

Lost Eden, Book 5

The Last Soulkeeper, Book 6

The Grounded Trilogy

Grounded, Book 1

Charged, Book 2

Wired, Book 3

ACKNOWLEDGMENTS

Different books serve different roles in our lives. Some books are like a warm bath, comforting and familiar. Some books scare us and when we close the cover we feel the thrill of knowing we are safe and alive. Some stories make us laugh. Others touch our hearts in ways we never expected.

As I come to the close of the Soulkeepers Series and Soulkeepers Reborn, I realize this series was sandpaper for me. Sandpaper is gritty. A sandpaper book challenges you. It sometimes makes you uncomfortable. But the wonder of it is that what's left behind is smoother for the irritation.

There are several parts of this book and this series that challenged me and sometimes made me uncomfortable. But I think this story has something to say about how perfectly imperfect we all are and what it means to have divine purpose despite our shortcomings.

I truly hope you've enjoyed Lucifer's Pride and the Soulkeepers series. My sincere thanks to all of the fans who have made these nine books possible, including Wil Shockley II for beta reading this one. Also to Nikki Busch editing and to Author Laurie Larsen, thank you for your skills, support, and guidance throughout the series.

GROUNDED

The Grounded Trilogy Book 1

Please enjoy this extended excerpt of Grounded, the Grounded Trilogy book one.

PROLOGUE

S*eptember 2062*

T*HE* *NIGHT* F*RANK* *FOUND* *HER* *IT* *WAS* *RAINING,* *A* *WRATH-OF-*God type of downpour Crater City hadn't seen in a decade. The power was out, but that was nothing new. The grid was unpredictable in any weather.

Later, he'd call it divine providence. If not for the rain, he wouldn't have grabbed his jacket to take out the trash. And it was the jacket that would save his life.

In the alley behind the fire station at the corner of Fifth and Lincoln, Frank escaped the endless drone of his fellow fire-fighters by volunteering to dispose of a smelly nest of takeout containers. Without power, the men didn't have the city's monitoring equipment to keep them busy. They became downright nostalgic by candlelight. Hell, if you let him, Jonas would drone on about his three freckle-faced girls until sunrise.

Frank could not deal. He didn't have a family. Not anymore.

He might not have noticed her at all in the blackout, but when he tried to lift the dumpster lid, a shock ran up his arm. The jolt made him drop the stack of waxed cardboard he was carrying, and he bent over to clean up the mess.

"What the—?" Frank crouched for a better look.

A newborn baby girl, in a worn pink T-shirt and wrapped in a plastic grocery bag, blinked at him from under the lip of the dumpster. Frank would have liked to think there was some compassion in the effort—that whoever left her meant for the thin sheath of plastic to keep her warm and dry, but under the abandonment law, it was legal to leave a newborn inside a public building. The fact that she wasn't safely indoors was a testament to what type of scum had abandoned her.

"Hi, sweetheart. Oh, you're cold. Don't worry, old Frank will take care of you." He lifted her into the cradle of his arms and shuffled under the awning of the alley door. By the light of the moon, he wiped the raindrops off her face with one burly thumb. Cuddling her tiny body against his chest, he enjoyed the innocent shine of her eyes and her slight weight in his embrace.

Frank's atrophied spirit stirred from a long, deep sleep. He smiled. And smiles were hard to come by since the day a semi-truck T-boned a Range Rover and turned Frank's family into just Frank. One tiny hand wrapped around his pinky finger, and that was that. She might as well have handcuffed his soul.

Shuffle-scrape. Shuffle-scrape. He searched the alley for the source of the sound. A sewer rat? Since the war, they grew as large as dogs. Better to be safe; consider the babe. He groped for the doorknob behind his hip.

A deep voice rasped from the darkness, "Don't! You've got

to get her out of here." From the shadows, a man stepped into the swash of moonlight; at least, Frank thought he was a man. The guy was a piece of raw meat with more bruise than face and open sores up both arms. Soaked to the bone, he wore bloody white hospital scrubs that clung like a second skin. The water sheeted off him, his breath a foggy reminder of the cold night air.

"Who are you?" Frank asked, tightening his hold on the little girl.

"Never mind that. They know we're here. It's just a matter of time. You've got to run. You've got to hide her."

"Hey, buddy, it's legal to abandon a baby here. Why don't we all go inside and warm up? There are places you can stay, get a hot meal."

"*Listen to me*," the man implored. "Everything you need is with her."

Frank ran his hand around the newborn. Sure enough, under her back the corner of a thick envelope scraped his palm.

"I'll take care of her," Frank said in his most reassuring tone. "We've got resources inside."

"*No!*" The man's voice broke and his eyes widened. Large, wounded eyes. Desperate eyes. "You can't tell anyone."

No stranger to desperation, Frank took pause. He'd been there once. The way the guy let the rain pound on him, with no attempt to move for the shelter of the awning, was a blatant cry for help.

"What's your name?" Frank asked.

The man eyed the street with twitchy apprehension.

"Come on inside," he continued. "Let's talk."

"They're coming," the stranger said, shaking his head. "We're out of time."

Damn, the guy's pale skin seemed to light up the alley. Or was he actually glowing? At first, Frank thought it was a trick of the moonlight, but the sky beyond the awning was no different than before. He closed his eyes, opened them again.

The sizzle of electricity echoed off the brick wall of the fire station. Was the grid coming back up? No, the source of the sound was the stranger! With each crackle, neon blue veins wormed beneath the man's translucent skin. Frank's mouth gaped. That was not normal. It sure as hell wasn't natural. He curled the baby closer and pressed into the door.

"You've got to get grounded, and fast." The man's stare bore into Frank. "You're a fireman. You know what happens when electricity and water mix. I can't hold back much longer."

Heat bloomed from the stranger's body, blue-white energy that extended a foot around his profile. The rain evaporated on contact, filling the alley with steam.

How hot must his body be to do that? Eyes narrowed against the glare, Frank pressed into the wall, forced back by the iridescent heat.

"Promise me you'll take care of her," the man begged.

One look at the baby girl in his arms and there was only one answer Frank could give. "I promise."

The stranger nodded. "Go. It's time."

If Frank had any ideas about handling the situation in an official capacity, those thoughts burnt up in the blue inferno that chased him from the alley. Hunched protectively over the babe, the blast singed his back just short of pain and infused the air with the acrid scent of scorched, flame-retardant fabric. Thank the Lord he'd put on his coat to take out the trash. Throat tight, he hurled himself behind the concrete wall of the covered parking garage bordering the fire station. Was the babe hurt? He peeled her away from his chest as he ran, relieved when she made a small mewing noise, like a good solid cry was coming on.

His faithful antique pickup waited in its usual spot overlooking Fifth Street. He fished the key from his pocket to let himself in and cranked the heater as the babe cried in earnest. "Cold we can deal with, baby girl. If you're hungry, you're out of luck for now."

Through the windshield, Frank's view was unobstructed as the stranger exited the alley, tendrils of steam heralding his blue glow. "Radioactive son-of-a bitch," he murmured, his head buzzing with theories about the stranger's condition. Toxic drugs, industrial exposure, alien DNA. Each as unlikely as the next.

The stranger stopped beneath the dead traffic light and faced a street abandoned due to the storm and the time of night. Abandoned, until a fleet of black Humvees roared up Fifth and unloaded a barrage of gunfire in the stranger's direction.

"Holy God in heaven!" Frank threw the truck into reverse, peeling out of the parking space. His transmission groaned as he forced the vehicle into drive and raced for the exit. In the rearview mirror, he expected to see the stranger's bloodied body in the street but slammed on the brakes at what he saw instead.

The man wasn't dead. He was a living lightbulb.

Holding the baby, Frank craned his neck over his shoulder for a better view. Lightning flew from the man's hand, igniting the first Humvee and catapulting another weighty vehicle into the air. A moment of flight and the fiery descent turned the jeep into a missile. The vehicle ripped through the advancing fleet, an oily, twisted mass of metal. Another lightning bolt flew, and then another. Like children's toys, the military vehicles popped skyward and folded accordion style, rolled and rumpled in the stranger's ire.

The glowing man stepped around the wreckage and advanced toward the next wave of Humvees.

Frank floored the accelerator, patting the now wailing baby as he exited on to Fourth Street at the back of the garage. He raced away from the flames and the rancor of burning rubber. Sirens blared from every direction but he did not stop. With nothing to lose, and no one who mattered to miss him, Frank ran.

It would be a long time before he stopped running.

❈ I ❈

LYDIA

S *eventeen years later...*

BISHOP KAUFFMAN OFTEN PREACHES WE ARE TO BE *IN* THE world but not *of* the world. I've never understood why he bothers. The only world I've ever known is Hemlock Hollow, and you can't be more set apart than us.

I press my cheek into Hildegard's tawny belly, and she stomps her hooves in disapproval. She's uncomfortable with my pace, but I don't slow my milking. I can't. I have my responsibilities, but there are also my priorities.

"Sorry, girl," I whisper. "We need to hurry."

I kick a clump of hay toward her head. The cow stretches her neck for a nibble, temporarily distracted from my tugging. The sky lightens beyond her hindquarters, distinct rays visible on the horizon. As planned, my bucket is full before the sun is up.

To Hildegard's relief, I set her to pasture and then return to the barn to get my bucket of milk. Mary Samuels arrives just as I'm leaving for home, rubbing her eyes and yawning. Behind her, the cow she leads looks as tired as she does.

"Already finished? Oh, to be a morning person like you, Lydia," she says. She straightens her apron with one dark brown hand, darker than usual due to her work in the sun this time of year. I curse the vulnerability of my fair complexion. Any other time, I'd enjoy a long talk with Mary, my dearest girlfriend, weighing the benefits of our various gifts, dark skin versus a morning disposition, but not now. Not this morning.

"Good to see you, Mary." Arm bent to keep the bucket a safe distance from my side, I hurry past her toward the house. Inside, I dump the fresh milk into the stainless steel receptacle we keep in our one and only modern convenience, a methane-powered refrigerator. Quickly, I wash my pail out for tomorrow and check on breakfast. The risen dough is ready for the bread pan. I've already gathered the eggs. My father will be in the field for at least another hour, plenty of time.

Without delay, I hasten toward the hay barn. Jeremiah sidles up to me, also finished with his chores. He wears the same black trousers and vest as all the other boys, but Jeremiah stands out to me. His eyes are the color of cornflowers and he's always smiling, even when none of his teeth show.

"Good morning, Lydia." He straightens his straw hat. His steps quicken until his feet slap the gravel ahead of mine.

"Good morning, Jeremiah." I match him step for step.

Lengthening his stride, he speeds up until he's ahead again. "Are you going to do the wise thing this morning and start breakfast early?"

"No, I don't think so. I think I'll be going to the haymow." I elbow past him.

"Yeah?" He smiles, breaking into a jog. "That's where I'm going, too."

Race on.

I launch into a full-out run, balling my long skirt in my hand. More of my tights show than is proper but I trust Jeremiah won't tell. Anyway, the shape of my calf might distract him. I can't allow him to beat me to the hay. Of all the mornings I've raced Jeremiah, he's only won twice, and I've never lived down either of those times. If he wins, he'll tell me with a quirky half-smile that maybe I've finally learned I'm a girl. He'll offer twenty times a day to help me carry the eggs or knead the bread, because the race has proven he is more capable. Not again. Not if I can help it.

My legs pump underneath me. I pant from the exertion, the air heavy with late summer heat and the smell of fresh hay. The pounding of Jeremiah's feet beside mine pushes me harder, faster than I've ever run before. Lucky for me, I'm fast for a girl.

We burst through the red and white doors of the hay barn at the same time and sprint past the mound of fresh hay to the worn oak ladder. I reach it first. With a smug grin, I skip rungs as I scramble up, Jeremiah nipping at my heels. His laughter behind me reminds me what I'll face if he wins. I tumble over the top rung and onto the loft, eyeing the huge pile of fresh hay beyond the unobstructed edge. The mound calls to me, but my head swims with vertigo at the space between the precipice and its welcoming fluff.

"You should still let me go first," he calls from the ladder as he pitches over the edge and onto the loft.

"Why? I beat you fair as feathers this time."

"To test the fall. A boy should jump first, just in case."

"Not a chance. You'll have to play the chivalrous male for

someone else. I'm going." I shuffle to the far wall and bolt for the edge before he can stop me.

"You're going too fast," he protests. "Slow down!"

I don't listen. I leap for the hay, stretching my body flat in the air. Wind rushes over my *kapp*. My stomach drops. The thrill and exhilaration catch in my throat. For a moment, I fear Jeremiah is right; I've jumped too far, too fast. Unable to gain control, I collide with the top of the hay and bounce across the pile, toward the edge. I dig my fingers into the bales and jut my leg out to the side to slow myself down. My momentum stops just in time, one arm and leg dangling.

Slowly, I roll onto my back. Jeremiah stands at the edge of the loft, eyes wide and arms crossed over his chest.

A self-satisfied grin creeps across my face. "I'm fine." I laugh. No matter how many times I make the leap, the fall sets my heart fluttering in my chest. I don't care if I do bounce off someday. I wouldn't give up this feeling, the free-falling excitement, for anything.

His lips part, and his tight, worried expression softens a little. "Thank the good Lord," Jeremiah mumbles.

"Well? Won'tchya jump, Jeremiah Yoder? Are you afraid?" I taunt him by lacing my fingers behind my head. Just resting in the hay. Not a care in the world.

His face relaxes into a lopsided grin. He answers by removing his hat and throwing himself over. He lands with a rustle a few feet away from me, and then rolls flush against my side. Propped up on his elbow, his cheeks pink from the exertion of the run, I am reminded of when we were children and would spend our days playing by the river. Not much has changed in seventeen years. We're simply taller and craftier than our younger selves.

Still, Jeremiah embodies everything sweet and good in this world. Of that I am sure.

"You could've let a man be a man, Lydia. What if we were courting? What about *demut*?"

Demut means "submissiveness" in the old language, Pennsylvania German. We still go to German School on Saturdays, although the realities of Hemlock Hollow dictate speaking like an *Englisher*. When Jeremiah says *demut*, he's referring to a wife's role with her husband. It's a way for him to tug at my heartstrings.

"I was protecting you from *hochmut*, Jeremiah." *Hochmut* means arrogance, about the worst trait an Amish can have. "And besides, by the time you choose to court me, you will have years of experience with my disposition and trust that I can leap just as far and as fast as you." As long as he's known me, I've been this way, a girl who likes to plow just as well as quilt and who has to win the race, every time. A risk-taker. Maybe being raised without a mother has cost me my femininity. I don't miss it.

He laughs in the deep baritone that reminds me of his father. Jeremiah is seventeen like me, but I can tell he will be a great man. He's already an accomplished carpenter.

"I brought something for you," he says.

"You did?"

From his hat he pulls a shiny piece of folded paper. My heart skips a beat.

"Eli brought it back with him."

Unfolding the slippery page, I examine a picture of a woman on a runway. If her skirt were any shorter it would be a belt, and the way her blouse sags off her shoulder makes me blush. In our *Ordnung*, our church law, we are taught to value simplicity. We strive to be plain. The woman's dress is sinful and contrary to everything I believe. Still, as a seamstress, I am fascinated. I trace my finger along the perfect stitching, the sheath of lace that falls just below the hem. Orange. Bold and unapologetic. What would it be like to wear orange?

"Do you think they all dress like this?" I ask. "Her shoes look painful."

"I don't know. But we could find out. When will you ask your dad about *rumspringa?*"

"Not this again. I've told you, there's no way he'll allow it."

"Come on, Lydia. Almost everyone in Hemlock Hollow lives outside the community as an *Englisher* before they commit to the *Ordnung*. They say it's better in the long run, in case you *have* to go someday. What they teach us in school is barely enough to get by in their world. Even the bishop encourages the tradition."

"I hardly think living as an *Englisher* is necessary to a happy Amish life. Besides, everything I need is here."

Jeremiah rolls his eyes. "Everything you need is here because other folks bring it back for you from the English world. I don't recall you spinning and weaving the cloth for that dress."

I shake my head. "You know my father. He lives the most modest life, and he hates the English world. There is no way he'll agree."

"Did you ask? Did you speak to him about it?"

"Not exactly. I know how he feels by hearing him talk about the others. Remember when Jacob left?"

"Yes."

"My father said, 'Such a waste of a good upbringing. It's like dipping a lily-white lamb in a tar bath.'"

"He did not!"

"He did. Every chance he gets, he reminds me of how he

lost my mother and brother in an automobile accident in the English world. 'The world outside ain't safe, Lydia,' he says. 'It's the devil's playground.'"

Jeremiah lets out a deep sigh that blows strands of hay over my shoulder. "I'm not goin' without you."

"Don't be silly. If you want the experience, go. I'll still be here when you get back."

His fingers hook into mine, and I stare up into his unbelievably bright eyes and clean-shaven face. What will he look like with the traditional beard of married Amish? Will his chin be as blond as his curls?

"There are more important things than *rumspringa*, Lydia. But I hoped we could experience the English world together. An adventure to talk about later when we're..."

"When we're what?" I flutter my lashes at him innocently, knowing full well what he means. We've been two peas in a pod since we could walk, and it's long been accepted that we would court. I can't help myself. I want him to say it. I want to hear the words.

Jeremiah lifts a corner of his mouth and then opens it to respond.

"Lydia? Lydia Troyer!" Katie Kauffman, the bishop's wife, calls from outside the barn.

Jeremiah rolls onto his back and flattens himself against the hay. Strictly speaking, we aren't supposed to be alone together unchaperoned.

I swing my head over the side. "Yeah?"

"What are you doing in there, child? I thought you were milking?"

"I finished. Having a rest."

"You must come. I'm sorry. It's your father."

I toss my legs over and jump to the barn floor, a good six-foot drop. "What about my dad?"

"He collapsed. Isaac Bender found him in the field. Rode all the way to the English neighbor on his fastest horse to call a doctor. They took him back to the house—"

I do not wait for the details. Without concern for social formalities, I dash for home, only yelling my thank you to the bishop's wife as an afterthought. As much as I complain about my father, he's all I have. I love him deeply and he's my only kin. Unlike most Amish, I have no brothers or sisters. When my mother was killed, she took with her any hope of more siblings. My father never remarried, and my grandparents, aunts, and uncles are dead. I have cousins, the Benders and the Kauffmans, but our house is rarely full.

I scale the wooden steps of our porch in one leap and grapple with the uncooperative doorknob. It turns much too slowly. Inside, a circle of Amish friends pray around my father. He's propped up with pillows on our sofa, eyes closed. The Benders, the Samuels, the Kauffmans—familiar faces pale against the dark wool of their clothing—whisper solemn appeals for health and healing. Thankful for the prayers and for the company, I place my hand over my heart.

Amish prayers are strong. God is listening.

The door slams behind me, and my father's eyes open at the sound. One of his hands twitches when he sees me; his mouth tugs unevenly to the left. I run to his side, pressing the twitching hand between mine.

"What happened?"

He mumbles an unintelligible response. Something is very wrong. Only half of his body moves and my usually quick-witted father barely acknowledges me. His eyes drift away from my face every few seconds.

The thunder of a car engine turns my head toward the front of the house; the English doctor has arrived. His name is Doc Nelson—he's treated members of Hemlock Hollow before in extreme circumstances. Isaac Bender opens the door before the doctor has a chance to knock and I move out of the elderly man's way without being asked.

After a thorough examination, Doc Nelson addresses the bishop. "I believe Frank has had a stroke. I need to take him with me to the hospital to confirm and to give him proper treatment."

My eyes meet Bishop Kauffman's, leader of our *Ordnung* and my oldest male relative, my father's cousin. For anyone to leave our community is against English law. In fact, most *Englishers* don't know we *can* leave. But with permission from a bishop, we still do. English law isn't our law. Amish understand that breaking the English law is a necessary part of living in a sinful world.

Even without speaking, the exchange between the Bishop and myself is clear to me. My father wouldn't want to be treated with English medicine, but he might die without it. The bishop must decide. He knows my father as well as I do, but the way he searches my face tells me he's waiting to see if I will voice my father's wishes. More importantly, I think he wonders if it's God's will that I become an orphan.

I've always had faith. Moments ago, I'd told Jeremiah that I would live and die in Hemlock Hollow. But now that it's my father who needs the English medicine, I'm not so willing to dismiss the value of the English world. The difference between Dad and me is this: he trusts that prayers will heal him, while I understand that God sent the doctor.

I remain silent and lower my eyes. It's what Amish women do when they submit to male authority. But by not speaking,

I'm sending the bishop a message, my desire for my father to be treated by the English.

"Take him, Doctor Nelson," Bishop Kauffman says. "Please."

I raise my eyes and breathe a sigh of relief.

With surprising speed, the men load my father into the doctor's black automobile. How is the world still turning? I can't lose him. *I can't.* Practiced prayers rattle through my brain as the only family I've ever known races away from me. All I can think is my father would find the car he's riding in as sinful as the hospital that, God willing, will save his life.

2

"You shouldn't be alone," Mary says to me. My dearest friend pulls me into a hug and rubs my back.

Martha, Mary's mother, nods. "You're welcome to stay."

After my father was taken to the English hospital, Mary insisted I come home with her. Her mother took me under her wing, fed me until I thought I might burst, and kept me busy the rest of the day at her shop, where I am an apprentice seamstress. I finished six dresses and two pairs of pants she'd started earlier. She worked me harder than usual to be kind, so I didn't have time to think about what happened. I am grateful for their charity but loathe to overstay my welcome.

"I want to sleep in my own bed and pray from my own Bible," I say.

"Well, you know best what you've gotta do. Door's always open," Mary's father says. "Benjamin and Samuel will help with your farm while your father is away."

Mary's two brothers nod in my direction.

"Thank you. I could never manage on my own."

With warm hugs all around, I leave, knowing a strong dose

of reality is in store for me without their distraction. Freed by the quiet of the walk home, my mind swims in a sea of insecurities, trying to make sense of my father's infirmity. He's always been my rock, my anchor. What will happen if they can't save him? Can I survive tossed about on the waves of my own independence?

I have a place, a secret place I go to think. My sacred space.

To get there, I cross through a field of summer wheat, caressing the soft bristles with my fingertips as the grassy stalks tug against my skirt. My hickory tree is at the edge of the wood. Struck by lightning, half the tree is dead and rotting, but the other half defies the odds, covered in lush green leaves. I run to its trunk and throw my arms around its bark as if the green branches could hug me, pat my back, and say everything will be okay.

The rotting side has a hollow heart that keeps my secrets. I plunge my hand into the hole, retrieving the treebox Jeremiah carved for me. It's made from hickory wood and the lid is carved in the likeness of my tree. Inside, there is a hodgepodge of mysteries. A flexible transparent rectangle Eli says is a phone. A piece of rubbery fabric Anna told me adjusts to size when made into a garment. There's a disintegrating paper cup with a picture of a kidney bean on it and the words Ready Bell Express. I add the photo Jeremiah gave me this morning, taking one more look at the woman in orange with her tall shoes. I sift through the box until my brain buzzes with thoughts of the outside world.

"Why do you keep that thing if you don't ever plan to go on *rumspringa?*"

I flip the box closed and turn to face Jeremiah, whose teasing tone does not match the grim tilt of his lips. He's as worried about my father as I am. I shrug. "I'm curious, I guess." It's a simple answer, although my feelings are far from simple.

"Come on, Lydia. Tell me the truth."

I stare at the box in my hands for a moment before answering. "Remember a few years ago, Benders had that dog with something wrong in its head?"

"Yeah, the biter."

I nod. "The Benders had to keep it chained so it wouldn't kill their sheep. That old dog would tug against that chain until his neck was bloody." I rub my neck. "Fur worn away by rubbing leather."

He nods.

"One day, the rain made the yard soft, and when the dog tugged against the chain, he pulled the spike from the ground, yanked it free from the mud."

"I hadn't heard. Did it kill a sheep?"

"You would have thought after all the tugging. But no. Instead he lay down at the edge of the yard with his head between his paws. The Benders found him like that, crying and shaking."

"What has that to do with *rumspringa?*" he asks through a smile.

I sigh. "Maybe I'm a bit like that dog. I want to know about the outside world, but I can't bring myself to leave home to do it. The English world is a novelty and a temptation. It calls to me, promising excitement and adventure." I shake my head. "But I'm thankful for the life I have. My father always says the dream of a thing is often better than the reality. The English world could never live up to my expectations."

He hangs his head. "Or maybe you're afraid it will."

I purse my lips. "Anyway, Dad will be back soon, I'm sure, and everything will return to normal."

"I'm sure it will, Lydia," Jeremiah says.

I hide the box again inside the hollow of my tree and then pull myself up into the lowest green branch. Jeremiah follows my lead and positions himself next to me. We sit in the shared silence of old friends. No words are necessary.

The red-molasses sun drips behind the twelve-foot wall that surrounds Hemlock Hollow. From here, the nuclear reactor in the Outlands is clearly visible. The towering concrete hunkers in the distance, both our blessing and our curse. There are guard towers on the wall, where my father says there used to be soldiers years ago, but the radiation made them sick and eventually the Green Republic couldn't get anyone to work there. By that time, the government thought all my ancestors were dead or dying. Some did, but the ones who lived learned to adapt. And because the Green Republic is afraid to come here, they haven't a clue about us. The reactor preserves our way of life.

"He's made of tough stuff, Lydia," Jeremiah says. "This is why we have the lessons. This is why we prepare. Your dad will blend in, get healed, and come home. Don't you worry." His hand comes to rest on the branch next to mine. Our little fingers touch. My cheeks warm and I have to look away.

"It's you who should be worried about what your mother will do if she catches you here after dark," I say to him.

He grins and jumps down from the branch. Tipping his hat, he says, "Good night, Lydia."

He disappears into the wheat. A few minutes later, I follow, arriving home by the light of the moon. I let myself into my house, hyperaware of the whine of the door hinges and the creak of the floorboards underfoot.

I fall into bed exhausted, but there's no rest for me. Nightmares fill my head. Nightmares of dark wolves chasing me.

* * *

IT'S TWO DAYS MORE BEFORE I HEAR ANYTHING. TWO DAYS I spend in prayer and fasting, even though Martha Samuels and others try their best to feed and comfort me. I don't want to be a burden. I do my chores and help with my father's. I stay in my own house.

When the knock comes, I approach the door, the weakest I've been since the time I fell into the river at nine years old. My limbs are just as shaky, and my heart pounds as it did when I had to tread water for hours to stay alive. I've never been sick, not even a cold, but maybe this is my first flu. I'm overdue.

On the other side of the door waits a slight man with minimal gray hair and a kind smile. He holds his hat at his waist.

"Bradford. Do you bring news of my father?"

"I do." His mouth pulls into a tight line. For a moment, I'm afraid to hear what he has to say.

Bradford Adams and his wife, Hillary, have been friends of Hemlock Hollow for some thirty years. The Adamses live a mile west of the wall, and it was their phone Isaac used to call the doctor. Bradford and Hillary are the only *Englishers* besides Doc Nelson I know and trust.

I remember my manners. A bicycle leans against the porch and there is no car in front of the house. "You rode your bike all this way." I motion for him to come in and sit down.

Bradford nods. "Out of respect for your traditions." The man limps into the house and takes a seat on the sofa.

By way of the kitchen, I return with some lemonade, pouring him a tall glass before plopping down ungracefully in the chair across from the sofa. "Please, tell me what you've learned."

"Doc Nelson called today. First, let me relieve your fears. Your father is alive. The doctor says he's progressing normally."

"Praise the Lord." I take a deep breath and let it out slowly. "When can he come home?"

"That's the trouble. See, your father had what they call a stroke. He can't speak or walk. The doctors on the outside can fix it. They have ways."

"I can take care of him while he recovers."

"Once they fix him you won't have to, honey. The only thing is, the treatment will take several weeks."

I shake my head. "No. Dad can't stay for that long. He wouldn't want to."

"It's too late to bring him back. As far as the *Englishers* are concerned, he's a plumber from Willow's Province. You have to understand, in the outside world, no one leaves the hospital before they're treated. If he leaves early, they might trace him back here. You and I both know that would be disastrous." He takes a sip of his lemonade. "They're moving him to a rehabilitation center in Crater City."

"Crater City? But that's so far away!"

"He's in good hands, but he will not be back for quite some time."

I press the heels of my palms over my eyes. I can't do this. I can't pretend anymore. As strong as I want to be, tears seep down my cheeks. I come apart tear by tear.

An arthritic hand pats my shoulder. "Don't cry, darling. If you want me to, I can take you in my car to visit."

It's a sweet offer, but it's unrealistic to expect Bradford to support multiple weekly visits to my father, especially considering I'd have to masquerade as an *Englisher*. The risk is too great. Even if I accepted, the time commitment would be burdensome on both of us. Crater City is more than three hundred miles away.

"I'm sorry. I need some time to think." I attempt to stand to show him out, but the walls start to wobble. My bottom hits the chair hard enough to slide the legs backward on the wood floor. I close my eyes. When I open them again, there is a glass of lemonade in front of my lips.

"For your father's sake, please take care of yourself," Bradford says.

"I'm so sorry. Don't trouble yourself with me. I'm just tired." I sip the lemonade and force a smile. "Thank you for coming. I'm going to rest now."

He watches me take a gulp of lemonade and shifts his weight from one foot to the other. The corners of his mouth sag.

"Really, I'm fine. I need rest, that's all." I give my most convincing smile.

"Okay. I'm going to go. Come see me if you need my help."

As soon as he leaves, I set the lemonade down and bury my face in my hands, giving in to the wave of grief that plows into me. The door opens again. I rub my eyes in a weak attempt to cover my tears. "Did you forget something?"

"It's me."

I lower my fingers.

Jeremiah frowns at me, a large basket hanging from his arm.

"I don't want you to see me like this."

He remains silent but sets the basket down. The next thing I know, he's swept me up into his arms. Carrying me to my bedroom, he props me up on every pillow he can find. Then

leaves the room and returns with the basket. "Dinner, compliments of *Maam* Yoder."

"Jeremiah, you didn't—"

"She insisted." Out of the basket, he pulls a soup urn and a
spoon and sits down beside me on the bed. He ladles the hot
soup and brings it to my lips. The savory liquid courses down
my throat, so delicious I moan.

"You're hungry," Jeremiah says.

"Chicken dumpling. Your mother's was always the best in
Hemlock Hollow."

Jeremiah feeds me again. While I chew, his attention
sweeps away from me toward the wall. "I've always loved
that quilt."

How embarrassing. The blue and gray log cabin style on my
wall was my first. "Don't tease me."

"I'm not. I love it."

"The corner is messed up."

He spoon-feeds me another bite of soup, locking eyes with
me. "I love it."

"Thank you," I say around the bite.

He rests the bowl on his leg. "Bradford told me about your
father's condition."

I nod.

"This is our chance. *Rumspringa.*"

I swallow the bite of chicken in my mouth. "Not this again.
Don't you understand? My father wouldn't want me to go."

"That was before, but now your father isn't here."

"Just because he's sick doesn't give me the right to disobey."

"You don't understand what I'm saying. He isn't here, Lydia.
He's out there. If we go on *rumspringa,* you can live where he is,
in Crater City. You can see him every day. Maybe this is God's
way of telling you it's the right time."

I try to derail his logic but come up short. Clutching the base of my neck, I attempt to calm my racing heart but the untrustworthy organ pounds against my palm, speeding at the thought of leaving home. Even after a few deep breaths my shoulders are still hunched in tight knots.

"I've known you since you could walk," Jeremiah says. "I think, maybe, it's not just about your father's wishes or about the dream being better than reality. I think, maybe, you might be afraid. A little bit?"

For a moment, I'm speechless as I ponder the accusation. Me? Afraid? "I trust my father and if he says the world outside is dangerous, I believe him. I want to visit him but I *am* afraid. I think we both should be."

"It's normal to be afraid. Everyone is. But we aren't the first Amish to do this. There's an English house that helps people like us with the transition. They provide papers, names. They'll help us find jobs at places that will be discreet about us. We'll get to see all of those things we've talked about. Remember how Eli told us about the television? Don't you wonder what that will be like? Or how it would be to flip a switch to light up any room, instead of hanging the gas lamp from the hook above the table? I know it's scary, but it might also be wonderful."

I squeeze my eyes shut and try to ignore the pounding in my ribcage. I picture what it would be like to live in a house with Jeremiah. Without the expectations of Hemlock Hollow hanging over our heads, we might finish what we started in the barn. His lips look soft, wanting. We've been inseparable for as long as I can remember, but we've never even kissed. In the English world there would be no limits, no chaperones.

My cheeks burn. Emotions swirl within me that I can't even name. I press my hand into my chest as if I can hold my heart at bay. Pressure on a wound stops the bleeding, after all. But a flood of memories comes back to me. Ever since I was a baby, my father has lectured me on the evils of the English lifestyle. This is one edge I'm not sure I can throw myself over, even if Jeremiah is holding my hand.

"Open," he says.

I obey, drinking in the spoonful of broth he brings to my lips.

"Good girl." Jeremiah drops the spoon into the bowl and sets the lot down on the bedside table. Then he leans over me. With a hand propped on the bed on either side of my chest, he accepts my eye contact as he would an outstretched hand. I relax into the down pillow. The sight of him hovering over me fills me with intense joy and a sense of security. If we had time alone, if we shared an uninterrupted kiss, would I feel for Jeremiah what a wife feels for her husband?

"Please, Lydia. Just this once, do as I say. Come with me. I want you to be the one I experience the world with. We're seventeen years old. A few months—just until your father has recovered—and then we'll come home."

The way he says home, his breath brushing my face, sends a shiver across my skin and makes my heart skip against my breastbone. He says home like the word is intimate: *our home.*

"Besides," he continues in a whisper, suddenly intent on my mouth. "Until old Frank is home, I have no one to ask to court you. And I will court you, Lydia, whether the English way, the Amish way, or both."

A curl of his blond hair falls across his forehead. I sweep it aside and caress his cheek with my knuckles.

Some decisions are carefully constructed towers of logic framed in lists of pros and cons, shingled in trusted advice. As I throw my arms around Jeremiah, pressing the apron of my dress against his vest, the choice I make is based on none of those things. It springs straight from my heart to my lips.

"Yes, Jeremiah. I'll come with you. I'll go on *rumspringa*."

The smile he gives me is as much a reward as the embrace that leaves me longing for more and anxious to begin.

❧ 3 ❧

Bishop Kauffman agrees to my *rumspringa* request with little concern. In fact, the way he claps me on the shoulder suggests he expected the turn of events. Literally, *rumspringa* means "running around," the only time in Amish life when the *Ordnung* overlooks transgressions. The Amish only baptize adults, so as a teenager I'm not bound to church law, but at seventeen, I'm considered old enough to make my own decisions. That means between now and the time I choose to be baptized, I am free of all expectations except those of my conscience.

But my conscience has a loud voice. My father has made sure of that.

"Lydia," Bishop Kauffman says, placing a calloused hand on mine, "where you are going, they don't have rules like we do. The reason we've come to this, living behind this wall, is because they chose a life without limits, without conscience, and we chose to preserve ours. I want you to go and experience that life so that you know what it is you're giving up, the good and the bad. But remember your roots. Remember who you are. You may walk through the valley of darkness, but remember you come from the light."

I smile and nod. "I won't let their world change me." As the words leave my mouth, I truly believe them.

His eyebrows dart toward the ceiling. "Oh, child, that's not what I'm saying at all. You *should* let it change you. When you leave here, there is no halfway. You will live, dress, and speak the English way. There's something wrong if living that life doesn't change you."

"Oh," I say. I knit my eyebrows.

He gives my shoulder a gentle shake. "It should make you more committed to our way of life."

I bob my chin. "Okay." My stomach twists with my impending reality. I will have to live English. All of my lessons, my schooling, it was all for this moment—so I could walk among them if I had to.

"Then, go. We'll take care of your father's farm while you're gone. I will miss you."

Tossing my arms around his neck, I squeeze hard enough for the hug to last until I return.

BALANCED BETWEEN RELUCTANCE AND EXCITEMENT, I PACK MY father's small brown suitcase. I start with a *kapp* to cover my head and the box of pins I use every morning to bun my hair under it. Will they make me cut my hair? Winding a loose tress around my finger, I watch the honey brown tighten like a noose against my pale skin. I bite my lip. I don't want to change my hair.

Head shaking, I resolve not to worry about a problem that hasn't even happened. *Keep busy*, I tell myself. The modest gray dress I pack is without zippers or decoration, and the tights I've sewn myself. Leather shoes made by an Amish neighbor go in next. It all fits easily. I won't be able to wear this clothing once I'm on the outside, but I want a change of clothes for the trip home. Plus, it feels good to bring something of my life with me into the void.

I clean my house spotless and turn off the gas that powers the lamps and refrigerator at the tank. Both run on methane collected from heating pig dung—an Amish invention. The Yoders will use our pigs' chips while I'm away. As for the water, I turn that off too and empty the pipes, in case I'm not back before the first freeze.

Everything is prepared, but I startle anyway when Jeremiah knocks. I scurry to the door, a mess of jittery limbs.

His smile melts when he sees me. "Are you all right?" He takes my waist as if he expects I might fall over at any moment. "You look pale."

"Just nervous," I answer.

"Do you need to sit down? Some water?"

"No, I'm fine." I turn to grab my suitcase. "Besides, I shut the water off."

"Just as well. I have a surprise for you in the buggy."

Through the door, I notice the Amish buggy in front of the house. *Huh?* "I thought we would be going in a car. Won't someone see us in that?"

"Baby steps, Lydia. Baby steps." He lifts the suitcase from my hand and leads me out the door. "The safe house is in Willow's Province, just outside the gate. The only neighbors are Doc Nelson and Bradford and Hillary Adams. No one will see."

It sounds risky, but I trust in his plan. Besides, the familiarity sets me at ease.

Jeremiah's horse, Abe, swats flies with his tail, the jingle of metal against leather mixing with the songs of sparrows in the summer wheat. It's all the encouragement I need. I climb into the cab and wait as he loads my suitcase. He takes the bench next to me and scoops up the reins. With a cluck of his tongue, Jeremiah spurs Abe into the road, where he quickens to a rhythmic trot.

"So, what is this surprise?"

Jeremiah raises an eyebrow. "Patience is a virtue."

"And so is initiative. Should I look for it myself?"

"No need. It's there." He motions behind me with his head.

I pull the covered pail that rests next to Jeremiah's suitcase toward the bench. When I lift the lid, the most glorious scent fills the cab. Two soft drinks are wedged next to a large, colorful paper bag with the Ready Bell Express logo.

"You brought fast food from the English world?"

He flashes me a conspiratorial grin. "Jacob met me last night to make arrangements and brought it. I thought you might like lunch. Reheated it this morning myself. Cheeseburgers, French fries, nuggets, and something called a pie that looks nothing like one. And soda, still cold from the fridge."

"You are my favorite person in the world right now." I kiss his cheek, then pull the drink from the pail. The ice-cold cola bubbles up the straw, courses down my throat. After the last swallow, I burp appreciatively.

I've only had soda pop once before, when Mary returned from *rumspringa* with a case of it. It was just a small taste because we all had to share. I slurp on the straw again, anxious to have my fill. Wedging the cup between my feet, I unwrap a cheeseburger, offering the first bite to Jeremiah, since he's holding the reins and can't feed himself properly. He wraps his lips around half the burger, only thwarted by the ridge of paper I'm holding.

"I see that large mouth of yours is *gut* for something, Jeremiah." I use the German pronunciation for emphasis, like a mother scolding her child. "Did ya leave any for me?"

"Not *gut*, Lydia. Good. From here on out, you have to speak like an *Englisher*. We can't slip into German, ever."

"Gooood," I drawl.

Waving a finger, he says, "When in the English world, act English. Always. Have you been looking through your book?"

He's talking about the book each of us is given with pictures of new technologies so that we don't embarrass ourselves the first time we see a dish sanitizer or an irradiator. Of course I've reviewed mine. As if the eight years of English culture we had to take in school weren't enough.

"How's this for acting English?" I shove the entire other half of the burger into my mouth until my cheeks bulge.

Laughing, he shakes his head. "There's more in there, you know. Please don't choke on my account."

I shift the half-chewed mass to my cheek. "It tastes funny. Mushy and bland. Is this beef?"

"I think so." Jeremiah glances toward the bag.

"So, how far is it?" I swallow and reach for another burger.

"Just a few miles past Bradford Adams's place. Jacob is coming home to be baptized. He's going to drive the buggy back for me."

"I guess the tar didn't stick," I say, looking out over the fields of crops that line both sides of the road. I can almost hear my father talking about Jacob. *Like a lily-white lamb dipped in a tar bath.* Is that what Dad will think of me when all this is over?

"I guess not." Jeremiah's quiet chuckle brings me back into the moment.

Abe's rhythmic *clip-clop* provides background music. This is how it is with Jeremiah. I'm not compelled to speak to fill the quiet. The miles skip by. Fields give way to hickory and birch trees and then the road melds into two dirt ruts. This isn't the fastest way to the wall, but it's the only way to the gate.

Hemlock Hollow borders the Outlands, territory ravaged by radiation during the war. Most *Englishers* won't live anywhere near the Outlands because of the radiation levels. There are rumors that certain animals have mutated. Dangerously large rats and bears with two heads are said to make their homes near the remains of the reactor. Once the wall went up, a bunch of men from Hemlock Hollow knocked a hole in the concrete, at the part deepest within the Outlands, and built a wooden gate. I don't know why the English didn't think we'd do that. Amish are talented builders and our faith makes us brave. If I were to guess, I'd say it was because they underestimated us and assumed we'd go quickly into death.

I think the rumors about the continued impact of the radiation are made up. While it's true, I've been told, that many people died that first year after the war from the sickness, people in Hemlock Hollow live long and happy lives now. For as long as I've been alive, no one has ever seen anything like a bear with two heads. Our homes are built as far away from the Outlands as possible, within the bounds of our walled existence. I don't really understand what radiation is or why the English are so afraid of it. All I know is, it doesn't seem to bother us any. Not anymore.

We reach the wall, and Jeremiah jumps out of the cab and swings the gate open. I take up the reins, guiding Abe through. He closes and locks it behind us. The forest is dark here, thick with trees that twist and tangle together. I scan both sides of the path for two-headed bears, then giggle at the ridiculous thought. Jeremiah climbs back in, and Abe breaks into a trot again.

"Why do you think Bradford and Hillary Adams choose to live so close to the Outlands?" I ask.

"My father says the houses are cheaper in Willow's Province. Plus, it's the place you live when you want the government out of your business. The Province is rural and keeps poor records. I'm guessing they aren't big fans of the Green Republic and decided to take their chances with the radiation."

"That makes sense. I think the radiation is hogwash anyway. Some invisible force that makes you sick? I don't believe it."

Jeremiah shrugs and laughs through his nose.

The forest opens up and Abe's feet *clip-clop* on paved road again. We pass the Adamses' small stone cottage. By the time Jeremiah guides Abe up a long driveway toward a sweet-looking yellow house with a white wraparound porch, I regret eating the second burger.

"Please tell me this is it. I think my stomach is rejecting the fast food." I blow my cheeks out as a wave of nausea washes over me.

"This is it, Lydia. Fifty-four Lakehurst Drive. Your temporary English home."

He pulls the buggy up next to a corroded blue hatchback and reins in Abe. Hopping out first, Jeremiah offers his hand to help me down.

"Thanks," I say.

On the surface, the house looks similar to the ones in Hemlock Hollow, but there are subtle differences. A glass cage over the door houses an electric lightbulb. There's no knocker.

Instead, the button on the frame is an electric doorbell. I've never used one, and I decide in advance that I won't push it. I'll knock on the wood with my knuckles. A string of party lights in the shape of chili peppers wrap around the porch railing. It's late afternoon, so they aren't lit, but I can picture what they must look like glowing in the darkness.

An Amish home would never have such decoration, not because of the electricity required to run them, but because it would be considered a form of vanity. It would be viewed as an attempt to make a house look better than its neighbor. An Amish community is grounded in sameness and humility. It's virtuous to hold others above self.

Still, they *are* beautiful; my eye is drawn again and again to the cherry red plastic hanging like ripe fruit from an electric vine. They seem harmless in this setting, where they can be enjoyed without judgment.

"Are you ready to go in?" Jeremiah nudges my elbow, his hands filled with our luggage.

"I'm sorry. Let me help you carry that." I reach for my suitcase, but Jeremiah shakes his head.

"No, I've got it. Can you knock on the door?"

I climb the two steps to the porch and pound my knuckles twice against the wood. The door whips open before I can make contact the third time. A boy in a T-shirt and cap holds his hands out toward me.

"They're here! Everyone, come see. The newbies are here," the boy yells.

I don't recognize the face in front of me, but I do recognize the voice.

"Caleb? Is that you?" I ask.

"In the flesh." He removes his cap to reveal a headful of spiky brown hair.

"We never heard what happened to you," I say.

"Well, I decided not to go back. I'm not surprised Hemlock Hollow didn't advertise my refusal of baptism. I'm the custodian here now."

"Oh." I balk at the permanence he puts behind the words and glance toward Jeremiah, who's joined me on the porch.

"Come on in, you two."

I follow Caleb through a sparsely decorated living room. A plain boy stands next to the sofa, hat in hands.

"Jacob!" I throw my arms around his neck for a quick hug then retreat a proper distance. Jeremiah ducks between us to shake Jacob's hand. "You look...exactly the same!"

The boy shakes his dark mop of hair and smiles. "Well, I didn't yesterday, but I'm ready to go home."

"Living English hasn't changed you, then?" I ask.

There is an awkward pause while Jacob studies the floor; the smile fades from his face. "Yes, Lydia. Living English has changed me. The people here don't value each other the way we do back home. People are tools here."

"Hey, that's your opinion, man," Caleb interjects.

"Yes," Jacob states. "That is my opinion." The smile returns to its proper place on his face. "Lydia, Jeremiah, *gut* to see ya again. I'll take Abe back for ya. Hope to see you both again soon." Without even a glance at Caleb, Jacob bounds to the front door.

I wave goodbye as he glances back and nods in my direction. What was that all about? He's lived here for months and not even a handshake for his host? I want to ask but it's none of my business. Still, tension hangs thick in the air as the door closes and Caleb doesn't acknowledge Jacob's leaving. Moments later, Abe's rhythmic *clip-clop* grows soft with distance.

After an awkward moment of silence, Caleb claps his hands together as if he means the sound to clear the heavy mood. "Let me give you guys the tour."

I exchange glances with Jeremiah. He shrugs.

Caleb holds his hands out toward a faded blue sofa with worn edges, a matching chair, coffee table, and end tables. "This is the family room."

"It's plain," Jeremiah says. He means it as a compliment.

"Glad you like it, because it's where we spend most of our time when we're home." Caleb turns around and points into an arched doorway. "That is the kitchen."

I step forward and peek in. The refrigerator is gigantic and strangely quiet compared to our gas-powered one. I recognize the irradiator and the dish sanitizer, but something is missing. "Where's the stove?"

"We don't use them anymore," Caleb says. "The new irradiator cooks the food while it sanitizes it."

"Oh." I run my fingers over the smooth silver top of the device, wondering if it will be difficult to use.

"Don't worry. I'll show you how it works later. Gotta warn you, the food tastes like crap."

I glance at Jeremiah, but he's opening and shutting the irradiator experimentally. Caleb does not expound on the quality of the food.

We follow Caleb back through the family room to a hall near the rear of the house. He points into a small rectangular room with a well-used twin bed and dresser. "It's not paradise, but it will have to do," he says to me.

"It's perfect." The quality of the furniture isn't important to me. I didn't come here to sleep, and I hope to spend as little time as possible in here anyway.

Jeremiah sets my suitcase down on the bed. I walk to the

only window and look out. Fields of corn go on and on, as far as I can see. I guess the English world isn't so different after all. If I wasn't so excited to be here, I'd be disappointed. "Looks like Hemlock Hollow," I say.

Caleb laughs. "You might not want to judge by that view." He motions toward Jeremiah.

"You're right next door. Let's get you settled in."

The boys slip from the room, giving me a moment alone.

It doesn't take long to unpack everything I own, and I begin to wonder where we're going to get our *Englisher* costumes. I return to the living room to ask. Caleb isn't there, but a girl in a tight T-shirt and jeans is reading a magazine on the sofa. She glances up at me.

"Lydia, I'm so excited to have you here." Her bright blond curls bounce over her shoulder with the movement of her head.

"I'm sorry, do I know you?"

"Don't you recognize me?"

I concentrate on the makeup-covered face in front of me. The girl's skin is flawless. Silver eyeshadow feathers across her lids and over her eyebrows toward her ears. It looks like she's wearing silver, wing-shaped glasses that have melted to her skin. The color contrasts sharply with her robin's egg blue eyelashes—long, thick lashes. A wide black line surrounds each eye and her lips are puffy and blood red. But under it all, I recognize the bow-shaped mouth and narrow nose. "My word, Hannah, is that you?"

The girl nods, bounding from the sofa and spreading her arms.

I accept her embrace. "You are so beautiful. Look at your hair, your makeup. It's like something from a painting... or a dream."

"You'll look like this too. It's expected here."

"Oh, I couldn't."

Hannah opens her mouth but is interrupted when Jeremiah and Caleb enter the room.

"Great, everyone's here. We can do the welcoming ceremony," Caleb says.

"What's the welcoming ceremony?" I ask.

Caleb and Hannah move to the windows and shut the blinds, plunging the room into darkness.

"Hannah, can I have a drum roll, please?" Caleb asks.

Hannah drums her fingers on the coffee table and trills her tongue off the roof of her mouth. Ritualistically, Caleb approaches the wall, chin held high with the exaggerated step-together-step of a formal occasion. His eyes fix on a switch. A *light* switch. Suddenly, I understand what all the fuss is about. This will be the first time Jeremiah or I have ever seen an electric light work.

Plain folk aren't against electricity per se. Our community is against dependence on an ungodly world. That's why it's okay for us to use gas to power our homes. Gas isn't connected physically to the grid, and frankly, we could live without it in a pinch. Still, whether it's the novelty or taboo that draws me in, I'm excited for this experience.

I smile, oddly breathless with anticipation as Caleb's finger hooks beneath the off-white plastic switch. Hannah quits her drumming with a fake cymbal crash. *Click.* The lightbulb in the lamp next to me glows for a moment. The bulb flares quieter than my gas version. But then bluish-white lightning arcs from where the lamp plugs into the wall, dancing for a moment in the storm of its own making.

ZAP! The bolt strikes me in the chest. Sparks fill my vision. A boom rattles my eardrums. Head snapping forward, my feet lift off the carpet and I fly backward until my shoulder blades slam into the far wall. *Crack!* My skull follows my momentum. Pain radiates from my heart to my fingertips as I am suspended for a moment, arms outstretched.

Jeremiah yells my name.

The white light retracts and my body crumples to the floor. I fall as if the hand of God has dropped me from heaven.

Continue the story. Get your copy at https://gpching.com/books/grounded/